OUTRAGEOUS FORTUNE

FORTUNE CHRONICLES 2

KATHLEEN MCCLURE
KELLEY MCKINNON

PUBLISHED BY OUTRAGEOUS FICTION

Edited by Lori Diederich
Cover by Youness Elh

ISBNs:
978-1-947842-22-9 (eBook),
978-1-947842-35-9 (paperback).

MORE OUTRAGEOUS FICTION

THE FORTUNE CHRONICLES

Soldier of Fortune

Fortune's Fallen

Outrageous Fortune

Change of Fortune

Fortune's Fool

THE ZODIAC FILES

The Gemini Hustle

The Libra Gambit

Thank you for choosing *Outrageous Fortune*.

If you enjoy the journey, please consider leaving an honest review. For individual creators like Kelley and I, your feedback is the best way to help other fans of quirky science fantasy discover our worlds.

And for more outrageous fiction, including new stories, exclusive content, and reader community, scan the QR code below to follow our Outrageous Crew on Ream. It's free, easy, and the best way to delve into our fantastical worlds!

Happy reading,

Kathleen & Kelley

https://reamstories.com/outrageouscrew

About the Fortune Chronicles

The Fortune Chronicles are a series of standalone adventures featuring a colorful cast of characters who wander through each other's narratives from time to time.

We hope you enjoy your visit to the distant future and the planet Fortune, where tech is low, tensions high, and heroes unlikely.

For the Meggido Forum, for allowing Errant her first flight.
Kelley

For Jil,
Mother of Dracos
Kathleen

—nor shall any government, institution, or individual engage in the study of ancient technology without express consent of Fortune's appointed Keepers.

— APIAN ENVIRONMENTAL ACCORDS, ARTICLE 12 SECTION 7

PROLOGUE

UCAS Kodiak
Approaching Nasa Escarpment
Treicember 21, 1442 After Landing

CAPTAIN JOHN PITTE ENTERED THE BRIDGE OF THE *Kodiak* with blood on his hands and fury in his eyes. He tried to control his limp, but every step he took felt as if his knee were stabbing itself from within.

Someday, he'd have to see about getting that shrapnel removed.

"Captain on bridge!" Sergeant Millar, the duty provost, announced.

"As you were," John said, brushing past the prov, his steps thudding unevenly on the deck as he approached the command dais where General Jessup Rand had stationed himself, hands clasped behind his back and attention fixed on the Nasa Escarpment, which loomed ever larger through the forward windows.

John, crossing the deck, took a deep breath of the familiar allusteel and oil mix, slightly tainted by the coppery odor of blood he brought with him. He felt the deck inclining slightly as the helm adjusted the *Kodiak*'s altitude.

Other than the thrum of the engines and accompanying clanks, pings, and clicks of the airship's workings, the bridge was quiet.

John was within a few steps of the dais when Rand finally turned to acknowledge his presence. Eyebrows rising, the general stepped away from the forward rail and crossed to the aft steps.

"Captain."

"General." John continued until he reached the foot of the dais.

Rand's dark face tipped down, then up. "You appear to be injured."

"Bad turn on the ladder," John said, looking up at Rand. As he did, he noticed a shadow emerging from the far side of the dais.

A shadow which resolved itself into Sergeant Jihan, General Rand's aide de camp.

"That was fast," John said to Jihan, whom he'd left on the *Kodiak*'s lowest deck not fifteen minutes past.

Jihan offered a salute but said nothing, adding to the heavy silence of the bridge, which pressed on John from all sides in a way utterly unfamiliar to him.

Possibly because it was no longer *his* bridge, not in any way that mattered, not with Rand in control of the *Kodiak* and the helm, elevator, and nav all being operated by Rand's officers.

Even Millar, the duty prov who'd called John's presence, had come aboard with the general currently studying John's uniform with obvious distaste.

Perhaps Rand objected to the sight of blood.

"You are out of uniform, Captain," Rand said, confirming John's supposition.

"And your man is out of order, General," John replied, his eyes darting to where Jihan stood at the foot of the dais. "Provost Millar," he called over his shoulder, "please place Sergeant Jihan under warrant for assault and conduct unbecoming a member of the Corps."

"Belay that, Millar," Rand called over John's shoulder. "Captain." He stepped forward but remained on the dais. "As I am certain Jihan would have told you, he was acting on my orders. It was your man, McCabe, whose behavior called for punishment."

"Punishment," John repeated.

"For dereliction of duty," Jihan inserted at the general's nod.

John didn't look at the sergeant. "Assuming I believed that, which I don't, since when did the Colonial Corps adopt the Coalition's use of the lash?"

"Since the dereliction in question endangered an entire airship," Rand countered.

"Gunner's Mate McCabe failed to report a faulty containment cell in one of his cannons," Sergeant Jihan inserted so promptly it struck John as rehearsed. "If I hadn't noticed the damage, the *Kodiak* might have been lost with all hands."

"You do get around," John murmured, sparing the general's aide a cold glance.

"The sergeant knows I like a full picture."

John turned back to Rand. "If such negligence occurred, it would still call for a full investigation and the convening of a court-martial, not the draco's tail in the cargo bay with no witnesses."

Rand's eyebrows rose. "I'd suggest you calm yourself, Captain Pitte."

"I believe myself to be quite calm," John said, briefly taken aback. He'd not raised his voice once, except to get Millar's attention.

"In that case you might, in your cool-headedness, recall that a commander has the right to enact field justice in a time of war."

"And as I am McCabe's commander, it was my right to make

that determination," John reminded the general . . . calmly. "Yet somehow neither these accusations nor this—field justice—came to my attention. Had my first officer not come across McCabe being dragged below decks, I'd still not have known."

Even as he said this, John saw something flash in the general's expression, something like satisfaction.

"And I remind *you*," Rand said, "that for the duration of this mission, a mission that involves recovering an entire company of deserters, the *Kodiak* and her crew are mine to command."

"With respect," John said, "in all matters *not* relating to your mission, such as the day-to-day running of the *Kodiak*, the 'ship and crew are *my* responsibility, and that includes all matters of crew performance."

And there John spied it, again, that flash of satisfaction in the other man's expression.

"It pains me to admit, but you may be correct, Captain Pitte," Rand said, glancing at Jihan, who moved from his position to stand behind John. "Mr. McCabe is of your crew, which makes him your responsibility and *your* failure. As such, I am compelled to order the surrender of your command—"

"Excuse me?" John stepped forward.

"—until such time as a full inquiry determines the level of your complicity in your crew's negligence," Rand continued, nodding at his aide.

Jihan reached for John's sword, but John snatched the sergeant's wrist. "No," he said quietly.

"Don't make this difficult, sir," Jihan said.

"Captain," Moncivais called from the radio alcove, "I'm receiving word of groundside movement from the crow's nest."

John shoved Jihan away. "What kind—"

"What kind of movement?" Rand cut in. "Where on the ground?"

Moncivais looked at John, who gave a short nod, and turned to

Rand. "Sir, crow's nest reports spying several individuals at the top of the Nasa Escarpment. She can't make a positive ID as the suns are setting, but they are there, and armed."

"The deserters. Just as I expected," Rand said. "Radio." He turned to Moncivais. "Contact Commander O'Bannion and tell her to have her jump teams standing by." As he spoke, he flipped the command intercom, set into the dais, to life. "This is General Rand to gunner deck. Charge all cannons and prepare to fire."

"*Cannons charging, aye,*" a tinny voice emerged from the speaker.

"Belay those orders," John called, earning a scathing glance from Millar and a confused "Sir?" from Moncivais.

"*Say again?*" came from the dais speaker.

"Did I hear you correctly, *Captain?*" Rand looked over his shoulder. "Do as you were ordered," he said to both the speaker and Moncivais before focusing on John. "You are treading on dangerous ground, Captain Pitte."

"Perhaps. But it strikes me odd that a company of alleged deserters would be standing in clear view of one of their own airships."

"We're being hailed," Moncivais announced.

John, Rand, and even Sergeant Jihan turned to the radio operator.

"Put it on speaker," John ordered, ignoring Rand's hiss as Moncivais flicked the speakers to life.

"*—hailing UCAS* Kodiak *under Captain Pitte, this is Corpsman Carver, 12th Company, 96*[th] *Infantry, please respond . . .*"

"It's them," Rand said, his satisfaction palpable. "We have him."

"We have a contact," John corrected. "Request the colonel's ident for verification," he said to Moncivais. "And to specify the nature of his mission."

"Jihan," Rand said.

Just that—just *Jihan*—and before John could blink he felt it, the cold intrusion of steel into flesh. He looked down to see the point of Jihan's sword emerging above his right hip.

"Consider yourself relieved of duty," Jihan murmured in his ear, then yanked the sword out.

The force of the weapon's removal caused John to jerk back, which caused his head to bounce up, so he caught sight of Moncivais, already half risen from her chair. He had enough strength to shake his head at her—*no point.*

"*Repeat, UCAS Kodiak, this is Corpsman Carver, 12th Company, do you read? Over.*"

John shook his head again as he heard Rand delivering targeting orders to the cannon.

"Captain John Pitte," Jihan intoned formally, "you are hereby placed under warrant . . ."

"All cannons take aim," Rand said.

"*Repeat, repeat, Captain Pitte . . .*" the young voice continued to call over the speakers.

"*Cannons taking aim, aye.*"

"You can't," John said.

Rand didn't even spare him a glance. "I already have," he said as another voice crackled over the speaker.

"*Hey, Kodiak, this is Colonel Gideon Quinn, 12th Company. Do you read? Over.*"

"Prepare to fire on my mark," Rand snapped into the radio as he stared through the windows at the escarpment.

"*Repeat, repeat, Captain Pitte . . .*"

"Mark," Rand said.

Don't, John thought, even as the whine of the plasma cannons filled the air.

John looked down at the thrumming deck, noting as he did the dark red drops vibrating as they fell, and then he too was falling. And then he was on the deck, the cold metal against his cheek contrasting with the warm blood seeping from his uniform.

Lying there, unable to move or speak, he heard Carver's voice again hailing him and then, last of all . . .

"All cannons, fire at will." Rand's voice, dark with triumph, followed John into the sanguine fog.

CHAPTER I

Dyar's Canyon
Eastern Allianza Territories
United Colonies of Fortune
February 9, 1449 After Landing

JOHN DUCKED A SIZZLING BOLT OF PLASMA, straightened, and glanced at the smoking hole left in the multi-hued strata for which Dyar's Canyon was renowned.

Admittedly, Dyar's Canyon was also renowned for its inhospitable fauna, alkali lakes, and treacherous electrical storms, but John felt a perverse fondness for the place. It was dangerous and beautiful and defiant and didn't give a lick for the humans who'd created it.

"What the fecking comb are you waiting for?" Jagati O'Bannion, John's first mate, asked as she ran past.

"Sorry," he said, racing after her, "but these people have no respect for nature."

"Report it to the keepers," she called over her shoulder as a series of shouts, followed by more plasma bursts, had both laying a quick burst of suppressive fire before slipping single file through the jagged fissure.

"Come on, come on, come on!" Jagati hissed as she clambered over a tumble of fallen stone.

"I'm come onning," John replied, one hand on the satchel he wore crosswise over his jacket.

He'd almost reached the top of the rock pile when another shot had him diving the rest of the way over, resulting in an awkward rolling-falling-bruising affair. He continued to roll to his feet with a fresh spate of twinges. "It's entirely possible," he panted, "that taking this job was a mistake."

From the steady stream of epithets drifting back his way, he could only assume Jagati shared his opinion.

"—ing, smog-eating, spawn of a hornet," she finished as he came even with her.

A sideways glance showed the raw umber of her skin matted with the same violet grime which coated their clothes and dusted the spiraling mass of her brown-black curls. Combined with her fierce expression, the end result was rather demonic.

At least she looked threatening.

If the back of his hand was any indication, John figured he came off like a victim of some unnamed, wasting disease.

"We're close to the LZ, right?" she asked, slowing as the canyon they traversed narrowed to the width of an airship's crawlspace.

"Almost certainly," he agreed, nudging her onward while he removed the satchel and held it at his side so he could fit through the cramped fissure.

"Almost?" Stuck sideways with her head turned forward, he could only imagine her glare. "Pitte."

"Best keep moving," he prompted.

She hissed but kept moving, and in a few minutes, which passed like only a few years, they squeezed through to the other side, where Jagati came to a halt and scanned the wider space.

"Pitte," she said again, which in Jagati shorthand meant *Tell me we're not lost. And if you can't tell me we're not lost, at least tell me we have a plan to become unlost. And if we don't have a plan to become unlost, feel free to present your ass for me to kick all the way back to the shadow traders' camp.*

Jagati's shorthand was an incredible time saver.

"We're not lost," he told her.

"Good."

"Except I think we should already have passed the column that looks like a mammoth's—"

"*Pitte!*"

"Oh, there it is." He pointed to the right, where the cold blaze of the noontime suns had flattened the distinctive geographic feature.

"Overcompensation," Jagati muttered, even as a rapid series of plasma bursts cut the suggestive formation down to size.

She ducked, glanced back, and cursed anew as a shadow trader emerged from the crevice.

"Almost there," John assured, ignoring the smoke curling up from a fresh plasma score on his right thigh.

"Can't be soon enough." She jogged past him, then paused. "Smog it, Pitte, you're—"

"Heads!" he warned.

She ducked, spun, and fired at the foremost outlaw. When the distant shape let out a short squeal and dropped, she backed up and tucked herself under John's shoulder.

Thus linked, they turned and ran for it while John fired off an occasional shot at their pursuers.

"That's the last tunnel." He jerked his chin forward, toward an inverted V of a passage which connected to the canyon where they'd left their airship moored.

An airship their crewmates should have fired up and ready to fly the second John and Jagati hit the gangplank.

She nodded and urged him faster. "This is more resistance than I expected. Do we even know what it is we're retrieving?"

"The client chose not to disclose that information." He disengaged his arm from her shoulder and limped into the tunnel. "When I asked, she said it was sensitive and started to cry."

"I hate when they cry," she said as she followed him into the passage. "Wait! I mean, don't wait, but . . . the client's a *she?*"

"Of course. Didn't I say?"

"Nooo . . ."

"Ah. Well then, yes—the client is a woman," he said. "Typical spoiled risto with more money than sense. I've no doubt we're risking life and limb for her great-grandmother's 7-Up reliquary."

"Could be worse," Jagati said. "Could be another one of those ancient torture devices."

"That was a shoe. An original Louboutin, as I recall."

"You say shoe, I say spiky pain-delivery device."

"At any rate," he said, "whatever is in this satchel meant enough for the client to offer treble the usual fee for a recovery."

"It's not enough."

John didn't reply but limped faster, bracing a hand against the side of the cavern until he stepped out into the bright light of day . . . and froze in his tracks.

Behind him, Jagati came rushing out, only stopping when she ran into his back.

"What's wrong?" she asked, squeezing past him. "Shouldn't we be boarding about now?"

"It was here," he said, staring at the wide, flat, and—most importantly—empty space before them. "It was right *here.*" He peered up, shielding his eyes from the suns, and Jagati followed suit.

"Smogging toxic Earth!" Jagati stomped her foot, raising a puff of purple dust. "This! Isn't! Funny!" She ran forward into the empty place once occupied by their vessel, then she—yes—cursed some more.

"Feel better?" John asked, limping up to join her.

Her lip curled in a snarl. "What do you think?"

"Just asking," he said, giving the tunnel they'd emerged from a meaningful glance.

She growled, then gave him a punch on the shoulder, then led the way to a craggy outcropping at the base of the canyon's northern wall. "I will kill them," she muttered as she began to climb. "I will kill them and dance in their blood. I may be sorry, later, but I'll do it."

John almost smiled but knew better than to say anything.

"Here," she called down, "toss me the case."

He unslung the leather carryall and heaved it up.

Jagati caught the strap and slung the bag over the top edge of the ridge. "There's level ground up here," she called down. "And it's defensible. Sort of."

He nodded and started to climb after her, but stopped cold at a sudden rattling of stone from the canyon wall to his right. Turning, he clung to the face with one hand and shaded his eyes with the other as he searched for the sound's origin.

What he saw made him release his grip on the outcropping and drop back to the canyon floor, where his leg almost buckled under him.

"What the hell are you doing?" Jagati asked from on high.

John, in the act of raising his hands, jerked his chin upwards.

As he had, she shielded her eyes from the suns and stared in the indicated direction.

There was a telling silence from above. It told him Jagati had also spied the sniper perched at the canyon's upper edge.

And in case there were any doubts, a splat of plasma seared the rock less than a foot from her shoulder.

"It keeps getting better," she said, slithering to the ground at his side. "Remind me what made us think this was a good career choice."

"Funny, I was just thinking the same thing, except without the 'us.'"

"What's that supposed to mean?" she asked as the first of their pursuers emerged from the triangular tunnel.

"Nothing."

"Don't say nothing when you mean something!"

"Fine." He shrugged, then went still as a warning shot from the sniper sizzled to his left. "What I mean is, I was doing fine before you came hunting me down in Nike."

"I did not hunt you down."

He looked at her.

"Okay, maybe I hunted you down, but you were *not* doing fine."

"I had a decent job."

"You were smelting scrap allusteel."

"It was good, honest labor," he insisted, staring at the oncoming shadow traders a moment. "I was doing fine."

"Sure you were." She squinted at the approaching group. "If by 'fine' you mean ready to drink yourself into an early grave."

"You're exaggerating."

"Not by much," Jagati muttered.

"Be that as it may, if you'll recall, this whole Errant Freight business was your brainstorm."

"Not just . . . Rory was there too, so . . . never mind." Jagati's shoulders hunched at John's sideways glance, then a rasp of boots on stone had him looking toward the shadow traders who had followed them through the tunnel. Five were spreading out to surround them, while a sixth walked up to face John and Jagati.

The man was taller than John, and slimmer, with angular features and a short-cropped wave of silvered black hair beneath the ubiquitous coat of Dyar's Canyon dust.

His eyes glittered with intelligence, and his bearing was pure risto.

"I believe there's been a misunderstanding," Jagati greeted the man as he came to a stop in front of her.

"And I believe a misunderstanding is when someone bumps into me and spills my wine," he replied with a cool Fujian accent.

"Funny, I was just thinking how I'd like to buy you a drink," she said as the shadow trader took her shooter and passed it off to one of his crew.

Letting Jagati continue to play the flirt, John tried to figure out what had happened to the *Errant*.

Perhaps Rory had spied trouble and taken it aloft.

Or maybe . . .

He grunted and doubled over as a fist to the gut interrupted his thought process.

"You would do well to pay attention," the tall man said as he disarmed John. "Thief."

"Okay, so . . . that's a no to the drink?" he heard Jagati ask as he pressed his hands to his knees and sucked in the cold desert air.

"I see you have a sense of humor," the shadow trader said to Jagati. "It may be difficult to imagine, but so do I."

"You do . . . have a way . . . with a punch line," John managed, straightening.

"*Seriously?*" Jagati shot a glare in his direction.

John recognized it as her *are you okay* glare and not the *you're a swarming idiot* glare. He responded with the *five by five* wink.

Seemingly satisfied, she returned her focus to the man in charge. "Heard any good jokes lately?"

"As a matter of fact," the man gestured towards his crew, "just recently, from another uninvited comedian we discovered in our territory."

On this cue, the five outlaws circling them parted like a chorus in the Shakespeare Circus to reveal two more of their number, plus one of John's.

Rory McCabe managed a wry grin and an awkward wave that showed some bloodied knuckles. "Hallo."

"Go on," the risto urged as Rory's guards shoved him forward. "Share the joke with your friends."

"Funniest thing," Rory said, "but this lot has themselves a lookout on the upper plain that gave them a brae view of the *Errant* coming in to anchor."

Which explained what had happened to their airship—up to a point.

"How is E—everything on the *Errant*?" John asked.

The risto grimaced. "Your 'ship is in excellent . . . decent . . ." He sighed. "She is in as good a condition as when we found her. One of my pilots is taking her for a flight as we speak."

"Daring," John observed. "I hope they keep an eye on the aft port engine pod."

"It's a wee bit dodgy," Rory confirmed.

"Maybe you should call your people back before something on the *Errant* blows," Jagati offered.

"That, I might be willing to discuss," the risto told her. "But first—where is it?"

"Where is what?" Jagati asked, then cursed as one of the shadow traders punched Rory in the kidney.

"Where," the man echoed himself, "is it?"

"Oh, *that* it," Jagati said even as John drew his breath to speak. "We dropped it a ways back, on the other side of the rock that looks like a mammoth's—"

"Deraun?" the risto interrupted.

Another of the surrounding party came forward.

"Yes, Tariq?"

"What did you see upon exiting Spider Crevice?"

"Wait." Jagati held up a trembling finger. "You telling me that teeny little tunnel had *spiders* in it?"

"Not the time," John murmured.

"After Rhys falling?" Deraun, a slight figure with pale hair and gray eyes glared at Jagati. *"Him,"* he pointed to John. "He had the cargo in his possession. He had it until he reached the Axis tunnel."

Tariq looked at Jagati. "Pity," he said, pointing John's shooter at her head.

"It's here," John said over Jagati's angry hiss. "We threw the satchel up behind those rocks." He pointed to the outcropping behind them.

"Check it," Tariq ordered Deraun, who started up the rock face.

"Wait," Jagati said, "what makes you so sure he's telling the truth? I mean, if I could be lying, so could he."

"Is this really the time?" John asked.

"I just want to know how it is everyone's always convinced you're the honest one."

"I know he is telling the truth," Tariq told Jagati, "because I can see what he values."

"What does that even—?"

"Got it!" Deraun's shout interrupted Jagati's question.

John turned to see the shadow trader holding on to the rock face with one hand and hefting the satchel in his other.

"So much for treble the usual fee," Jagati muttered.

"Bring me the case," Tariq ordered Deraun, stepping back as the slender outlaw's descent sent a small avalanche of pebbles skittering to the canyon floor.

As they watched, Jagati fogged the air with a series of ripe curses, most of them aimed at John, who was watching Tariq and the shooter still aimed at Jagati's head.

"Does she truly not know?" Tariq asked softly.

John turned from the gun to Tariq. "Know what?"

"Ah." Tariq smiled. "I see."

"What are you two gabbing about?" Jagati asked.

"Nothing, apparently," Tariq replied, his attention sliding away from John, at which point John's hand snapped up to grab

Tariq's shooter and point it upwards, causing Tariq's finger to tighten on the trigger. The plasma burst hit Deraun, who gave a sharp cry and fell the rest of the way down.

John, meanwhile, used the gun to spin Tariq into the rock wall, barely registering the crack of the other man's head striking stone as he wrested the shooter free. From beyond, he heard a series of shouts and thuds and angled to see Rory snapping an elbow into his left-hand guard's arm to send her sword flying into the nearest shadow traders, who scattered to avoid being sliced by friendly cutlery.

At the same time, Jagati lunged for Rory's right-hand guard, throwing a right cross at his jaw while Rory drove his boot into the same man's knee.

An ominous *splat* of plasma from above reminded him of the sniper, so John hauled Tariq forward and held the weapon to the shadow trader's head. "I think you know what to do," he said.

"Hold your fire!" Tariq's voice echoed through the canyon, and John had to admit he was impressed at the speed with which the order was obeyed.

Combatants from both crews froze and turned.

Jagati, straightening, shoved the shadow trader she'd been wrestling with to one side while Rory crawled out from under the guard who'd been about to deliver a punch.

Then a rebellious sizzle of plasma creased the air, leaving a glassy scar centimeters from Jagati's elbow.

"I'd listen to him," John called out.

Tariq merely nodded once, and the rest of his crew lowered their weapons.

"Weapons on the ground, if you'd be so kind," John ordered.

They did as he said, again impressing John.

Unlike many a shadow crew, Tariq's people were loyal to him rather than the cargo.

"Don't forget your man on high," John murmured, indicating the sniper.

"Woman, actually," Tariq corrected before calling out, "Ysabel!"

At the top of the northern face, a figure grew from the glittering purple crag and raised two empty hands before one foot shifted forward and, seconds later, a long-range crysto-plas repeater thudded to the canyon floor, raising a cloud of dust around it.

"And leave us," John added.

Tariq sighed but nodded.

Slowly, Tariq's people backed away, and even the sniper faded from view.

Those on the ground paused only long enough to scoop up the wounded Deraun before making a subdued trek back to the angular tunnel.

"Thank you," John said to Tariq.

"Think nothing of it," Tariq replied.

"I'm kind of surprised," Jagati said, retrieving the satchel from where Deraun had dropped it. "You don't strike me as the type to give up so easily."

"But I have not given up," Tariq observed with what appeared to be amusement. "This current reversal is only temporary."

"How so?" John circled around so he could face the other man, the gun now trained on his opponent's heart.

"Have you forgotten where you are?" Tariq asked. "We stand in the middle of Dyar's Canyon, which is as inhospitable a desert as the Morton Barrens. Perhaps worse," he added, considering, "as the Barrens have no alkali lakes to tempt a man when the thirst inevitably drives him to madness. It is an ugly way to die, alkali poisoning," he said as if discussing the relative merits of clover versus sage for honey. "Fortunately for you, this will not happen."

"I'm glad to know that," John said.

Tariq smiled. "It will not happen because long before the

thirst or the madness take you, my people and I will hunt you down and skin you for the sheer pleasure of it."

"Skinning?" Jagati echoed, retrieving her own shooter and helping herself to one of the fallen rifles. "A'ight, maybe we messed with your airship a little," she recalled. "And shot a couple of your guys, but—"

"Not helping," John cut in.

"I'm just saying," she shrugged, "skinning seems kind of extreme."

"In my line of work," Tariq told her, "one either lives by extremes or dies by them."

"Now that's what I call a motto," Rory said as he removed the battery from Ysabel's rifle. "You should put that on a mug," he added, setting the rifle down and moving on to disable the next fallen weapon.

"It's a difficult life, I'll grant you that." John drew Tariq's attention back to himself. "But it is also a given that objects of value, once stolen, may just as easily be stolen back. Most in the shadow trade consider it the price of doing business."

"A point of view," Tariq agreed. "But not one to which I ascribe."

"Too bad." Jagati shrugged. "I'm not much looking forward to being skinned."

At her negligent tone, Tariq's eyes narrowed.

"And here it comes," John murmured at the same time a low drone, as of thousands of bees on the swarm, presaged the approach of a small airship. It flew low, almost brushing the high ground, so when it came over the open air of the canyon, the rope ladder, which it had been dragging along behind, fell within reach of those waiting below.

Tariq looked from the hovering *Errant* to the ladder Jagati, with the satchel, had just grabbed hold of and back to John. "How?"

"I'd tell you," John said, "but I'd hate to spoil the mystery."

"Do you even know what is in that case," Tariq asked as Jagati made her ascent.

John waited for Rory to follow Jagati up the ladder before responding. "Do you?"

"I know what it is worth to me."

"Then we have something in common," John said.

Tariq's head tilted as if considering John's statement. "I very much doubt that."

"Ladder's clear!" Rory called from above.

"And I've got you covered!" Jagati's voice followed.

At Jagati's bellow, John holstered his shooter and began to climb, leaving Tariq, his riddles, and his threats on the cold ground below.

CHAPTER 2

John reached the bay door and found Jagati's extended hand. "Thanks," he said, grunting a bit as she hauled him into the cargo bay, hard enough that he almost landed face-first on the deck.

It was interesting to John how the air of the bay seemed colder than the air outside. "Something I said?" he asked, righting himself before turning to help Rory pull in the ladder.

Rather than respond, Jagati slung the shadow trader's rifle she'd appropriated over one shoulder, clomped past John to the opposite bulkhead, and activated the bay intercom.

"Eitan," she called into the mic, "we're all aboard and good to go."

"All aboard, aye," the voice of the *Errant*'s fourth and final crew member crackled through the speaker. No sooner had he spoken than the drone of the engines increased to a high-pitched whine and the airship surged into a steep ascent.

This gave John and Rory an interesting few moments as they were still pulling in the ladder, but with the aid of the handrails on either side of the opening, they managed to muscle the last rungs inside before slamming the door shut. They spun the lock in place, and almost immediately the acrid scent of the canyon was replaced by the sickly odor of burned flesh.

Rory's eyes dropped to John's injured leg.

"Do we have the cargo?" John asked Rory.

"Safe and sound." Rory nodded to where the leather satchel sat, nestled in the pile of coiled rigging.

"Barely." Jagati muttered.

"Best check on Eitan," John told Rory. "And thank him for the save, however he managed it."

"Aye to that." Rory headed to the forward companionway.

"And stow the cargo," Jagati added as he passed by.

"Leave the cargo," John countered, directly.

Rory, who had already turned and snapped up the satchel's long strap, wordlessly dropped it, spun on his heel, and made for the companionway at double time. On the second step, however, he looked back at John. "Best not linger over your argument," he said. "That leg needs cleaning, and sooner rather than later."

John's eyebrow quirked up. "Who said there'd be an argument?"

"Her face," Rory said with a jerk of the chin toward Jagati.

John looked at Jagati. "Ah. I see."

"Oh yeah," she said.

But Rory was already on the move, dashing up the stairs as fast as his long legs would take him.

John waited until the thud of boot-steps faded before looking at Jagati. "So, what are we arguing about?"

Her eyes widened, and her hands flew out in a frustrated gesture older than Fortune. "I can't believe you even have to ask."

His head tilted. "Given I can't sense thoughts like Eitan, I can't believe you can't believe I even had to ask."

Her wide eyes narrowed. "Keep it up, Pitte, and this argument will turn into a fight."

"First landers forfend," he murmured. "But truly, I would like to know what it is you're angry about. Because I know what I'm angry about—"

"You?" Jagati's jaw dropped. "You have no reason—"

"—which is the way you regularly take ridiculous risks—"

"—to be angry, when it's you—"

"—lying about the satchel's whereabouts when—"

"—lying down and offering your throat up to some smogging risto thief just because—"

"—he had a gun to your head!"

"—he had a gun to my head!"

On that last simultaneous exclamation, both froze.

At some point, John realized, they'd moved, each crossing to the center of the bay as the argument escalated, so by the time they'd reached the sticking point they were face-to-face, which meant he spied the moment she registered what he'd said, even as the memory of Tariq's words fell silent between them.

I can see what he values.

As he watched, her expression went blank.

"He wasn't going to kill me," she said with a certainty John couldn't fathom.

"How could you possibly know that?"

She opened her mouth, then closed it, then shrugged. "I just do."

John tried to read her expression, but all he could make out was *Closed for Business*.

"Anyway," he said, "he was very serious about the satch—"

"We should see what's inside that swarming case," she said at the same time.

They stared at one another, then as one turned and walked— or, in John's case, limped—to the disputed satchel, still perched in its nest of ropes.

John hefted the bag by its worn leather strap while Jagati unbuckled the flap and peered in.

"Well?" John prompted. "What is it?"

"A lockbox," she said, pulling out the object in question and holding the case up for him to see. It wasn't particularly noteworthy, just a simple, molded metal box, roughly the size of a document case, or perhaps a jewelry chest.

"Locked, I presume."

She ran her fingers over the latches. "Yes. Dammit." She gave the box an annoyed shake before John could stop her. "I bet Tariq knows the combination."

"We probably shouldn't go back and ask for it."

"Probably not," she agreed. "But maybe we could break into it? Or Rory could, I bet."

John considered the possibility. No doubt if he set Rory loose, the clever-minded mechanic would find a way into the box. "I'll consider it. But for now . . ." He held out the open case.

With obvious reluctance, Jagati slid the box back into the bag, and John slung it over his shoulder. "So," he began.

"Right," she said, then stepped back, possibly to make room for the awkward silence rising between them.

Rather than wait for it to grow, John threw her a bone. "Eitan will need the coordinates to Nike graphed—"

"Rory won't settle unless that leg's looked after—" she said, her words once more overlapping his.

They paused, eyeing one another warily.

"I'll just," he jerked a thumb upwards, "go to the medbay."

"And I'll get up to the bridge," she said, spinning and striding to the stairs with an eagerness perhaps more desperate than Rory's had been, minutes before.

John waited for her footsteps to recede, in part because he wanted to give her a decent lead and in part because his leg ached fiercely.

As he ascended, however, he felt the echoing pulse of another ache . . . an old one, and familiar, and caused by no visible wound.

But because this pain was old and familiar, he expected it

would soon sigh its way back to the hollow space beneath his heart where it dwelled, and there remain.

No bother to anyone at all.

Rory didn't slow his pace until he entered the rear of the suns-washed bridge, where Eitan Fehr sat at the helm, pushing the airship's engines to their limits.

As Rory's eyes adjusted to the brighter light of the bridge, he saw his crewmate's shirt had a rent in the left sleeve and his hair, a mass of black he most often wore in a tail, hung loose to his shoulders.

He took another moment to slow his breath and check for bodies—always an option when Eitan was involved—and on finding none, turned his attention to the bridge itself, where he found a fresh gash alongside the navigator's table to port, a new ding in the elevation relay's brass surround, and a burn scar in a starboard girder.

"I apologize for the mess," Eitan called over his shoulder, as if reading Rory's thoughts—which was not entirely out of the question.

"'Tisn't so bad," Rory replied with a shrug. Still, his fingers brushed over the blackened girder on his way to the helm, where he stopped behind the empty co-pilot's chair. "I'm to thank you for the save," he said. "So, thanks for the save."

Eitan's response was a crooked half nod, which showed a hint of bruise above the neatly trimmed beard.

Rory wasn't fluent in Eitan's nods, but this one came off like a *you're welcome*, so he turned his attention to the control panel. "Port aft engine is running a mite hot." He nodded to the engine's output indicator.

"I noticed," Eitan said. "Still, I'd like some distance between us and those shadow traders before we drop speed, if you think she'll do?"

Rory considered the question. If the *Errant* were crystal-powered, he'd have already shut down that engine. But *Errant*'s liquid aluminium batteries were far less volatile than the crystal cells which powered the vast majority of colonial 'ships. "She'll do better if you bump up the output in the other three," he decided.

Eitan made the necessary adjustments while Rory glanced over the pressure gauges arrayed along the forward panel, above the ballast controls. "Cells eighteen and twenty-three are low," he noted while Eitan nudged the elevation levers back with his left elbow to increase their ascent. His right hand remained on the yoke of the steering column, holding their course steady as they rose.

Rory glanced down at the other man. "So how did you manage it?"

"Manage what?"

Rory's eyebrow arched. "Playing daft buggers, are we?"

Eitan smiled.

"Fine." Rory raised his hands in surrender. "How did you retake the 'ship?"

"I was in the training room when the shadow traders boarded, so I took the aft ladderwell to the bact-tank."

"And I'll grant that's impressive," Rory said, "but there were three shadow traders still aboard when I was hauled away, all armed to the teeth."

"Four," Eitan corrected.

"Four," Rory echoed.

Eitan's glance slid sideways. "Do you truly wish to know?"

"No," Rory said after a moment's consideration, "I don't imagine I do."

Eitan nodded, toggled the engines back to a less strenuous output with his left forearm, then elbowed the elevation levers forward, leveling the 'ship. "Were you planning to see about the pressure in cells eighteen and twenty-three?"

"Yes," Rory said, pulling his eyes up and away from Eitan's maneuvers. "Right. Carry on, then, and I'll just—do that." Feeling the blithering idiot, he turned to leave the bridge. "Except," he stopped halfway to the door and turned back, "I can't help noticing you've lost your prosthetic . . . again."

"I did not lose it." Eitan glanced down at the space where the hook had been buckled on his left arm, then back to the window. "I know precisely where it is."

At which point Rory mentally juggled the image of Eitan and four shadow traders, all armed to the teeth, who were no longer aboard the 'ship. "I don't want to know that either, do I?"

"I am certain you don't."

Rory sighed. "Aye, well, I'll get to work on a replacement. Would you be wanting to go back to the prongs, then?"

"Whatever suits," Eitan replied. "I have no preference."

Of course you don't, Rory thought. *Because you'll just lose that one, as well.*

He should probably stop trying but, truth be told, seeking a viable solution for Eitan's lost hand was about all that was keeping Rory from being swept away in his own loss, or the woman who shared it.

And since he could do naught to bring Liam back for Jinna, Rory would keep making new prosthetics for Eitan.

At the moment, however, Rory had an airship to keep aloft, so on leaving the bridge he headed for the midship envelope hatch, where he donned one of the breathers left hanging next to the starboard ladder before climbing up to crank open the locking wheel.

Pushing open the hatch, he was glad of the breather as the cold touch of leaked anterrium instantly frosted over his exposed skin.

He climbed quickly into the envelope, dropped the hatch

closed behind him, zipped up his jacket, and pulled on the insulated gloves he kept tucked through his belt.

He looked down through the grating at his feet, where dozens of pipes sprouted from the central tank and climbed, like organized vines, up the frame's interior. Thinner shoots split off from these vines to feed anterrium into each individual cell.

It was the tank Rory addressed first, double-checking the gauges set into the container to confirm the readings he'd seen on the bridge. Once he had, he twisted closed the valves that supplied the two compromised cells, then hefted the patch kit from its niche under the grated decking.

This would be the third time he'd patched up number twenty-three, and the second for eighteen.

Perhaps once they received their payout for this job, he could squidge enough of the ready out of John to replace some of the older cells.

That hopeful thought—along with the focus required to size, cut, and affix patches in the numbing cold of escaped anterrium—kept Rory's mind occupied enough that thoughts of Jinna popped up only six times.

Seven at most.

———

Eitan, left elbow hooked around the yoke, was tapping the elevation gauges when he heard Jagati step onto the bridge.

"Problem?" she asked, crossing to the nav table.

"The gauges are placing us at eight hundred meters elevation," he told her. "No, wait. Now we seem to be at three hundred meters."

"I think we would have noticed if the 'ship had dropped over a thousand meters," she said after a beat.

"Almost certainly."

"Probably the gauges are acting up," she offered.

"Most like," he agreed, giving up on the tapping and giving the panel a concerted thump with his fist.

"Better?" she asked.

"Back to 2,050 meters, more or less," he said, relaxing back into the pilot's seat. "But once we dock, we should ask Rory to check the gauges—after he gets the aft port engine running sound and cells eighteen and twenty-three patched."

"Always something," Jagati replied, pulling out the appropriate charts while he again took hold of the yoke with his right hand.

As she worked, Eitan avoided thinking about the hand that wasn't there or the false prop Rory would soon build to fill the empty space.

"Lost another one?" Jagati asked around the pencil stuck in her teeth.

He didn't have to ask what she meant. "Not lost so much as sacrificed."

"Mmph," she hummed, before removing the pencil. "You know, you could always tell Rory to stop making replacements."

"I came to a similar conclusion," Eitan admitted, wondering at how closely Jagati followed his thoughts. "But if I did, what would he do with his spare time?"

Her response was a dry chuckle and then, to his quiet relief, she let the matter drop.

While Jagati was plotting the *Errant*'s course, a supremely angry Tariq El Karim was climbing the gangplank of his grounded *Al-Djinn*. Brushing the patina of purple dust from his coat, he looked over the cargo bay and noted that, aside from the acrid stench of crystal det and a strip of blackened metal where the bay door's lock had been, there was no other sign of intrusion.

As far as he could see, every crate, canister, and barrel

remained undisturbed, all safely secured under their flight webbing.

Interesting, as many of those crates, canisters, and barrels contained high-value goods—goods a crew flying a wreck like the *Errant* should have found tempting.

Instead, Captain Pitte had used his small window of opportunity to steal one middling-sized box, which had been hidden in one of the dozen smuggler's hides the *Al-Djinn* boasted.

Which meant, Tariq further thought, that Pitte not only knew what he wanted but where to find it.

The intimacy of Pitte's knowledge struck Tariq like a hot fist, spurring him up the ladder so quickly that the remaining dust wafted around him in a violet haze, as if he were himself the spirit of air and fire for which his airship had been named.

He didn't stop until he reached the entrance to the starboard pod on the third deck, where he looked inside to see the *Al-Djinn*'s mechanic already head and shoulders deep into the engine's guts.

"How bad is it?" he asked.

"Not as bad as it could be." Jacques O'Malley slid out from the open casing. His expression, what little was visible above the ruddy beard, was perplexed. "Kinda surprising, considering anyone with the smarts to break into the pod's guts could'a done a lot worse. Instead, they just disconnected the overhead coupling," he pointed to the part in question with one hairy paw, "and pulled out the secondary and tertiary buffers but—and this is what's so swarm about it—they left both tubes standing outside the pod, nice as you please, so's we'd see what they did."

"Very polite of them," Tariq murmured.

"I'll say," Jacques agreed, immune as ever to his leader's sarcasm. "Be easy enough to steal the buffers, then let us try to power up, which would pretty much be the end of all our troubles."

Tariq considered the mechanic's statement. "So you're saying they wished us no harm?"

"Nothing permanent," Jacques confirmed. "My take? They just wanted us grounded long enough to make their getaway."

"Which, as it stands, seems to have worked."

"As my old gran used to say, some days you're the dire wolf, some days you're the dodo," Jacques said, giving his beard a scratch.

"Tariq."

At the sound of his name, Tariq turned to see Ysabel, his sniper and second in command, waiting in the passageway behind him. He was surprised to see her so soon, as she'd been leading the search party for the missing men.

"You found them?"

Ysabel dipped her close-shaved head in a single nod. "All four. On the island."

Jacques peeked out of the pod. "That'd be right cramped."

Tariq had to agree, as the island was in fact more of a boulder with aspirations set in the middle of an alkali lake. It was large enough for one man to lie down, if he kept his knees tucked in. Four would have been challenging.

"And they were alive?" Tariq asked.

"Mostly."

By the first landers, it was like pulling teeth with this one. "And what is that you are holding?" As he spoke, Tariq indicated the hand she'd kept low at her side.

"Franco had a souvenir from the *Errant*," she said, handing over the object.

Tariq held up the wicked-looking hook attached to a soft leather cuff with a series of buckles sliced apart. The leather, he noted, bore a few suspicious red-brown spatters.

Jacques leaned further out of the engine pod. "That'll leave a mark."

"It did," she confirmed.

"Where?" Tariq asked.

When she failed to answer, he looked at her, at which point she dropped her gaze to an anatomical region that had Jacques going pale, and even Tariq experienced a brief chill.

"Liliane says Franco will still be able to sire children," she said.

"That's assuming he can find a woman willing to let him try," Jacques said after a beat, bringing something close to a smile out of Ysabel.

Tariq, however, found nothing amusing in the situation. "Did any of them say how they lost the *Errant?*"

Her head shook once, left to right. "Only Franco was conscious when we rowed out to them, and he passed out in the boat."

Which Tariq found understandable. "I will speak to them when they wake."

"Liliane has Franco pretty morphed up."

"Then I will speak to him last. Meanwhile, Dyar's Canyon is no longer a haven for us. Ysabel, spread the word. I want the caves emptied and everyone aboard the *Al-Djinn* within the hour. Jacques," he turned to the mechanic, "can you get her flight ready within that time?"

"Could do," he said, scratching the beard. "Could do faster with a pair of spare hands," he added.

"I can assist," Ysabel said before Tariq could ask. "As soon as I speak with the others."

"Good." He turned away. "If anyone has need of me, I will be on the bridge, plotting out our course."

"You don't mean to follow them?" Ysabel asked.

Tariq glanced back. "I don't need to follow them. I know precisely where they are going."

The stoic sniper and quizzical mechanic shared a glance. "Okay, I'll bite," Jacques said. "Where are they going?"

"Nike."

"And now I will bite," Ysabel said. "Why Nike?"

"Because," Tariq explained, "Pitte knew not only where in all of Fortune to find us, he also knew the best time to break into the *Al-Jinn*."

"The dawn storms," Ysabel guessed, referring to the electrically charged dust storms which swept through the canyon at sunrise, without fail, from Treicember through March.

During the storm season, Tariq kept the *Al-Djinn* powered down, and any crew not on sentry duty atop the canyon walls sheltered in the nearby caverns.

"And not only was he aware of the storms," Tariq said with a nod, "he and his crew bypassed a small fortune in easily disposable cargo in pursuit of that case. Which leaves me wondering how Pitte knew so much about us."

"Someone had to have told him," Ysabel said, baring her teeth.

Tariq nodded. "And only one person outside the crew knew where we would be and what we carried."

"Oh," Jacques said as he caught the falling quarterstar, "no. No smogging way."

Tariq understood the sentiment, and yet . . . "Can you think of anyone else?"

"But why?" Ysabel asked, shocked enough that her brow actually furrowed. "And after she went to such trouble to steal it?"

"That, I don't know," Tariq admitted. "But I intend to find out." With that, and a brief glance at the hook, he turned away. "If anyone has need of me, I will be on the bridge, charting the fastest route to Nike—where I expect to have a very long conversation with my wife."

CHAPTER 3

JAGATI SPENT MOST OF THE NEXT HOUR CHARTING A course for Nike, one twisty enough to keep Tariq off their backs.

Once it was complete, she'd left the bridge to find Rory climbing down from the envelope, en route to the aft port engine pod.

She offered to help, but Rory assured—maybe a little too emphatically—that he'd do better alone. His assurances, only slightly insulting, left her free to head to her quarters, where she planned to shower off the remains of Dyar's Canyon and do some hard thinking.

By the time she emerged, the dust was nothing more than a smear of violet on the shower floor, and she'd come to a decision.

She quickly dressed and headed up the passageway to John's quarters. She raised her knuckles to the door and rapped softly. When he failed to respond, she tested the brass knob and found the door unlocked, so she pushed the door open and heard the shower running.

Congratulating herself on her excellent timing, Jagati slid inside and closed the door behind her before the chill of the passageway could infiltrate the small, steam-warmed space.

She looked to her right, where the steam originated from, and found the bath's pocket door had been left half open, revealing a few inches of the cabinet-sized shower stall's flexi-glass screen.

As she looked, a flash of dripping elbow appeared on the other side of the screen, followed by a portion of equally wet torso. Her heart kicked into overdrive, and her eyes locked on that torso, which showed the angry line of an old sword wound, the remnant of what had been a very bad day, just above his hip.

A hand slicked with soap—sage, her nose told her—slid over the scar, and then John shifted again, leaving her looking at nothing but fogged flexi-glass.

With a relieved huff, Jagati turned her attention to the rest of the room.

Unlike the captain's quarters on the *Kodiak*, John's berth on the *Errant* wasn't appreciably larger than any of the others, which should make the search easy.

It also made his obsessive neatness even more obvious.

The jacket he'd worn down in the canyon had already been wiped clean and now hung neatly on one of two hooks to the right of the closet, next to his gun belt and sword.

Since they were nowhere in evidence, she assumed his dirty and bloodied clothes were already in the drawer-like hamper, installed in the bulkhead under the hooks, where they would remain until whoever was up on the laundry rota collected them for washing and mending.

His bed was made to Corps standards and—Jagati looked at his desk—not a single object was out of place.

And, she thought with disgust, *there's no sign of the swarming box we retrieved from the* Al-Djinn.

She bit back a curse and looked under the bed, then straightened and crossed the room to peer inside the closet.

The deck juddered beneath her feet, and Jagati reached out to steady herself, but rather than the smooth bulkhead, she grabbed the battered leather of John's jacket. Instinctively, her fingers clutched at the sleeve, taking obscure comfort in the sturdy leather.

The jacket had been a gift from her, presented to John on the day they'd taken formal possession of the *Errant*.

Though Jagati never said so aloud, the rugged brown leather suited him far better than the rigid lines of his Air Corps jacket ever did.

And now she was romanticizing a coat, for keepers' sake. Disgusted with herself, she turned her attention to the closet's interior.

If she were John, where would she hide the satch—

"Looking for something?" John asked.

The hand resting on the jacket became a fist as she realized the water was no longer running. "Yes," she said, forcing a smile and turning to face John, who stood at the door to the head and, *hoo boy*, wore nothing but a towel held negligently around his hips, just below the memorable scar. "I, ah, I thought maybe you'd borrowed my gun belt," she explained, forcing her eyes to meet his.

"Your gun belt," he repeated, his expression mildly curious. "You mean the one you're wearing, or a different one?"

Shit, was she wearing her gun belt? She looked down. Of course she was, because where else would she keep her shooter? *Stupid, stupid, stupid* . . . "Fine," she waved her hands in the air, "I wasn't looking for my gun belt."

"I thought not," he said, curiosity deposed by a hint of amusement.

"I was looking for—" she began.

"You were looking for—" he overlapped.

"—the box," they both said at once.

Jagati clenched her teeth. "Tell me this isn't going to be a thing."

"This?"

"This talking at the same time thing."

"I'm sure I couldn't say," he murmured. "I'm too busy wondering if *this* is going to be a thing."

"This?" she asked, backing up a step at his expression, which was now neither curious nor amused. "What *this*?"

To her annoyance, the amusement returned. "This thing where you sneak into my quarters."

"I wasn't sneaking," she countered. "I knocked!"

He tilted his head. "I didn't hear a knock."

"Guess the water was too loud."

"Or the knock too quiet."

"Maybe. Whatever. Anyway, if you don't want someone sneaking into your room, you should lock the door."

"I thought you weren't sneaking?"

She thunked her hand to her head. "Okay, maybe I was sneaking. A little. But it was for a good cause."

"The cause being to take the box," he noted, leaning one shoulder against the bathroom's doorsill.

"Not take," she said, huffing. "I just—look, we both agreed it would be a good idea to let Rory try to open it, didn't we?"

"I said I would think about asking Rory to look into the issue," he countered. "Was that not proactive enough for you?"

"It's not that." She shrugged and looked down, noting the livid burn creasing his left thigh just below the towel. Her eyes darted toward his desk while her face warmed. "Not exactly that," she said to the writing box, set dead center of the desk. "It's just, breaking into the case would skirt too close to your personal boundaries."

"My boundaries?"

"Your sense of what's right and what isn't." She waved a hand in his direction. "And breaking into someone else's property isn't. Face it, Pitte, you're an honorable man."

"Why," he mused, "does that sound like an insult?"

"It's not an insult." With a shrug, her focus shifted to the pocket watch he never wore but kept in a little wooden bowl near the writing box. "It's just, being an honorable man isn't the greatest survival trait on Fortune."

"And because I am such an honorable man, you decided to protect my interests by taking the issue of the lockbox—the lockbox, I might add, that I stole from another airship—out of my hands."

"Listen, I get you're mad . . ."

"Who said I was mad?"

I can feel it, she thought. "Your speech pattern gets even more formal when you're pissed," she said.

"That must be disconcerting."

"You have no idea." She turned to glare at him. "Anyway, this is a ridiculous way to have a conversation. Would you mind at least getting dressed?"

"I wouldn't mind, but you're standing in my closet."

"I am not." *Am I?* Swarming apiaries, she was. "Fine." She started to push her way out when a knock on the door, followed by Rory's head popping into the room, sent her all the way back into the closet's narrow confines.

Please don't see me, please don't see me . . . wait, why does it matter if he sees me?

"Sorry, didn't mean t'interrupt your shower," Rory's voice filtered through the pair of muslin shirts that had fallen in front of her. "I must not have been thinking, what with being busy patching gas cells and skelping dodgy engine pods into order since we boarded."

"Not at all," John replied, his voice pleasant. "How can I help you, Rory?"

Jagati stifled a sigh. It wasn't that John didn't catch Rory's sarcasm, but by being *him* and seeming to accept everyone else's words at face value, it completely took the lift out of the opposition's airship.

As was proven by Rory's *un*-stifled sigh and the rattle of paper.

"It's this note. The one you left in the shop with the cargo."

Cargo? She just barely stopped herself from thumping her head against the closet wall.

"What about it?"

"Well, I get that you want the box open, but the question is, do you want it fast or pretty?"

What's the difference? Jagati thought.

"What's the difference?" John asked.

"The difference being, if you're wanting it pretty, it'll take as long as it takes, and being it's a tri-level Kairos lockset, it'll be pure luck if I manage it before we reach Nike."

"And fast?"

"I seal up the machinist's room, fire up the cutting torch, and sure as Ben's your uncle, I'll be through the case in an hour, two at most. But it'll make a hash of the case, which might be a problem if you're not wanting the client to know we've opened the thing. And if whatever's inside is heat sensitive, or flammable, or—"

"I understand," John cut in. "How about this: go for pretty, but if it doesn't seem possible by the time we set down in Nike, we'll consider fast."

"Aye to that," Rory replied, and the door clicked shut. Jagati was just stepping out of the closet when it opened again. Cursing loudly in her head, she ducked back again.

"One more thing," Rory said.

"There's still enough in the clean tank for fifteen minutes of running water," John said with the barest hint of impatience. "Eitan may want a few of those minutes, but there will be another full tank bact-scrubbed by 2800, latest."

Of course, he'd check the progress of the bacteria tanks. She rolled her eyes. Just as he'd leave a reserve for the rest of the crew.

"And that's grand," Rory replied after a beat, "but I meant to ask if you'd cleaned that wound properly."

"Oh." As John spoke, she imagined his eyes dropping to the

burn on his leg. "No. I mean, yes. It's fine. I'm fine," he said. Rory must have looked unconvinced, however, because John continued. "I promise, there's not a hint of grit or thread or anything but leg in my leg. Keepers' truth."

"If you're certain, then . . ."

"I am."

"In that case, I believe I'll take myself off and use up seven and a half of those minutes of water."

Inside the closet, Jagati listened to the door close again. This time, however, she counted to twenty before easing past John's shirts to see him still leaning in the open bathroom door, waiting.

She crossed her arms over her chest. "So, you asked Rory to open the box."

John simply watched, a small smile tugging at one side of his face.

"So," she said again, "I guess I'll go now."

"I think you're forgetting something."

"What? Nope. I've got all I came in with." *Except my dignity.*

"Not that kind of forgetting." He straightened and took the two and a half steps necessary to meet her. "I was thinking of something else. Something more . . . personal."

"Personal?" Was her voice squeaking? Her voice never squeaked.

"Yes." He leaned closer, tilting his head down the inch or so necessary to come close to hers. "Something like," he was so close she could feel his breath over her lips, "an apology."

"An a—*what?*" Her head snapped up, and her fists clenched, and it was only fear that socking him would lead to a lost towel that kept her from following through on the punch that was forming. "Why?"

"It's what one generally does after being caught breaking and entering—"

"There was no breaking. Entering, yes, but no breaking."

"*And* attempting to steal—"

"Not. Steal. Not—you know what? This is a stupid conversation. One I am going to end. Now. By leaving."

John took a half step back and, with the hand not holding the towel, gestured to the door.

Shaking her head, Jagati slid past him, yanked open the door, and was out in the passageway before she could do something she really regretted, like slugging her captain.

Or worse.

Since her brain refused to settle on what constituted "worse", she decided to forget the entire affair.

It was time to relieve Eitan at the helm, anyway.

CHAPTER 4

AFTER THREE DAYS OF HARD FLYING, JOHN OPTED TO shut down the engines and drop a high anchor over the Avonian territory of Lycos.

His plan was to lie low for a few hours, giving both 'ship and crew a chance to recover and Rory, in particular, more time to work on the mysterious case, which he'd been poking at for almost the entirety of their flight.

John had called him out of the machinist's room on day one, to deal with the aft port pod, but other than that, the mechanic's time was given entirely to matching wits with the tri-level Kairos combination lock.

Eitan, on day two, observed that the case had become Rory's white whale.

Jagati then asked what a beluga had to do with a briefcase, at which point John had excused himself from the conversation.

On day three, soon after dropping anchor, John knocked at the door of the machinist's room, intending to tell Rory he was free to give up on keeping things pretty and to cut his way into the damned case.

The door opened, and John barely resisted stepping back from the rumpled, wild-eyed manifestation of a Campbell Islander that appeared. Over Rory's shoulder, John saw the lockbox sitting in the middle of the worktable, surrounded by what appeared to be Rory's entire collection of lock picks.

"What is it?" Rory demanded, his accent thicker than Jagati's version of porridge. "Can ye nae see I'm working, here?"

"As a matter of fact, I can," John replied, meeting the younger man's manic gaze with his own steady regard. "I thought you'd want to know we're at high anchor, five hours out of Nike."

"Yes? *And?*"

"If you'll recall, we determined you had until we reached Nike to try and open the box without damage."

"Yes, but we've not yet reached Nike, have we?"

"Perhaps not, but we are—"

The door slammed in his face.

"—close," John finished even as he heard the door's bolt snick home. "So, I'll come back later, shall I?" he called through the barrier.

The response, muffled as it was by three inches of allusteel-encased bamboo, might have been an acknowledgement, a curse, or an anatomical suggestion John believed to be impossible.

John figured he could try to force the issue—he was the captain, after all—but they had the night.

If Rory couldn't defeat the Kairos lock by morning, John would order him to pull out the cutting tools.

He turned from the door and headed toward the ladder, only then noticing the odor of burning threading into the cargo bay.

Apparently it was dinner time.

Since he doubted Rory would be amenable to another interruption, John left him to it and headed to the aft ladder, climbed one flight to the starboard passage, and then continued forward, past the medbay and training room, until he reached the galley, where the sconce lamps were glowing warmly, a pot of tea was steeping on the table, and the air was redolent with the bitter tang of smoke that confirmed it was Jagati's turn to cook.

"Excuse me," Eitan said, easing past John to take a seat at the table while Jagati slammed a pot down next to the platter of aurochs kabobs. John poured the tea while Eitan and Jagati served themselves, then filled his own plate, discovering that the pot contained steamed kale.

At least, John thought it was steamed kale. Mostly what he got from the first mouthful was singed green.

For a time, they ate in silence, with only Eitan displaying any appetite, ingesting the unevenly grilled aurochs and mystery greens with a single-minded efficiency that spoke of a man not yet accustomed to regular meals.

"I don't like it." Jagati finally broke the oppressive silence while shoving the food around her plate.

To her left, Eitan disposed of the last cube of blackened meat, put down his chopsticks, and used a crumbling bit of flatbread to scrape up the drippings.

"Then why did you make it?" John asked, giving up on shoving his own food around and instead shoving the entire plate to his right.

Eitan, without looking up, retrieved the chopsticks and started working his way through John's untouched meal.

"Not the dinner." She took her fork and stabbed a bit of green, which she then pointed at John. "This job."

"Which part?" he asked as, to his right, Eitan's dark eyes slid up from John's plate, then immediately slid down again.

"All the parts." Jagati swung the fork around. "Starting with this nameless client."

"Sameen," John said, picking up the pot and warming his tea. "Her name is Sameen."

"*Just* Sameen?" Jagati asked, her voice pitching unusually.

He set the pot down and picked up his mug. "That's the name she gave me, yes."

Jagati's eyes narrowed as she turned the fork around to take a bite, at which point she seemed to actually *see* the kale, and instead let the clump fall back to the plate where it landed with an unappetizing *splat*.

Eitan looked up hopefully, so she pushed the plate to her left. "It's all yours," she said and while Eitan claimed the spoils, as it were, turned back to John. "So let me get this straight: a woman you've never met hired us for a retrieval, supplied all the details about the location of the item—including where it would be hidden aboard the shadow traders' 'ship and the best time to retrieve it—but not her surname, what the item is, how many shadow traders would be involved, or how desperate they'd be to keep it."

John sipped his tea. "That about sums it up, yes."

She slumped back in her chair. "And you were satisfied with that?"

"I wouldn't say satisfied, precisely, but—"

"Because generally, when we take a client, we get a few more details."

"And how has that been working for us?" John demanded, thumping his mug onto the table as a long-contained frustration bubbled to the surface. "A year's worth of jobs, and we're barely keeping the *Errant* aloft, much less earning enough to feed the crew."

Both glanced at Eitan, who was just finishing up John's plate.

Jagati turned back to John. "Still—"

"We were going to lose the 'ship," he said then, as Eitan's surprised gaze joined Jagati's appalled stare, continued. "The *Errant* was going to be impounded by the Nikean Transport Authority and held for auction unless we made good on our quarterly freight levy. And perhaps we might have managed the levy if we hadn't already used up the profits from Raul Nyevsky's hemp shipment on a month's moorage in Stolichnaya during that last winter storm, or had to give up a part of the profit from Noam

Carrera's leather shipment because of the bolts we lost while fighting off those pirates. And should we talk about the fine for Yu Shaori's bees that she never mentioned were contraband?"

"I might live a full and happy life never talking about those bees," Eitan put in, as it had been he and Rory who'd been tasked with smoking the swarming beasts back into submission.

"Could have been worse," Jagati said, raising her own mug. "Could have been spiders."

Eitan's head tilted. "Who in their right mind would be shipping contraband spiders?"

"My *point*," John cut in before an entomological debate ensued, "is the bees and the fines and the storms and the pirates all happened, and in every one of those jobs we knew what the cargo was and everyone's surname."

"We didn't know the bees were contraband," Jagati reminded him.

"But we did know more than we expected about Raul Nyevsky, thanks to Eitan."

"Raul and his sister," Eitan confirmed, smiling at the memory.

Jagati's glare turned his way. "Seriously?"

"A very warm family," Eitan said with a shrug. "And Stolichnayan winters are very cold."

John's eye started to twitch. "I am simply saying we knew a great deal about every one of those clients and still lost money, which led to us being unable to pay the Nikean levies, which led to me standing in front of the docking offices arguing with the NTA official when Sameen stepped in and offered to settle our debt as down payment for this job."

"And you said yes?" Jagati asked, sitting up and leaning forward to rest her crossed arms on the table. "Just like that? Without telling me—consulting with the rest of us?"

"Yes," John said. "Because it was say yes or forfeit the *Errant*," he continued, his voice tight. "And because, when a woman wearing a necklace that costs more than our combined earnings over the past year appears with a generous offer and a single name, I didn't feel I had any choice but to take them both."

"A woman like that," Eitan offered quietly, "could likely afford better."

"I've no doubt she could," John agreed. "As I have no doubt she knew that in hiring me she was hiring someone too desperate to ask questions. And she was right," he admitted, deflating as he spoke. "I didn't ask a single one, and it nearly got us killed. So if either of you are rethinking my position as captain of the *Errant*, suffice it to say, I won't hold it against you."

There followed a pause, during which Eitan and Jagati shared a look before turning back to John.

"I hope you're not expecting me to take the job," she said. "I hated the idea before, and hearing what you've had to deal with—the levies, the admins, the well dressed women?" She shuddered. "Thanks but no thanks."

John looked at Eitan.

"As much as I enjoy a well-dressed woman, my skills are more confrontational," the other man said.

"Perhaps Rory?" John suggested. All three gave that a thought.

"No."

"Nope."

John himself considered. "Perhaps not."

"So we're agreed," Jagati said, slumping back in the chair. "You're stuck with being the captain."

"Ah, well, if you say so."

"I do."

"Though perhaps," Eitan ventured, "once we receive the payment for this job, we should take a more formal approach to managing our capital. Create separate accounts for the business and the crew—even make a few investments." Eitan paused as John and Jagati openly stared. "I studied economics for two terms in university."

"Of course you did," Jagati said.

"Did you happen to study engineering whilst you were at it?"

All three turned to where Rory stood in the galley's port arch, the much-disputed box under one arm.

"Rory." John rose from the table. "Did you crack the combination?"

"I did," he replied, though he sounded less exhilarated than John would have expected.

"And?" Jagati asked, also rising. "What is it? Art? Jewelry? A shoe? One of those fart sounding things?"

"I think that was a kazoo," John murmured.

"Whatever." She waved him off, though at the time she had been unreasonably obsessed with the item. It had been one of their first retrievals, undertaken on behalf of a Dolian risto with a fondness for Earth instruments. "C'mon," she prompted Rory, "what is it?"

"That's what I'm trying to say. I've no idea what it is. Here, see for yourselves." Rory strode to the table, and John hastily shoved the teapot and mugs aside to make room for the case which, as advertised, didn't have a mark on it.

"Pretty," Jagati observed.

Rory didn't appear interested in compliments on his handiwork. Instead, he focused on the case itself, now sitting on the cleared space between John and Jagati. He angled the box so Eitan, on the opposite side of the round table, could see as well, then grasped the case's two front corners and lifted the lid open in a manner that came off as more dare than flourish.

"So," he stood back, shoved his fists in his trouser pockets and glared at everyone, "that's it."

The other three looked inside the box. And kept looking.

"Okay, so—not a kazoo," Jagati said. "Unless they come in box shape?"

"Box shaped with keys on," John said, angling his head to get a better look. "Numbered keys," he added, nodding at the columns of black and silver keys set into the black allusteel casing. They only ran from 0 to 9, but others, these black and copper and bearing various mathematical signs, filled the two rows across the top and the rightmost column.

More numbers were engraved on what looked to be a long row of spinning drums, visible through a slat above the topmost row of symbols. A toggle on one side indicated the thing was powered. By crystal, aluminum or solar cells, John couldn't determine.

"See what I mean?" Rory leaned over the table. "I've never seen the like."

"I have," Eitan said, speaking for the first time since Rory had entered the room.

"Is it some kind of new teleph machine?" Jagati reached for the object.

"Wait," John placed a cautioning hand on her wrist. "Is it a weapon?" he asked Eitan. "Some sort of explosive?"

"Should we contact your friend?" Jagati turned to Rory. "Jinna was demolitions in the Corps, right?"

"Was," Rory agreed. "But as she's over six months along, I'd prefer not to expose her to a potential boomer."

"You do not need to contact Jinna," Eitan said. "It is not an explosive, though some might argue it is a weapon, of sorts."

"Of what sort?" John asked.

Eitan looked up. "It is a piece of ancient Earth technology."

"Really?" Rory asked, hands coming out of his pockets to lie flat on the table as he leaned closer in. "Brilliant!"

"But there is no ancient Earth technology on Fortune," Jagati said.

"Even if there were, this device is of recent manufacture," John pointed out.

"And of Colonial make," Rory added, straightening. "This toggle, these keys," he pointed to the parts in question, "all out of the Macintosh catalogue, and the case is Tenjin-quality allusteel."

"I grant you, the device itself is new, but the design is *ancient*," Eitan said. "I have seen diagrams of machines similar to this *and* read papers on how they were used." His eyes moved from Rory to Jagati and landed, finally, on John. "I *know* what this is."

"All right," John said, though as he met Eitan's gaze, a chill skittered up his spine. "What is it?"

"That," Eitan said, "is a calculator."

CHAPTER 5

"I'M SORRY," RORY TURNED TO EITAN, "A WHAT, again?"

"A calculator," Eitan repeated, his voice steady despite the fact that, for the first time since joining the crew, he found a meal weighing uneasily in his stomach. Which, given the crew's cooking skills, was saying something. "A machine once used on Earth for advanced mathematics."

"Like an arithmometer?"

"Only in the same sense that the *Errant* is like a weather buoy," Eitan replied to John's question before pointing to the copper-colored keys. "On the Earth-made calculator, these keys allowed the user to perform advanced computations, not only multiplication or divisions but also statistics, probabilities, exponential functions."

"And I bet that would be impressive if I understood what half of it means," Jagati observed.

"It means we have a problem," John murmured.

"Why?" Her glare shifted from the calculator to John. "Because knowledge is power and power corrupts?"

"I've always thought that was bollocks," Rory said, cracking his neck. "Three days," he muttered as all three turned to stare. "Three days hunched over a tri-level Kairos."

"We get it," Jagati said. "You're a miracle worker. A genius. A god among dodgers."

"I was na' asking for—"

"We have a problem," John cut in, "because this kind of tech is outlawed."

"But the Apian Accords only forbid tech that can be used as weapons," Jagati countered. "Computers, artificial intelligence, programmable weaponry. It doesn't say a thing about fancy adding machines." She waved a dismissive hand at the device.

"Believe me," Eitan said, "this is precisely what the Apian Accords speak of. These buttons?" He pointed to three that read HEX, OCT, and BIN in turn. "These represent three numerical systems the Earthers used to create computer code. Primitive, compared to what our ancestors had available to engineer and colonize Fortune, but . . ." He withdrew his hand and looked at John. "You are right to be concerned. The mere knowledge of such a device is forbidden. I don't care to imagine what might befall anyone the keepers found in possession of an operating model. A stint in the Barrens would be the soft option," he said, shooting a warning look in Rory's direction.

"Which begs the question," John said, turning to face Eitan, "given those prohibitions, how did you come to see these designs in the first place?"

"I—" Eitan paused, rubbed at his beard with the stump. "I learned about them at university."

"Chandrasekhar offers a course on illegal tech?" Jagati asked.

"Oronhyatekha University required a term on the ethics of Earth technologies," John told her.

"As did Chandrasekhar," Eitan nodded. "But this was something different."

"Different how?" Jagati asked.

"During my fourth term, I became involved with a group with

technochrist leanings," he confessed. "They were interested in expanding on the university's teachings, as they believed Fortune's children deserve full access to Earth's technological legacy."

"And?" Jagati prompted when he hesitated.

"These students were in contact with an underground archivist who had in his possession the design specifications of several Earth-made devices, supposedly salvaged from the first landers, before the transports were destroyed."

"Such as the specs for a calculator?" Rory surmised.

"Such as," Eitan confirmed.

"Brilliant," Rory muttered, then grabbed Jagati's forgotten mug, drained the dregs of her tea, then made a face because it was of course stone cold by now. "So," he said, setting down the empty mug with a thump, "what do we—"

"Toss it," Jagati cut him off. "Dump it in the Oracle and forget we ever saw the smogging thing."

"We can't," John said, then looked at her. "We *can't*."

"If you're worried about the keepers catching us for illegal waste disposal—"

"Not just that," John said. "The real issue is that too many people already know about this, and they know we have it. We can't just toss the thing without painting a target on our backs."

"Smogging wonderful," she said with an ill-tempered shrug.

"It's nae all bad," Rory said. "I mean t'say, as long as it's here, can we not take it out for a spin?"

"*No.*"

"Not a chance."

"Are you crystal mad?"

"There's no need t'get snippy." Beset from all three sides, Rory removed his hand from where it had been about to flip the power toggle. "It might not even work."

"How would you know one way or the other?" Jagati asked.

"I've a head for maths, myself," Rory said. "With Eitan's help, I'm betting we could determine if it's operating to spec."

"No doubt we could," Eitan said. "But I am with Jagati in this. We should destroy the device. Now. Before we set down in Nike."

"If we destroy it, we won't be able to set down in Nike," John said. "Or anywhere else. Sameen *hired* us—"

"*Sameen* set us up to retrieve contraband tech," Jagati tossed in. "To my mind, that means we owe her smog-all."

"And there will be other jobs," Eitan added, bolstered by Jagati's support. "Fortune is large. Larger now the war is over."

"Not large enough to outrun a bad reputation," John countered. "And when word gets out the *Errant* doesn't deliver? We were scraping the bottom of the hive before this. What happens when the jobs dry out altogether?"

Eitan shook his head. "It would be worth the risk."

"Worth our lives?" John asked. "Sameen isn't the only player involved. Tariq is also out there, and he seems more than willing to kill for that machine."

"There are worse things than death." Eitan straightened, his fist clenching as he faced the captain.

"Yes," John agreed. "Watching others die needlessly, for instance."

"Boys," Jagati moved to stand between John and Eitan, "you're both a queen's dream, so why don't we all step back and take a breath before Rory gets hurt."

"Oy!"

"And not that I don't agree with you, because I do," Jagati turned to face Eitan, "but isn't this a pretty extreme reaction, given your interest in the tech, back in the day?"

He shook his head. "Back then I was young and arrogant enough to believe Fortune could be trusted with Earth's knowledge," he told her. "But now . . . suppose the calculator works as intended? Would the users be satisfied exploring Euclidean geometries? Would they delve into the possibilities of base 60 maths or attempt to map the route of infection of Midasian Fever? Or would Sameen, or Tariq—or whoever Tariq meant to sell it to—use the device as the jumping point for the next technological advance? And what, do you suppose, that next advance might be? Programmable detonators? Guidance systems for airborne missiles? Earth had those, and more. What would the Midasian boffins turn their minds to, do you think? Because if we allow this machine into the world, I promise we *will* find out."

"All of which, I'll grant, is a valid argument," Rory said, "but it also assumes this particular calculator is the prototype. We've no way of knowing, do we, how many of these wee mechanicals have been built?"

"I wish that made me feel better," Jagati said.

"And even if it is the only one," John picked up Rory's argument, "the draco's effectively out of the shell. Someone has already built this thing and could easily build themselves another."

"Not easily," Eitan shook his head. "You have no idea what went into this—"

"I would if you'd let me open it."

"—the manufacture of the processors alone would be next to impossible," he overrode Rory's comment.

"What's a process—"

"Even for someone with the design specs?" John spoke over Jagati.

"Even so," Eitan confirmed while Jagati gave John a hard poke in the shoulder. "The specs I saw back in Chandrasekhar were created based on records from Earth, designed for Earth-made supplies and power sources. Meaning the someone who made *this* calculator had to retro-fit the internal workings to suit what is available on Fortune."

"*And* do it without anyone knowing it was being done," Rory added with more than a hint of admiration.

"Would that be hard?" Jagati asked. "The keeping the work a secret bit, I mean."

"Try ordering a coil of fine-extruded copper," Rory told her. "'Tis easier to buy a full crate of crysto-plas chargers for your shooter."

Again, silence fell as all four stared at the seemingly innocuous device.

"What we need is more intel," John finally said.

Eitan turned to face the other man. "Were you not listening? There is no amount of intel significant enough to justify keeping this machine intact."

"And while your opinion is valued," John replied, "I am still the captain of this airship, and that means it is on me to decide how this issue is dealt with." He paused, met Eitan's gaze. "Unless you've changed your mind about my abilities in the past fifteen minutes?"

Eitan's hand clenched at his side as he faced John who—damn him—stood quietly waiting, until Eitan let out the breath he'd been holding and shook his head.

"Very well," John replied, showing neither relief nor satisfaction which, Eitan had to admit, was an enviable quality in a leader.

John then looked to Rory, who shrugged his acquiescence, and at Jagati, who waved her hands in brief surrender.

"So," she asked, "how do we play this?"

"As I said," John looked around the table, "we can't make a firm decision without more intel and, at present, there is only one person I know of able to provide it."

"You mean to keep the meeting with Sameen," Eitan guessed.

"I do."

"You mean *we* do," Jagati stated firmly. "No way you're meeting this broad without backup."

"That may be wise," John said, to her visible surprise. "Meanwhile," he looked to Rory, "I know you were planning to check in with Jinna but . . ."

"*But,* you'll be wanting me to stay behind and watch the 'ship."

"Not at all. But I was hoping you'd be so kind as to deliver a package on your way to see her?"

Rory's eyes widened, then narrowed. "A package?"

"Did you forget someone's birthday?" Jagati asked.

"No," John said to Jagati, "and yes," he told Rory.

"And what's to be in this package?"

"It doesn't matter," John said. "All that matters is that the package itself is about that size," he indicated the open box on the table.

"*That?* What? *Ahh . . .*" Eitan watched Rory grin as the crystal sparked. "You're wanting a decoy, then."

"Only as a precaution," John said.

"Why?" Jagati asked. "I mean, we left Tariq in the dust, so who are we worried about?"

"I'm not certain we can discount Tariq. He strikes me as the determined type," John said, then looked at Rory. "You'll need to be convincing. If anyone's watching, we want them to believe the calculator is in your possession."

"What fun," Rory decided.

Finally, John turned back to Eitan. "And I'd like you to act as his backup."

Oddly relieved to have a purpose in this morass, Eitan nodded.

"And grateful I'll be," Rory said, "but shouldn't whoever's playing backup be a mite more discreet?" He looked at Eitan. "I've never seen you so much as cross a room without bodies tripping over themselves to get your teleph exchange."

"It is not that bad," Eitan protested.

"Actually," Jagati said, "it's kind of that bad."

"Forgive me," he offered his own small smile. "I should perhaps say it does not have to *be* that bad."

"Uh huh," Jagati's eyebrow rose. "So, you're saying you have an off switch?"

He considered that. "I suppose that would be the best way to describe it, yes."

"Oy then, is this a sensitive thing?"

"Yes, it is a . . . sensitive thing," Eitan told Rory. "One I would be more than happy to explain to anyone who wishes a primer on neurochemical attractors and the conscious suppression of—"

"No, but thank you for offering," John said.

"I'm good," Jagati added.

"I'd like to know," Rory pointed out. "But it can wait."

"Glad to hear it," John said, then looked at the calculator. "Now I just need to find somewhere to hide this thing."

"You are not bringing it to Sameen?" Eitan asked.

John shook his head. "As you said, we don't know what anyone might do with such a device so, for now at least, our best option is to keep it safe."

As he spoke, a complex, five note trill sounded from the galley's radio box.

"That's Nike field's call sign," Jagati noted.

"I radioed earlier with a request to contact us when they have an open dock," John said, and looked at Rory, who offered a wry fist to the heart in salute and crossed to the other side of the galley. While Rory took the communication, John gingerly lifted the calculator from its nest of cork. "Lighter than I'd have thought," he told the others before giving his head a shake. "I'll get this hidden, then we can raise anchor."

As John departed, Eitan could sense Jagati wanted to follow and see where John hid the calculator. He rather thought she might give in to the urge—Jagati hated missing out on any kind of action—and so he was surprised when, rather than slipping out of the galley after the captain, she nudged him in the shoulder.

"So, you were part of a radical technochrist student movement in college?"

Despite the gravity of the situation, Eitan felt the smallest tug of a smile. "I was experiencing a rebellious phase."

"Yeah?" Her eyes slid sideways. "What was the rebellious phase's name?"

He looked away, shook his head, then looked back as he accepted that Jagati often saw more than even she thought she saw. "Galileo," he said quietly, remembering. "He was quite . . . persuasive."

"I bet he was," she said, then slapped him on the shoulder and started for the door. "I guess we should get the pre-flight going."

"Of course," Eitan said, but as he had spent many years avoiding thinking about Galileo Kane, it took him a moment to catch up and follow her out of the galley.

They'd just reached the forward passage when they heard Rory's distressed shout. "Oy! Who's to do all these dishes, then?"

CHAPTER 6

AN HOUR AFTER THE *ERRANT* SET DOWN IN NIKE, RORY tracked Eitan down. He started with the crew quarters on the third deck, then headed for the public rooms on the fourth. He checked the forward lounge and galley before striking comb in the training room, which was snugged handily between the galley and the medbay.

On entering the room, Rory inhaled the expected odors of leather, metal, and sweat along with the unexpected ghost of last night's burned kale, which tended to permeate everything.

As Eitan was in the middle of some complicated sword form, Rory leaned against the door and watched as the other man moved through the kata with a slow, steady fluidity . . . until he flung himself into a spinning-kicking-slashing affair, leaving Rory with the unfortunate sense of invisible body parts flying across the mat.

Swallowing the bile accompanying the idea, Rory watched as Eitan came to a standstill, swinging the blade in salute to whichever absent master had taught him.

He'd doffed his shirt for the exercise, so was bare to the waist and gleaming with sweat, causing Rory to swallow again.

"Did you require something?" Eitan asked, his expression distant, as if still engaged with his imaginary enemies.

"As a matter of fact, no," Rory replied, waiting while Eitan returned his blade to the weapon's rack, exchanging it for a towel. "But I did come up with something you might like." He held up what looked to be a few bits of leather, metal, and buckles. "I got to tinkering between goes at the lockbox."

Eitan's distant expression took another few steps back. "Rory . . ."

Rory held up his free hand to stave off judgment. "It's not what you'd be expecting," he said and, since the sword was safely in its rack, stepped into the room and held the device up for Eitan to see.

Eitan stared, silent a moment. "Is that . . ."

"A dagger you see before you?"

Eitan looked up.

"Sorry, hard to resist that one."

"Perhaps you should have," Eitan said, but his attention was clearly caught. "How does it work?"

"Like this." Rory held the contraption flat to the inside of his own left arm, bare beneath the rolled-up shirt sleeves. "It stays snug under your sleeve," he explained, fastening the buckles, "and if all goes well, no one will ever know you're carrying."

"The sheath is backwards," Eitan pointed out. "I would be unable to draw the blade."

"A little patience, if you don't mind." Rory pulled the last tongue through the last buckle. "Now, supposing you're in a tussle, aye? And you've need of a secondary weapon . . ."

"Have I lost my primary weapon?" Eitan asked, continuing to towel himself off.

"What?" Rory looked up. "I don't know. Why?"

"Just curious."

Rory rolled his eyes. "Just give this a watch, will you?"

"Carry on," Eitan said with the barest hint of a smile.

"Right, so, there you are," Rory assumed his version of a fighting stance. "Enemies from all sides and you with naught left to fight with."

"Naught beyond my arms, my legs, my elbows, my head, my—"

"*My* turn," Rory cut in. "Any road, you're surrounded, outnumbered, outgunned . . . the usual," he said with a quirk of a grin. "But just as the drones think they'll take you down easy, you give your left arm a tap, thusly, and—" Rory suited action to word, and the blade he'd set in a spring-loaded sheath shot out past his open palm. "Presto," he said with a flourish that almost resulted in him slicing his own palm open.

Eitan remained where he was, towel seemingly forgotten in his hand, staring.

Rory straightened and held out his arm. "Of course, on you there's no hand to get in the way. And, ah, unlike a prosthetic which is always there, you've only to press this—" he set his right palm against a raised plate at the top of the sheath, and the dagger retracted. "Neat as you please."

Still, Eitan remained silent.

Rory let out a soft huff as his hopes of finally constructing a device that would truly suit his friend deflated. "Well, t'was only a thought," he said, beginning to unbuckle the brace. "If you've no use for it—"

"*Use?*" Eitan shook his head. "Rory . . ." he flipped the towel over his shoulder and approached the mechanic to grip him by the arm. "This?" he looked down at the spring-loaded blade. "*This*, I like."

Some hours later, when the suns were dipping to the west, Jagati and Eitan stood at the base of the gangplank watching Rory cross the airfield carrying a worn canvas pack.

Jagati had to admit she found Rory's performance convincing. His body language played as furtive enough to appear suspicious without tipping into pantomime. In fact, he was so committed to the act she almost hoped they were being watched.

Then, as Rory passed into the next docking ring, sunslight sparking off the pack's buckles, Eitan stepped forward to follow the mechanic.

Which was when Jagati discovered Eitan hadn't been kidding about the off switch, because it didn't matter how hard she tried —and she tried—her attention slid away from Eitan the way a magnet's north pole slid off the field created by another magnet's north pole.

Even though she *knew* he was right there in front of her, the best she could manage was a glimpse of the dark brown coat or a flash of the silver hoop in his ear before her attention was pushed away toward the heavy freighter one slip over, or up to a flock of pelicans swooping overhead, or back down to that fraying lace in her boot she kept meaning to replace.

The entire experience left her unbalanced and edgy, and more than happy to return to the *Errant*.

Once inside, she climbed up to the bridge where she found John seated in the co-pilot's seat, wearing the radio headset while he rubbed the knuckle of his right thumb over his brow, as he did when tense or irritated. Or both. "Yes," he said into the mic, "understood."

Jagati gave him a questioning look, and he dropped the knuckling hand as he mouthed *Sameen* at her before continuing, "I'll be there by twenty-three thirty hours—" He paused, as if interrupted. "Ah, forgive me," his gaze dropped to the deck, then rose to the bridge's sloped ceiling. "that would be half-nine."

Jagati's lips curled in a sneer. Apparently Sameen wasn't familiar with the military's twenty-eight hour clock.

While John's expression grew more pained, her sneer thinned to a frown as her brain flashed back to the memory of John in a towel.

Nope. Not going there.

Cutting the image off at its knees, she crossed to the starboard locker to pull out the reason she'd come to the bridge in the first place—her long-range crysto-plas repeater rifle. It was the favored weapon of the Air Corps jump teams, and the one with which she was most familiar.

"Of course," John was saying, still engaged in the radio conversation, then paused for whatever Sameen had to say next. "Ah." He glanced up to where Jagati had propped herself against the nav table to check the rifle's sights. "Yes, well . . . I, ah, I look forward to it. Yes. Thank you. Yes. Yes . . . *goodbye.*"

On that last, he quickly pulled off the headset and dropped it into its bulkhead cradle.

"She has her own radio set?" Jagati asked.

"Rich people," he said, though he was still staring at the headset as if afraid it would bite.

Interesting, she thought. "So, what's the plan?" She flicked the fire control from single bolt to burst and back, taking a visceral pleasure in the heavy *chink* of the metal as it shifted beneath her fingers.

"Sameen gave me an address." He held up a torn-off triangle of graphing paper bearing the imprint of his handwriting which, like everything else about the man, was immaculate. "A private residence on Donne Street. She specified I should come alone," he added, crossing to the weapons locker. He pocketed the address, then selected his favored shooter, sliding it into the under-arm holster he wore under his jacket.

"Not to worry. I can cover you from a distance," Jagati said as she double-checked the rifle's battery charge. "Unless she tries to get you naked. That happens, you're on your own."

"I hardly think she'd be interested in—it's more likely she

doesn't want to risk any interference in the retrieval of her property."

"Who says she can't multitask?" Satisfied with the rifle's readiness, Jagati hefted the gun and looked up to see John exiting the bridge, hands raised in surrender as he muttered something unintelligible.

"What?" she called after him. "Was it something I said?"

Inside the airfield tram, Rory parked on one of the inward facing benches and opened the newspaper he'd purchased from the stand near the docking office.

He wasn't so much interested in the news as he was in keeping a barrier between himself and the man who'd tailed him from the airfield gate—a burly fellow with a robust ginger beard and an affable expression.

In normal times, Rory doubted he'd have given the man a second thought, but these weren't normal times, thanks to the device-which-must-not-be-named. So Rory did give the man a second thought, and then a third when, as Rory paused at the gate's kiosk to purchase the *Suns Times*, the man dropped down to tie his shoe.

A move which would have proven more convincing had he not been wearing laceless boots.

A hum and a bump caused Rory to glance up from an advert for Tenjin Research to see the tram had begun its journey, and it took all his will to *not* look at the bearded fellow, who was seated at the rear of the trolley.

He also had to keep himself from seeking Eitan, whom he knew to be following, even though he couldn't see him, per se.

At one point, he felt sure he'd spied the hem of Eitan's coat, but in retrospect, it could as easily have been a leaf skittering over the tarmac.

Rory huffed and turned the page of the newspaper, more determined than ever to learn just what Eitan meant by an off switch.

For now, however, he just hoped an armed and dangerous Eitan really was here, following the man who was following him.

At that thought he smiled because, even without knowing all the hows and wherefores, Eitan's trick would make a fine story to tell Jinna once this charade played out.

For now, he gave the paper a rattle and turned his attention to the doings in Nike.

Though in retrospect, Rory wondered if he shouldn't have picked up one of the dreadfuls at the airfield kiosk instead, given he was living out the plot of one, this very minute.

Not long after Rory's tram departed, John locked down the *Errant*, then he and Jagati made their own way to the airfield gates.

A light rain had begun to fall, and John took a lungful of moist air as he considered the airfield which, in the wet and fading light, put him in mind of an underwater seascape, the airships drifting at anchor transforming into a host of great underwater beasts tethered to the ocean's floor.

He said as much to Jagati, who scowled, then pointed out that underwater beasts wouldn't be tethered anywhere.

"Unless you believe all those drunken sailors and their mer-stories," she added, hitching her waterproof duffle up on her shoulder. "In which case, a'ight, maybe a mer would have the stones to tame an ichthyosaurus or a whale or—except, wait, would mers have stones? And if they did, where . . ."

"Never mind," John said.

"But now you've raised the philosophical question, I want to know."

He glanced sideways. "The philosophical question of the existence of submarine humanoids or that said submarine humanoids have stones?"

"Both."

It was, of course, a ludicrous conversation, but one that allowed both to appear unconcerned by the other bodies headed toward the airfield's tram station, any of whom might be after the calculator.

If any of them were, John hoped they believed the calculator was inside the satchel slung crossways over his jacket—the same he'd taken out of Dyar's Canyon—and not inside the *Errant*.

"I still don't like leaving the 'ship unguarded," Jagati said under her breath, as if she'd been reading his mind.

"No help for it." He lengthened his stride as he spied an approaching tram.

"Only because you insisted on Rory playing decoy," she pointed out, keeping up.

"Better a decoy in the city than a sitting duck aboard the *Errant*," John pointed out, then stopped because she had stopped too. "What?" he asked while, around them, cargo handlers and airship crew and newly arrived travelers continued on toward the tram.

"You wanted him safe," she said, her tone almost accusing.

"Of course I did. I have found, over the years, it's best to keep my crew alive. Which is also why Eitan is following him," he added with a little hurry up gesture, which she ignored.

"Did you really think we needed a decoy?" she asked. "Or were you just trying to keep Rory out of the crossfire?"

"Which answer will get us on that tram the fastest?"

She glared.

He gave up. "They're both true," he said. "Dyar's Canyon proved two aren't enough to keep the 'ship secure, even if one of them is Eitan. But," he added, "I also believe what I said about

Tariq not giving up, which means a decoy is valuable. So . . ." he gestured toward the airfield gate. "Can we go now?"

In answer, she shook her head, sending a spray of fine drops out in an echo of the rain, then turned to jog toward the waiting tram, leaving John to follow.

CHAPTER 7

To Jagati's disgust, the tram was already full by the time they boarded, so she and John were stuck standing next to each other for the rattling trip into Nike proper.

She didn't mind the standing so much as the poking elbows, misplaced boots, and general odor of wet wool that drifted through the tram car.

Plus there were two Corps enlisteds on liberty who kept shoving her into John as they debated the most likely spots in the city for a gal to enjoy herself.

The taller of the two had made eyes at John almost as soon as he boarded and taken his good-humored shake of the head with an equally good-humored shrug of regret.

Jagati wondered if John would have been more open to the enlisted if they weren't dealing with the wasp nest Sameen had dropped them in.

Then she wondered why she was wondering about it.

Then she wondered why her spine contracted every time she thought of Sameen.

"Something on your mind?" John asked.

"Just wondering if it ever doesn't rain in this city," she lied.

"There was one day, in April of '46 if I recall correctly," he said. "Not only did it not rain, the suns remained visible for the entire day."

Her gaze slid over to see him staring out over the sea of heads. "I know you think you're funny, but you're not."

"I know," he said, turning to face her. "I also know it's not the weather you were thinking about."

Her face warmed. "It's not?"

Behind her, the lusty sergeant's partner made a suggestive comment, and both women laughed. Jagati ignored them. "And what would I be thinking about, since I am so transparent?"

"Charitably?" He shrugged, no small feat in their current, contained circumstances. "You're thinking I put all of us in the line of fire for the sake of money."

"Not quite," she said, angling to face him. "I know it's not the money, or at least not the money for money's sake. But you did it without telling me, which back in the day, you'd never have done. Even when you were in command of the *Kodiak*, you never kept secrets from me."

At which point she caught the edge of something in his eyes before he looked away.

"What?" she asked.

"Nothing."

She had to work to not clench her teeth. "Stop saying nothing when you obviously mean *something*."

"Fine." He turned to meet her expectant gaze. "Suffice it to say that everyone has secrets."

She looked away but couldn't stop herself from asking, "What kind of secrets?"

"If I told you, they wouldn't be secrets."

"Listen, Pitte—"

"It was nothing you'd find interesting."

"Lipton Street!" the conductor called as the tram jerked to a stop, effectively putting an end to the discussion.

The doors opened with a blast of damp, and a horde of passengers, including the two enlisteds, poured out onto Lipton Street.

Taking a deep breath of the rain-drenched air, Jagati dropped into a now-empty seat and slumped back. She set the duffle at her feet and let her eyes half-close, as if she had zero interest in the world around her.

A half second later, John sat down next to her. "Anything?" he murmured.

"Shiny bear-dog, 13 o'clock," she replied under cover of a yawn, referring to a man with gleaming gold-brown skin and a slick black coat. "Boarded right before us, well dressed but the lump under the arm says he's got a shoulder rig too. You?"

"Russet coat, seven hundred." He coughed, the covering hand indicating the tall, slender woman in a flowing coat, whose close-shaved skull set off striking ebony features and a set of cheek-bones that could cut allusteel. "Followed us on."

"Weapons?"

"Left sleeve; best guess a knife or a shock stick."

She grunted acknowledgement and hoped the presence of two potential shadow traders on their tram meant Rory was safe.

"So, where are you meeting this Sameen of yours?" she asked, pitching her voice loud enough that both Cheekbones and Shiny could hear.

Was it her imagination, or did Cheekbones stand up straighter at hearing the name? She let her gaze drift over to Shiny and saw his eyes come to focus on Cheekbones, at which point they narrowed, as if not pleased with what they saw.

"She's not *my* Sameen," John said in response. "*I feel like a dodo stuck between a dire wolf and a draco,*" he added under his breath.

Jagati didn't disagree. "How are we going to ditch two of them?"

He looked out through the window, noting their location.

"Coming up on Coleridge," he said. "I think we need to do the thing."

Her hiss ruffled his hair as he mentioned the contingency plan they'd cooked up in case they were followed. "I don't wanna do the thing."

"Coleridge Avenue," the conductor called.

"Too late," John replied as the tram heaved to a halt.

A glance at Shiny told Jagati he was preparing to move.

"Wait for it," John murmured.

"Waiting," she mumbled back while Cheekbones settled back on her heels in the loose-limbed preparedness Jagati had often seen Eitan display just prior to ruining his opponent's day.

Around them, a trio of passengers debarked, then a half dozen young people boarded.

"All aboard for Bard Street and the Shakespeare Circus," the conductor called.

"*Now*," John hissed, and Jagati followed him as he surged off the bench and swung for the exit.

Since he was closest, John blocked the door of the tram open while Jagati jumped past a flummoxed young woman to hit the pavement running.

"Terribly sorry," she heard John apologizing to the woman before jumping out after Jagati to land on the wet pavers with a splash.

She turned and caught his elbow as he stumbled, and they both took off running.

From behind, she heard a series of curses and the splashing thud of boots on pavers.

She didn't look back to see who'd followed them off the tram. "We could head into the park," she said, spying the wildlife center to their right.

John shook his head. "Too isolated."

"Exactly. No collateral to damage."

He glanced her way. "I don't want any shooting."

"Then why did you have me bring the rifle?"

"In case there's no other choice. For now, we stick with the plan and try to lose them." He elbow-bumped her to the left, toward a building that looked like someone had planted a garden of minarets atop a warehouse.

Under the minarets, crystal-powered chaser lights spelled out Xanadu in a rainbow of colors.

Below this display stood a double-doored entrance, through which Nikeans of all ages streamed.

"Next time," she said as they joined the relative safety of the queue, "we go for the shooting option."

"Next time you can shoot me first," he replied. "It would be less painful than all the arguing."

"Tempest Park!"

At the conductor's announcement, Rory folded the paper he'd been pretending to read and stood, rocking with the rest of the passengers as the tram came to a stop.

As the door opened, he heard the patter of rain on stone and huffed a sigh. "Lovely," he muttered and folded the paper into the pack before slinging it over his shoulder.

Once on the walk, he shoved both hands into his jacket pockets and headed down Tempest Park Avenue, in the direction of a line of shops.

As he walked, the smattering of rain increased to a downpour, leading to a host of umbrellas popping open.

Having no umbrella of his own, Rory eased closer to the clustered buildings, less in hope of staying dry than avoiding being smashed by the competing umbrella canopies.

As he made his way along the avenue, the street lamps flickered to life, their reflections in the wet pavement shining like opals.

And where did that bit of fancy come from?

Rory shook his head and wove his way down the street, paying no more heed to the shop displays than he did the poetically glistening cobbles.

Only once did he stop, pausing in front of the tea stall for several moments, as if considering a cuppa in the dry.

In fact, he only wanted to confirm he was still being followed and, sure enough, there was the cargo worker, russet beard dripping, seemingly engrossed in a crate of pomegranates, four shops back.

There was no overt sign of Eitan, but if he tried to view the street only from the corner of his eye, Rory could see the occasional rushing pedestrian swerving to the right or umbrella twisting left of their path, as if avoiding an Eitan-sized puddle.

It was not a reassuring view.

It became less reassuring when the red-bearded man looked up and suddenly he and Rory were staring at one another through the curtain of rain.

"Ha," Rory's breath plumed out in a rush of nerves.

Redbeard's own mouth twitched in a rueful grin just before Rory spun on his heel and sped down the street, hitching the pack higher on his shoulder as he wound through the press of foot traffic, eventually ducking into an alley to his right.

. . . and skidded to a halt about halfway down as he discovered this wasn't the alley he'd wanted, because the alley he'd wanted opened onto Marlowe Street.

This alley, which was more a narrow crevice between two buildings, led to a dead end.

Worse, there wasn't a single door to be seen.

"How do they take out the rubbish?" he wondered aloud, just before the telltale splash of large boots and the spark-to-thrum sound of a shooter powering up told him the gig was up.

With a sigh and a mental shrug, Rory turned to find Redbeard approaching, shooter in hand. "Can I help you, then?" he asked.

"Pretty sure you can," the man said, stopping short of the bright patch of light in which Rory had come to a halt. "First let's see your hands. Slowly," he added, gesturing with his shooter. "We don't want any unfortunate surprises, do we?"

"That we do not," Rory agreed, removing his hands carefully from his jacket pockets and spreading the fingers wide to show them empty. "How's that?"

"Perfect," the ginger replied, all amiability. "Now, I'll thank you to hand me that pack you're carrying, eh?"

"Ah, that might be a wee bit of a problem," Rory said.

"It'll be a much bigger problem if you don't give it over."

"That . . . is a very good point," Rory decided, shrugging so the pack's strap dropped from his shoulder to his hand, but even as he prepared to throw it, he spied something—someone—else in the shadows behind the ginger.

"Hand it over, kid," Redbeard wiggled his fingers and twitched the shooter suggestively. "You've been doing great, so far. Don't smog it up now."

"Believe me, the last thing I want to do is make any trouble," Rory said, then pointed at the figure behind the would-be robber. "But he might."

"Aww, lad." Redbeard shook his head. "You don't really think I'm gonna fall for the 'there's someone behind you' trick? I may be from Moosehead but even I . . ."

Rory jumped at the *thunk*, then again as Redbeard slumped to the pavers. "Well, that was—" he began, then blinked as the hooded figure came close enough for Rory to realize it was not, in fact, Eitan who had come to his aid. "Ah." He took in the shooter which had just impacted Redbeard's skull and was now aimed at himself.

The hooded person reached out his other hand and wiggled his fingers, reminding Rory that, despite the sudden change in cast, this was still a robbery.

"Right," he said and, mindful of the shooter, tossed the pack over.

The hood's waiting hand snatched it out of the air by one strap and, in the same motion, slung it over his shoulder.

Package delivered, Rory waited for the hooded one to make his exit, but instead, after the slightest of pauses, he came another step closer, close enough Rory could see the steady glow of the shooter's charge indicator.

Which was when Rory realized that robber 2.0 might not be as amenable to a peaceful resolution as his predecessor.

This, he thought, staring down the weapon's gleaming barrel, *would be a smashing time for Eitan to show up.*

For Eitan, the tram ride had been quiet but educational.

He'd boarded directly after the red-bearded fellow who was obviously following Rory, then followed him to the back of the tram.

Thanks to the off switch Jagati had joked about, he'd moved through the other passengers without difficulty, as wherever he went, their eyes immediately turned away.

Since the tram was full, Eitan took a risk by settling next to Rory's shadow, close enough their wrists touched and, during that brief connection, Eitan sensed the man's name was Jacques, that he worked for Tariq, and that he wished he were still aboard the *Al-Djinn* with a glass of Campbell's Best.

Though tempted to try for a deeper read, Eitan knew he was already in an ethically gray area, so he broke the tentative contact and removed himself to a space near the rear door until they reached Tempest Park, where first Rory and then Jacques debarked.

Eitan followed Jacques off the tram, then took shelter in a

mass of wet pedestrians, all the while keeping a firm grasp on the "off switch."

He only wished maintaining the veil *was* as simple as flipping a switch.

Unfortunately, the trick of hiding in plain sight required not only the act of diverting attention from oneself, but the ability to monitor one's own movements through space at the same time.

All of this he'd learned long ago, from the same lover who'd introduced him to the technochrist movement.

But, like everything else Galileo had shared, the veil carried a price.

In this case, in the form of backlash migraines if the veil was used too often, or for too long.

Eitan hoped he could avoid that cost, today.

Certainly, the weather was challenge enough, as the part of him tracking his physical self noted the rain increasing, along with the number of pedestrians opening umbrellas.

Perhaps he could drop the veil and trust the rain as his cover?

Even as he thought this, Eitan found himself in the path of a woman so laden with parcels under her umbrella he doubted she'd have seen him even without the veil.

Twisting aside to avoid a head-on collision, someone slammed into him from behind, hard enough to make him stumble.

He bit back a curse but, on righting himself, let the curse fly, because as he straightened, the rain-drenched street in Nike melted and reformed into the steaming heat of equatorial Adia.

And while some distant part of Eitan *knew* he still stood on Tempest Park Avenue, icy rain dripping down the back of his coat, the rest of him was stepping onto the thick red dirt of the Domino arena, sweat sheening his skin, the dull roar of the Adian cheers echoing overhead and the stench of blood and the perfume of the coliseum's flowering vines filling his senses.

The whirlpool drag of memory was so complete, Eitan didn't

even feel the hard crack of his knees on the walk, or the sharp cries of fear as he, no longer hidden, dropped to the ground.

CHAPTER 8

John stepped up to Xanadu's ticket counter, dug a ten-star bill from his pocket, and tried not to wince over even this small expense.

"Skate size, love?" the attendant asked, taking the cash.

"I am *not* putting on skates," Jagati hissed over his shoulder.

"That would be a 50 and a 40, respectively," he said with a polite smile.

"What did I just say?" Jagati poked him in the shoulder.

"That'll be five starbucks." The woman pulled two pairs of the wheeled allusteel skates from under the counter and a five-star from the till. She set the skates down and placed the five-star in his hand, explaining, "These are the latest thing, just pop 'em over your shoes and Ben's your uncle."

"Thank—" John began.

"As far as I'm concerned, you can take those death shoes and roll them right up your . . . hey!" Jagati protested as John grabbed her arm and both pairs of skates, then propelled her inside the flashing, dancing lights of Xanadu.

Underfoot, the floorboards vibrated with the music pumping from an organ the size of the *Errant's* gondola, a deep counterpoint to the clangs, crashes, and chimes reverberating from the game area to the right of the rink.

It was loud enough that John could barely hear Jagati's cursing.

At last, they reached the refreshment area, where the noise softened and the air took on the scents of cider, chai, popcorn, and wasabi nuts, reminding John they hadn't bothered with dinner before leaving the 'ship.

Finally, he stopped at the entrance to the rink.

"Here we are," he said.

"What?" she shouted, hitching her duffle higher on her shoulder.

"I said, here we are!" he shouted back, holding up the skates and jerking his chin over the wall to where it seemed the entire population of Nike was swarming around the waxed-bamboo rink.

"No," she said, her expression going flat. "You can't make me."

John leaned close enough to tell her, without shouting, "There's an exit behind the organ on the far side of the rink."

She angled her head to speak into his ear, and her breath tickled his skin. "Then we can walk across the rink."

"It's against the rules to be on the rink without skates," he replied, angling so his breath sent some stray curls fluttering.

Their eyes met, held, then she jerked her head back. "I can't believe you're worried about the rules at a time like this."

John caught sight of movement from the entrance. "At the moment I'm more interested in being somewhere they can't go."

Jagati turned to look over her shoulder, and he saw the moment she clocked their two pursuers from the tram.

Both the tall woman and the well-dressed man had arrived, the woman circling the gaming wall near the entrance, the man standing at the foyer door, scanning the tables.

They kept checking each other's progress, confirming John's

suspicion they weren't working together. Still, John doubted the pair's mutual suspicion would keep them from spotting him and Jagati for much longer. "We need to move," he said, holding the skates out to Jagati, which she finally accepted.

"I hate you," she said.

"Noted," John replied, then held her duffle while she crouched to snap the skates over her boots, then he let her lean on him while he put his own skates on. Straightening, he adjusted his satchel and looked at her. "Ready?"

"Smog no," she replied, wobbling as she slung her duffle over her shoulder. "But let's get this over with before I decide it's easier to shoot somebody."

He nodded and, keeping careful hold of her elbow, led her through one of several open sections in the wall and onto the rink. "You're doing great," he assured, holding her upright as her legs tried to slide in opposite directions.

"You are a lousy liar," she replied before snarling, "Why are you good at this?"

"My former landladies enjoyed the occasional evening at the rink," he explained, pulling her in close before she did a header over another inexperienced skater as he flailed past.

She almost stopped at that. "Your landladies were over a hundred years old," she pointed out.

"Only Sadie, and she wasn't yet a hundred when Xanadu opened," he said just as her feet got out from under her and she dropped hard on her behind.

"I hate this," she said again as John spun around in front of her. "*Hate.*"

"I know." He reached down hauled her up so they stood, face to face, surrounded by skimming, rolling, swooping Nikeans.

Though he'd have expected her to let go, she kept hold of his hands, so they stood entirely still in the flurry of motion, in their own little pocket of privacy.

It was, he decided, a rather pleasant moment.

Then Jagati's face twisted. "We've been spotted."

So much for the moment.

———

"Look at that, will ya'?" A rough voice sliced through Eitan's nightmare. "That's a spike overdose if ever I saw one."

Eitan winced at the harsh accent, which landed hard enough to shake the sweating illusion of Adia.

"Then you ain't seen a spike overdose," another voice drawled. "Look at them eyes, black as a no-moon's night, they is. That there's a bad milk'n'honey trip."

Shuddering, Eitan moved his hand, gratified to feel the cold wet paver, though he still felt the heat of Domino, the grit of the sand beneath his feet, the weight of the chain on his left wrist—

His heart stuttered, and he shook his head violently as the weight of that chain, the pulse throbbing in that wrist, tried to pull him back to the arena.

"Will ye look at the poor lad, Sadie." Another voice, this one cracked with age, pattered into the mix. "Time was them's as were usin' kept to Wolstonecroft and no bother to anyone."

"I see's 'im, Ronette," an equally aged voice replied. "Pity, though. He'd be right handsome if he weren't a fumer."

"Excuse me." Yet another voice—this one young, female . . . and familiar—overtook the murmuring disapproval. "Coming through, thank you, excuse me . . ."

"Have a care, miss," the milk and honey proponent warned. "This 'ere fella could be dangerous."

"I'll be fine," the familiar voice promised, and then Eitan felt the brush of a hand on his face.

"Eitan." The voice spoke his name softly. "Can you hear me? It's Rory's friend, Jinna."

"I—"

"Mebbe we should call the coppers . . ."

"Or a cog."

"Or the keepers."

"Belay that," the young woman snapped, and it was the martial authority of her voice that helped Eitan shake off the remains of the nightmare.

"*Whoa!* Easy! Easy soldier!" The woman shuffled back, her umbrella swaying as Eitan shoved himself straight up from his knees.

His gaze shot from two wizened aunties to the disapproving glare of a man in an apron to the small woman with long red hair, who he did, indeed, recognize. "Jinna," he greeted, then, "Little Mother." He glanced down, then up. "I'm sorry to have frightened you."

Jinna grinned. "Not so frightened," she said, waving to disperse the hovering witnesses, who went muttering on their way. "And not so little anymore, either." Then her gray eyes sobered. "What happened to you?"

"I don't know." He paused, closed his eyes, tried to remember. "I was on the tram," he murmured, his memory pulling up images of the ride, and Rory, who was carrying a pack because . . . because . . .

"Decoy," Eitan murmured.

"I'm sorry, what?" Jinna asked.

He opened his eyes again to see Jinna's red hair, triggering the image of a man with a red beard.

"Jacques," he said, turning to look down the street, but there was no sign of the bearded man.

"Who?"

He looked at Jinna. "A shadow trader. He was following Rory."

"Wait. Rory's here?" She glanced around. "And being followed? Where is he?"

"I don't know. I need to get to—" He cursed and, waving his left arm in a frustrated gesture, took off down the street at a run.

Jagati gritted her teeth, trying to stay upright on the stupid skates while John guided her over the stupid rink.

They'd rounded about a third of the oval, and she figured if they stayed with the flow of traffic, they might make the exit without her falling again.

A glance over her shoulder—which almost led to a face plant on her part—revealed that their male shadow, Shiny, was watching them from the partition.

"Keep moving," John prompted. "There's nothing they can do in this crowd."

That seemed optimistic to Jagati, and she started to tell him so but he shoved her to the left, abandoning her while he sped forward. "Hey!" she yelled, arms flying out and feet swerving in opposite directions. "You are *dead* to me!"

"I'll be right back," he called, leaving her free-rolling into the nearest wall which, thankfully, had a bar affixed to it, presumably for beginner skaters to hold onto. Once anchored, she spun around to see John weaving through the other skaters, picking up speed as he neared Shiny, who was now standing *on* the rink—without skates, Jagati noticed.

Then John rounded the narrow end of the oval, and she could see when Shiny's eyes met John's.

All around, the other skaters slowed or quickened, angled away or around, making whatever adjustments were necessary to remain upright and in motion, unaware any danger existed beyond the common risk of a bruised behind.

Which meant no one but Jagati saw Shiny's gloved hand dive under his black, rain-specked jacket, as if reaching for a weapon.

It also meant that when John slammed shoulder first into Shiny, sending him to the floor with a skull-cracking *thunk*, it registered as nothing more than another obstacle to be avoided.

She was just about to cheer when she felt the distinct chill of metal against the base of her skull, telling her that: one, Cheekbones had snuck up on her while she'd been watching John take out Shiny; and two, Cheekbones had a shock stick.

"It's not active," a deep voice told her. "Yet."

By then, John was slowing to a stop in their quiet little sector of the rink.

"You're not wearing skates," he greeted Cheekbones.

"Guess she didn't care about rules," Jagati quipped.

Rory, standing in a blind alley with a live shooter pointed at his heart, wondered where this second thief had come from.

Then he wondered how things had gone so swarm, so fast.

Lastly, he wondered what had happened to Ei—

"You already have what you want," Eitan's voice sliced through the patter of rain. "Take it and be glad of your life."

"Yes!" Rory raised his fist in victory but just as quickly dropped it because the hooded man now stood behind him, one arm wrapped around his throat and the shooter pointed at his head.

Which was bad, and also confusing, because Rory hadn't seen the man move, and he'd been staring straight at him. *How could I have missed that?*

Someday, perhaps, I shall explain . . .

The voice—which was not a voice at all—slid through Rory's thoughts, and suddenly he understood.

This thief was a sensitive.

And you are more perceptive than you look.

"Oy, then . . ." Rory bristled, but the shooter's muzzle pressed into his temple and his protest died on a tongue gone dry as Dyar's Canyon, rain notwithstanding.

Eitan, however, continued his approach, even now stepping past the unconscious Redbeard.

"You'll stop where you are," thief number two warned in a rich voice, heavy with a Guinness accent.

Eitan, hearing that voice, actually stumbled to a halt, which caused Rory's jaw to drop because Eitan was not the stumbling sort.

"Better," the thief said. "Now, whatever weapon you are carrying, drop it."

With visible care, Eitan withdrew a shock stick from under his coat and dropped it to the pavers with a clattering splash. He held out his empty right hand and his left arm before saying, "You do not want to hurt him."

"I wouldn't be so certain of that," the thief said before adding, "It's good to see you, Eitan."

"Wait," Rory heard himself say. "You know this wasp?"

"Leo," Eitan said to the thief, which pretty much answered Rory's question. "You don't have to do this."

"Actually, I do," the thief—or Leo, rather, scoffed as he dragged Rory forward and past Eitan, angling to keep Rory between the pair as he went.

"Please," Eitan said, also turning to follow Leo's progress. "Let him go."

"I might have," Leo said. "But now, thanks to you, he knows my name."

"So do I," Eitan pointed out.

"And so do I," a new and distressingly familiar voice called from behind Rory.

"Smogging toxic Earth," Rory muttered.

"I know a few other things, too," Jinna continued. "I know you're threatening someone who matters to me, and I know how to drop a body with a shooter from fifteen meters—and you are *way* closer than fifteen meters."

"Syl?" Leo asked, his voice suddenly much less assured.

"What?" Jinna asked back.

"Who?" Rory tried to look at the man holding the gun.

"Let. Him. Go," Eitan said again, causing both Rory and Leo to tense.

"What he said," Jinna added.

"If you insist, little sister," Leo said, then shoved Rory straight at Eitan, who dodged.

Jinna cursed while Rory stumbled upright and spun in time to see Eitan shoving Leo into the alley wall, his right arm trapped between their two bodies, both men struggling for control of Leo's gun.

Jinna started forward, Redbeard's shooter in one hand and umbrella in the other.

"Don't!" Rory, Eitan and—surprisingly—Leo shouted in a three-pronged warning that startled the pregnant woman to a halt.

Just in time too, as Leo's shooter fired a single burst of plasma that sizzled in the rain before striking the pavers.

The smoking hole at Jinna's feet set Rory's heart racing again and had him sending her a flapping *back-off* wave as he ran to assist Eitan.

A useless move, for at the same time Eitan's left arm twitched and Rory heard the *snicking* release of the spring-blade he'd given his crew mate only a few hours past.

"Stop," Eitan ordered softly, pressing the dagger into Leo's side. A breath of silence followed, and then . . .

"Consider me stopped," Leo said, letting his right hand go lax, allowing the contested gun to clatter to the pavement.

Sometime during the struggle, his hood had fallen away, revealing a marble-pale face and dark eyes beneath a mass of curling black hair.

"Wow," Jinna said, and Rory had to agree as, seen together, Eitan and Leo looked less like combatants and more like matinee idols in the middle of a scene.

A very intimate scene, judging by Leo's next words.

"It has been a long time, *delbar-am*."

"Oh," Rory said, and Jinna's breath audibly hitched as the term for one's dearest beloved fell between the two men.

"A long time indeed," Eitan responded in a voice barely audible above the falling rain, "for you to become a killer."

"This, from the man who ran away to war?" Then Leo's lips turned up and his eyes dipped. "Is that a dagger in my side, or are you just happy to see me?"

"Seriously?" someone who was neither Rory nor Jinna nor Eitan said aloud.

Everyone, including Leo, turned to where Redbeard, the original thief, was pushing himself up from the alley floor. "Piece of honeycomb, she says. Won't be a bit of trouble, she says," he grumbled, grabbing a bit of nearby wall and hauling himself to standing. "Like taking a pack from a skinny mechanic. No offense meant," he added, glancing Rory's way before he looked at Jinna. "I don't suppose you'd care to hand me back that there shooter?"

"Sure. And would you like a side of hummus with that?" she asked sweetly.

"So that'd be a no."

"That'd be a no, yes." She sighed. "No."

Rory almost smiled, but there were still Eitan and—

"*Leo,*" Eitan breathed the name. "What on toxic Earth have you gotten yourself into?"

"I would love to explain, really," Leo said, "but—"

I am afraid there is no time.

Rory blinked as Leo's spoken voice tripped into the hollow internal speech from earlier, followed by a soft sigh which was, in turn, followed by a rough curse, and lastly by Leo murmuring, "Brave little sister." Then he shook his head and found himself staring at Eitan as he slammed his palm flat against a wall now decidedly absent of Leo.

A frantic survey of the alley showed Jinna, umbrella, gun and all, looking in confusion at the red-bearded thief, now flat on his ass in a puddle.

"Bloody smogging wasps in the hive!" Rory cursed, slapping his thigh and kicking at a puddle. "How does he *do* that?"

CHAPTER 9

"You will give me the satchel," the woman said to John.

"No he won't," Jagati muttered as the organ's music, which had been playing incessantly, went silent.

"She's right," John agreed, "I won't." He eased closer as, around them, the skaters began to slow. "And beyond that, I can promise you won't be committing any murders here."

The woman's eyes narrowed. "You are so confident in my restraint?"

"No." He shook his head. "I'm just watching the clock."

At which moment the piercing screech of Xanadu's loud-speaker filled the air.

The woman holding Jagati jerked in a whole-body wince and Jagati, as John had hoped, dropped straight down, removing herself from the threat of the shock stick, and allowing him to pull her to safety.

"Honored guests of all ages," a voice blared over the loud-speaker as they made their retreat, "it's that time!"

"Time for what?" Jagati asked, keeping a loose grip on John's left arm as he led her toward the crowd gathering in the center of the rink.

"Everyone come to the center of the rink for the Hokey Pokey!" the announcer continued.

"That," John said, easing them both to a stop. As Jagati wavered, he watched several of Xanadu's employees approaching both their pursuers and escorting them off the rink. "Looks like it does pay to follow the rules."

"Whatever." Jagati shrugged. "So what's a Hokey Pokey?" she asked as the organ player started up again.

"It's a dance . . . of sorts."

"It sounds filthy," she muttered. "Is it filthy?"

"Sadly, no."

<hr>

"I thought you said that dance wasn't filthy?" John heard Jagati ask as they shuffled through the back door into Xanadu's storage shed, comfortable in the knowledge their pursuers were still being lectured by Xanadu's security team.

"What?" he asked, crouching to unbuckle his skates.

Jagati parked on a nearby crate and proceeded to shed her own skates. "You said it wasn't filthy."

"You mean the Hokey Pokey?"

"Please stop calling it that, and yes, the . . . *that*. 'Put your tail feather in and shake it all about'?" She kicked off her right skate.

"I don't know as I'd call that filthy . . ."

"Whatever you call it, we are never—and I repeat, *never*—going to speak of this." He glanced up to meet her glare. "Ever."

"Understood," he said as they unbuckled their second skates. "Can we at least mention the limbo?"

She made an inarticulate noise.

"I guess not." He grabbed both pairs of skates and set them

on top of a box of spare wheels, then gestured toward the shed's outer door. "Shall we?"

"Shall we what? Oh, right, Sameen," Jagati thunked her palm to her forehead as she answered her own question. "How far are we from the meet?"

"One district over and several blocks in." He adjusted the satchel. "It'll be a wet walk," he noted as they stepped out into a rain much heavier than what they'd seen before entering Xanadu.

"At least we're not on wheels," she said, hunkering into her coat.

"It could have been worse," he said, squinting into the downpour.

"How?"

"They could have been ice skates."

"Who would do that?" She asked, waving her arms so that John had to weave to avoid getting thwapped. "Who would put skates on ice?"

"There's rather a lot of ice involved in Moosehead winters," he pointed out. "Maybe the colonists who first settled the north needed a way to pass the time." He glanced her way. "Didn't Dodge City have any skating rinks?"

"The day Dodge City installs a roller—or ice—or whatever the hells kind of rink, is the same day I'll be emigrating to Adia."

His eyebrow arched at the extremity of her distaste. "You know you don't live in Dodge anymore, don't you?"

"It's the principle of the thing."

Eitan was staring at the wet brick before him, still coming to terms with the absence of Leo, when Jinna asked, "Can someone tell me what just happened?"

"*Leo* happened," Rory replied. "Assuming Leo is his real name?"

"Galileo." Eitan let his head rest against the cold brick as he sighed the name. "Galileo Kane. Leo was what I called him in . . . in private."

"Aye, well," Rory continued after a beat, "it seems yon Galileo's a sensitive and likes to muck with a body's mind, stopping smogging time—"

"He did not stop it." Eitan shoved himself off the wall and turned to see Rory, Jinna, and—keeping a respectful distance from Jinna—the red-bearded Jacques.

"Then what did he do?" Jacques asked.

"What he said." Jinna agreed.

Eitan looked at Rory, who shrugged.

"He blanked our perception of time's passing," Eitan explained, ducking to retrieve his fallen shock stick. Leo's gun was, of course, gone with Leo.

There was a beat, as if all three were considering that explanation.

"Could *you* do such a thing?" Rory asked, at last.

"No," Eitan admitted, carefully studying the stick for any signs of damage. "Galileo tried to teach me, as he taught me to use the veil—the off switch," he amended, glancing at Rory. "But I could never learn the way of blanking time."

"Off switch?" Jacques muttered.

"I got this," Rory told Eitan. "The off switch is a sensitive trick of diverting attention away from themselves." He glanced at Eitan. "Right?"

"Close enough."

"So that's why I didn't see you or that Galileo fella tailing me," Jacques growled. "And may I add," he continued, glancing at Eitan, "it's a sad statement of our times when you can't even trust the ex-boyfriend not to make off with your score."

From under the umbrella, Jinna looked at the ebullient Jacques. "Who *are* you?"

"This is—" Eitan began.

"This here is the scunner that tried to rob me before Galileo took over the job," Rory cut in.

"Oh?" Jinna's eyes, and Jacques's gun, were now aimed at the failed thief.

"Jacques O'Malley," the bear of a man introduced himself. "And in my defense, I was only stealing back what his boss," he pointed at Rory, "stole from my boss, first."

To which Rory and Eitan could only share a glance and a shrug.

"I could shoot him," Jinna offered, giving her umbrella a playful twirl.

Jacques, for the first time, looked nervous. "Now then . . ."

"I suggest you leave," Eitan told him.

"Good idea," Jacques agreed but first looked at Jinna. "I'd be grateful to have my gun back," he told her. "She's a favorite of mine, been with me since the Corps."

Jinna studied Jacques for a moment, and as she did, she spun the weapon over her finger, three times forward, three times back. Then she tucked her umbrella between her chin and shoulder, freeing her left hand so that when she sprang the power casing, the crystal cell dropped into her open palm.

She pocketed the cell and tossed the powerless shooter to Jacques.

"Thank you, kindly," he said before turning to Rory. "No hard feelings, friend?"

Rory's eyes narrowed. "I might harbor one or two."

"Yeah?" Jacques tipped his head and scratched his beard. "And whose idea was it to sabotage the *Al-Djinn*?"

"Then again, ill feelings are bad for one's health," Rory replied without missing a beat.

"That's what I thought." Jacques grinned.

"Go," Jinna said.

"Of course. Msrs," he said with an impudent bow to all three, before turning and striding jauntily out of the alley.

Once the shadow trader departed, Eitan slid the shock stick in its holster before tapping the pressure plate on the spring dagger, causing it to slide back into the sheath. "I should go as well."

"Go where?" Rory asked.

"Wait, who is Syl?" Jinna asked, at the same time.

"Back to the *Errant*," Eitan told Rory, then looked at Jinna standing under the umbrella, her red hair slick over her shoulders. "Syl is the name of Galileo's sister," he said. "She might have grown up to look like you," he added, recalling the picture Leo kept with him, always.

"Would have?" Jinna prompted as he trailed off.

"Syl . . . died very young," he explained.

"Oh," Jinna said, her voice soft.

"Right." Rory cleared his throat and, Eitan could tell, tried not to hover over Jinna. "I suppose we should both get back to the 'ship."

"There is no need," Eitan assured, catching the disappointment on Jinna's face. "Our mission was a success, so you may as well enjoy a visit."

"Mission?" Jinna asked, homing in on Rory.

"I'll explain later," Rory promised.

"You can explain now, while you walk me to Kit's. I was on my way to work when I saw Eitan collapse on the sidewalk," she continued.

At which point Eitan decided it was time to activate the off switch again.

"He what?" Rory asked Jinna before turning to glare at Eitan. "And now *he's* done it!"

"Okay," Jinna said, angling to peer around Rory, "that's— odd."

"And then some." Rory continued to glare into the alley, not knowing his eyes were consistently turning away from where Eitan stood, not a meter away. "Where's he got to, then?"

"He's probably headed back to the *Errant*, like he said," Jinna replied, her eyes sliding around Eitan without even a hitch. "Which means you can either follow him, and impose yourself on a man who's just had a very uncomfortable meeting with an old flame, or . . ." She reached up and grabbed Rory's chin, angling his eyes down, toward her. "Or you can come to Kit's with me, and I'll buy you dinner." She dropped her hand and waited, peering up from under her umbrella.

"Oh." Rory cleared his throat, then glanced back down the alley, where Eitan was by now holding his breath. "Well," he huffed, and turned to Jinna. "I could do with a meal and a cuppa. But I'll do the buying, and thanks."

Quietly blessing Jinna's perceptiveness, Eitan waited in the shadows for the young couple to clear the alley. Only after they'd turned the corner did he drop the veil and follow.

And as he headed back to the tram stop, he hoped Jinna and Rory could manage to salvage some joy from the evening.

Who knew, but they might actually take some time to delve into whatever feelings the pair clearly held for one another.

Meanwhile, the idea of a meal was promising, even if he would need to prepare it himself.

Considering what supplies remained on the *Errant*, he raced to board the tram that was waiting at the Tempest Park stop and quietly blessed his luck in finding an open seat near a large party of students, identifiable by their bulging book satchels and vigorous opinions, who occupied the rear of the tram.

He'd only just settled in his seat when the backlash migraine —which he hadn't managed to avoid after all—struck like a white-hot spike between the eyes, causing a nauseating explosion of colors to splash across his vision while a cacophony of voices scraped at his hearing, only occasionally resolving into actual words.

"—all right?"

"Come on, Tiago—"

"—just another drunk."

"—you'll miss your appointment—"

And then, to Eitan's everlasting relief, a wave of darkness rose, and he heard and saw nothing else.

CHAPTER 10

Jagati kept a weather eye on John who was
trying, and failing, to hail a cab as they jogged away from Xanadu;
as far as she could tell, his knee wasn't going to give way again,
but he was definitely favoring it.

Which was why, when they came upon an empty rickshaw
parked a few streets away from Xanadu, she yanked him to a halt.

"No driver," he pointed out, only slightly winded.

"Maybe the driver's just taking a break," she said, even as the
door of a nearby tea shop opened and a woman emerged, wolfing
down a scone and slurping from a flask. On spying the bedraggled
pair, she came to a stop, swallowed a lump of scone, and pointed
to the "Out of Service" sign hanging over her cycle.

"Ah," John said, turning to read the sign. "Well . . ."

"We'll pay double the normal fare," Jagati said, already
climbing into the hooded cab, setting the duffle at her feet.

"Jagati—"

"In that case, where are you headed?" the driver cut in,
popping the last of the scone into her mouth and pocketing the
flask.

Jagati looked at John who shook his head. "18 Donne Street,

4th District," he told the driver, climbing into the hooded cab and landing next to Jagati with a squelch.

"And don't spare the crystal," Jagati added.

"You got it, sister." As if to prove her point, the driver revved her cycle and shot from the curb so quickly Jagati let out a little *whoop* of glee. Then she grabbed the side of the cab as the driver held to the brief, speeding to the center of Nike with little regard for the rain, posted limits, or any other vehicles on the road.

By the time the cab squealed to a halt in the rarified inner 4th District, Jagati was wondering if there had been something stronger than tea in the driver's flask.

Then she looked at 18 Donne Street and forgot all about the trip.

She wasn't sure what she'd been expecting of Sameen's neighborhood, but this demonstration of understated wealth wasn't it.

She climbed out of the rickshaw and stared at the gated residence while John paid the fare.

"So, your Sameen is a risto," she muttered as he joined her on the walk.

"She's not *my* Sameen," he muttered back as their driver sped off.

"Whatever." She hitched her bag higher on her shoulder.

"At least the rain's eased off," he observed.

"And it's a quiet street." She indicated the sparse number of houses which meant, in turn, fewer neighbors potentially spying the two half-drowned aeronauts approaching number 18. "I haven't seen anything like this since I took liberty in Tendo," she added, studying the graceful Fujian lines of Sameen's house.

"It is impressive," John murmured before adding, "But this . . . doesn't seem to fit her."

She looked over to see him studying the house, his eyes troubled. "Why not?"

"I don't know," he admitted. "It just doesn't." Then he

exhaled a foggy breath and started toward the gate. "Let's get this over with."

She followed, spying an outbuilding to the left of the house. She tapped John and pointed to the line of windows in the smaller building, then a giant bow window in the main house. "If you can get Sameen in front of that ginormous window, I can cover you from that shed. Or is it a stable?"

"No clue, and I'll do my best," he said, then reached for her, causing her to jerk back until she realized he was pulling a stray leaf out of her hair.

"Ah," she brushed a hand over the damp coils, "thanks."

"Think nothing of it." He flashed a smile that didn't reach his eyes and angled for the front door, leaving Jagati alone and feeling oddly incomplete, as if something that should have been said, hadn't.

John turned in time to see Jagati disappear into her chosen lookout, then stepped onto the brightly lit porch where he shook off as much water as he could, adjusted his satchel, and finally gave the knocker a brisk double tap.

Waiting for a response, he wondered if the knocker, a bronze djinn with wings of fire, was of Sameen's choosing or happenstance.

Then the door opened, and all his attention shifted to the woman standing before him.

Blond, well-rounded, and disarmingly small—she only reached John's chin in height—Sameen gave an immediate impression of soft femininity, an impression aided by her choice of a loosely sleeved, soft green gown that fell to the ankles of her bare feet.

She smiled up at him, pulling the door open with a soft chiming sound thanks to the collection of thin, hammered bangles on one wrist.

Mentally, John compared the Sameen in the doorway to the sobbing bundle of nerves he'd met at the airfield.

That Sameen had been clutching at his arm as she begged him to retrieve her property, while *this* Sameen assessed him with cool eyes the same shade as her gown.

"Captain Pitte," she greeted, every centimeter the welcoming risto. "Or may I call you John? You've gone to such trouble for me; it seems foolish to adhere to formalities."

"I'd prefer it," he said, offering a smile as she stepped back, allowing him entrance to the foyer. "Given you never told me your surname."

"Oh, but surely I told you?" Perfectly arched brows, only a shade darker than her hair, pursed thoughtfully.

"I'm certain I'd have remembered."

"Well of course you would," she said, the thoughtful expression falling away like a veil. "I can't imagine what I was thinking at the time, not that I was thinking at all clearly." She waved a delicate hand, and again the air resonated to the jangle of the thin bangles while she, John noted, continued to not share her last name. "Which makes me fortunate you're as trustworthy as you appeared. Another aeronaut might have taken my money and run for the Adian border."

"Maybe not that far," he said, turning his attention to the surrounding space.

Like the outside, the house's interior reflected Fujian sensibilities. Smooth plaster walls and bamboo floors—none of the typical stone Avonians favored—and with a lamp of copper and sepia glass gilding the space from above.

On the right, he noted an arched door, closed but with a sliver of light visible along the door's base.

Straight ahead, the foyer spilled into an open darkness. All John could make out were humps of furniture and beyond that the shadow of another wide arch.

Against the wall on the left, a stair with wide, shallow treads rose to the shadowed second story, and to the left of that another arched door, this one open, through which he could see a well-lit room featuring a series of floor-to-ceiling bookshelves.

Though he knew Jagati had eyes on that room, the door to the right intrigued him, so he turned toward it.

"Let's go to the library, shall we?" Sameen stepped between John and his goal. "More fitting for business than the parlor." As she spoke, she slid her arm through his and guided him to the left.

With no sound reason to argue, he allowed her to draw him into the library.

"Do you like it?" she asked, pausing inside the door.

"It is impressive," he responded truthfully. But as much as he might admire the design of the octagonal chamber, he felt again a sense of wrongness about the place, and not only because the fireplace hadn't been lit.

The cold, and the lack of snapping flames, only highlighted how quiet the house was.

So quiet that the silence seemed to push back against the squelch of his boots and the soft chime of Sameen's bracelets.

And then there was the dust.

Not the actual dust, for only the thinnest patina of neglect coated the visible surfaces, but more the flavor of dust in the air, as if Sameen had just returned from a long absence and had yet to fill the house with her presence.

Sameen, however, continued into the room with no sign of discomfort, leading him past a pair of armchairs with a low table between them and the sofa on the opposite side.

John looked over the furniture, well made and comfortably worn. "I didn't know you had a child."

That gave her pause. "A what?"

He nodded toward the couch, where a tin airship peeked from under one of the cushions.

"Oh." She waved it off. "That belongs to the cook's son. He's always leaving his toys every which where."

John glanced back at the little airship, then followed her to the slate-topped mahogany desk. On the desk sat a closed writing box not unlike the one he kept in his quarters aboard the *Errant*.

Behind the desk, the large multi-paned window Jagati had pointed out was framed by thick-woven curtains, through which he could just make out the stable where Jagati hid. Turning from the outside view he spied, just peeking from the edge of the curtain, a well-worn pair of crutches.

"Now, John," Sameen said, rounding the desk. "Shall we get down to business? I have your payment," she added, lifting the lid of the writing box, thus blocking his view of her hands.

"Of course," he said, giving the box a brief glance. "But first, perhaps you can satisfy my curiosity."

Her eyes shot up, and there was that sharpness again, but it disappeared quickly as she murmured. "I'd satisfy more than that, if you were so inclined."

"Maybe later," he said. "After you explain why you asked my crew to retrieve unlawful technology."

"Unlawful?" Her brow furrowed, and she took on an expression of confusion. "I'm afraid I don't understand."

"Then either you are a fool, or you think me one," John said.

"I'm no fool. But I have to admit, I rather hoped you were." And as she spoke, her hand emerged from the writing box holding not a stack of starbucks but a Cooper mini-bow.

Which might have been bad for John had he not, in the same moment, drawn his own gun.

"Ah," she said.

"Indeed," he replied.

"Coopers are famed for their accuracy," Sameen pointed out. "Shot for shot, they'll hit their target more often than any plasma shooter on the market."

"At a distance," he countered. "But with less than a meter between us, I'd say it's even odds we both die."

"As much as it pains me to admit it, I believe you're correct."

"So, shall we call this a draw?"

"That would be terribly civilized," she agreed. "However, that just won't work for me—or my client."

"Client?"

"Yes. And he's quite determined, to put it mildly. So be a good boy, John, and hand over that satchel."

"I'd rather not."

"Of course you wouldn't."

"So," he said after a contemplative pause, "now what?"

"Now? We do this the hard way." As she spoke, her glance darted over John's shoulder. "Isn't that right, Colin?"

Colin? John blinked but didn't look.

"That's right, Mary," someone with a lower-comb Nikean accent replied from behind John. "But then, I prefer it the hard way."

"He really does," Sameen—or Mary, rather—said to John.

"Best put the shooter down, mate," Colin said, "else you'll see how hard I can make it."

"Why would I give up my leverage?" John asked. "Seeing as I can get at least one shot off before either of you take me out."

"True," Mary said. "Except for the part where it isn't you he'd be shooting."

John had a sudden vision of Jagati in Dyar's Canyon, Tariq's shooter to her head.

"Go on," he heard Colin say, "tell the man what's what."

"But I don't know what is what," a small, almost piping voice responded to the prompt.

Not Jagati, John thought, but worse.

Much, much worse.

Not bothering to cover the wince, John put the shooter down and turned to face Colin who, he probably shouldn't have been surprised to see, was actually the shiny man from Xanadu, holding the gun he'd failed to draw on John, earlier.

And standing in front of Colin stood a small boy with wavy black hair, bronze skin, and eyes of an amber John had seen before.

"Tell me," he said to the child, "would your father happen to be named Tariq?"

The familiar eyes blinked up at him. "You know my papa?"

"We've met."

CHAPTER II

Walking into Kit's Diner, Jinna took a deep breath of warm air infused with the scents of spices, maple and bacon.

Rory, entering in her wake, took an appreciative sniff. "Now that's the ticket," he said with a grin of anticipation.

Then again, she'd never known Rory McCabe to be shy around food, this despite having the physique of a scarecrow.

As the scarecrow was busy shaking off the rain, she stepped out of splash range and turned her attention to the diner and felt a rush of relief to find the place empty.

The tables and booths on the left side of the diner were clean and bussed, and the counter, with its rotating stools, gleamed under the overhead crystal lamps.

Better still, she saw no sign of Sol, the diner's owner.

Both circumstances meant Rory would have the chance to dry off and stay as long as he wished.

"Been slower than sap in Treicember since tea time," Luis, the day cook, said as he emerged from the kitchen. He shed his apron as he came around the counter, the prosthetic leg he'd earned during the battle of Santandar putting a slight hitch in his step.

"Sol sent Ryan home before he left, and told me to head out when you came in."

"You're not planning to leave Jinna alone for the night?" Rory asked, looking up from the boot he'd been shaking.

"Ignore him," Jinna told Luis. She slipped out of her coat and hung it and the umbrella on one of the hooks provided for the purpose as she asked, "What's on the menu?"

"There's the butternut squash soup on the stove. Fixings for ranger sandwiches and plenty of batter left in the cooler for griddle cakes." As he spoke, Luis gave Rory an approving glance. "I've already swabbed the kitchen," he continued, turning back to Jinna, "filled the condiments and done what dishes we had, so closing shouldn't be too difficult."

"You're a queen's dream," Jinna told him as she headed for the counter.

"So all the lads say." Luis shot Jinna a salute, and with a last, lingering glance at Rory, who was busy brushing rain from his jacket, flung on his coat and stepped out into the night.

"Nice fellow," Rory commented, vigorously scrubbing his hands through his hair.

Jinna shook her head at his obtuseness, pulled her apron from behind the counter, and looped it over her head. As she reached around to tie the apron back, she felt a little quiver from within and let out a gasp.

"What is it?" Rory asked, dashing to her side. "Are you not well? Maybe you should sit down."

"I'm fine." She sidestepped his efforts to push her toward a stool. "It's nothing. Well, not nothing; it's the baby. Here." She grabbed his hand and pressed it over the swell of her belly.

He blanched at the touch, but before Jinna could regret the impulsive gesture, the flutters increased and Rory's expression shifted from shock to warmth, and his palm against her side relaxed.

Under the twin pressures of the child within and the man without, Jinna experienced a long, slow turning of her heart.

Then the flutter subsided, and in a breath, his eyes shuttered and his hand fell away.

"That's—grand," he said, stepping back. "Liam would have loved it."

Which was true, Jinna thought. Liam would have loved it, as much as he'd loved everything else about the idea of becoming a father.

He just hadn't loved it enough to resign from the Air Corps, and then the *York* had gone down and. . . "Here." She turned and reached over the counter for a clean towel, which she then flung at Rory. "Take this to the bathroom and dry yourself off. I'll get some griddle cakes going."

"I'd be fine with the soup," he protested, but Jinna was already around the counter and diving into the kitchen before she gave in to the urge to punch him.

Or before he could see the first tear spill.

By the time Rory returned, not quite dry but no longer dripping, Jinna was setting a plate piled high with griddle cakes and bacon on one of the tables, along with a steaming mug and a pitcher of syrup.

There was another mug on the counter, telling Rory that Jinna had at least made herself a cuppa, but for all that, she appeared worn, her pale skin dark under the eyes.

"Maybe you can join me," he offered, grabbing her mug and carrying to the booth.

"I don't think I—"

"Please?" he pressed, setting the cup down. "There's enough to feed three on that plate."

Even as he said the words, he regretted them as, until a few months ago, there might well have been three people at the table, enjoying a meal together.

Jinna's expression froze, then softened as, no doubt, she had the same thought. With a sigh, she looked over the empty diner, the rainy night, and the lack of any pedestrians outside. "Just this once," she agreed with a shrug and, grabbing a spare set of flatware from the next table, slid into the booth opposite him.

Rory moved the plate so they could both reach it, and she poured the syrup.

And if both of them were thinking of the empty Liam-shaped space next to her, neither mentioned it.

Taking his first bite, Rory let out a soft moan. "Keepers," he said, going back for more, "I keep forgetting what real food tastes like."

"You eat pretend food on the *Errant*?" Jinna asked, crunching a bit of bacon.

"Not so much pretend, but it's certainly abused," Rory said, swirling a bit of bacon in the pooling syrup. "Of all of us, John's the best cook, but there's not a lot he can do with the dried proteins and rehydrated veg we generally stock."

"You'll all have to come to the diner more," Jinna said, frowning at the griddle cakes.

"Something wrong?" Rory asked.

"No," she said, her voice distant. "Just wondering if we have any almond butter in the pantry. I bet it'd taste great on these." She blinked, then looked up. "Cravings," she explained. "It's a thing. Last week I couldn't stop thinking about dried raspberries. It was a rough couple of days, because even dried, they're hard to get this time of year."

"But aren't dried raspberries very—"

"Sour?" she cut in, taking another bite of griddle cake. "And then some, but I *had* to have them. Luis took pity on me and went on a raspberry safari." She paused, took a sip of tea. "Fortunately he scrounged enough to sate the cravings. I can only hope that one's over with." She looked down at her belly. "Try for something a little more accessible, okay?"

There was a moment of silence, during which Rory realized he was waiting for the baby to respond. "Well," he said, cutting off another bite of griddle cake, "besides sour fruit issues, how have you been? You're staying safe?"

She shrugged, focusing on catching a stray bit of bacon with a bit of griddle cake as she replied, "Since my job no longer involves dismantling bombs—or setting myself up to get robbed, like some people I know—I'd say I'm pretty safe."

"I explained that on the way over." Or most of it. He hadn't mentioned what, exactly, Galileo and Jacques had been after. The fewer people who knew about the calculator, the better. "And let's not change the subject. Have you had time for yourself, or to make any friends?"

"Yes, big brother," she said, setting down her fork and reaching for her tea. "Keeper Talia's been introducing me around on service days, and—"

"You're still performing service?" He frowned. "I'd have thought you'd be excused by now."

"I'm at least two months away from being completely useless," she told him, giving him a light kick on the shin. "The district keepers found me a spot doing some gardening in one of the agricenters. Plus, Luis is a gem, and Mia comes round more often these days. You remember Mia?"

Rory thought of the wild-haired street-thief. "I don't know as I like you keeping such close company with a dodger."

"You mean a dodger who's not you?" she teased.

"I'm not sure I'd have approved of you being my friend, either, back in my dodging days."

"And yet, you still taught me to pick a lock."

"I shouldn't have done that," he said. "I don't want to be a bad influence."

"I wish you did," she murmured, but before he could question that, she changed the subject, asking after John and Jagati and the problems of keeping the *Errant* aloft, which flowed into stories of the diner and her dreams of someday having her own tea shop.

"I know we'll be okay early on," Jinna said, laying a hand over the mound of her stomach, "but when I'm ready to work again, I don't know that I want to be beholden to Sol for a job."

"Is he such a tyrant, then?" Rory asked, automatically bristling.

"Oh, he's not a matinee villain or anything," she said, placing all the flatware on the empty plate. "It's more that he isn't in the business for anything but the business, if you know what I mean?"

"No joy from the work."

"Exactly," she said, pointing a finger at him before angling to scoot out of the booth. "I've done my bit for Corps and colonies, now I want to do something that feeds people . . . well, obviously." She grinned. "But really, I want to do something that gives people a lift, that takes them out of their troubles, gives them comfort."

"It's a good thing to want," he said. "If Liam were here—"

"Don't," she cut in. "Do not make Liam a part of this."

"I can't help it," Rory said. "I can't not think of him, or how if I hadn't resigned from the Corps when I did—"

"If you hadn't resigned," she cut in, "you'd have gone down with the *York* too. You'd both be gone, and I'd—" She cut herself off, shaking her head violently. "We are *not* talking about this."

"Of course," he managed.

"Good," she said, and after a beat added, "I'll get you some more tea," before disappearing into the kitchen.

Rory glanced up at the clock and was wondering how much longer he could reasonably linger when the diner's door swung open and a chill breeze flew in with two newcomers, one of whom he recognized as Mia, the dodger Jinna had spoken of earlier, alongside a man wearing a battered infantry long-coat.

Jinna emerged from the kitchen and beamed at Mia. "Honey from the keepers," she said as the man glanced Rory's way.

Rory nodded to the soldier, then turned his attention to his empty cup while Mia and Jinna caught up, their voices too low for Rory to hear what was said.

He roused himself as the dodger and her friend passed by his table.

"Oy there, Mia."

"Oy back, Rory," Mia replied, drawing a smile from Rory.

The pair took a booth a couple tables back, and Rory, almost against his will, felt his eyes drawn back to Jinna as she rounded the counter.

Enough, he thought and, fumbling into his jacket, found a damp wad of cash which he shoved under the plate before rising from the table just as Jinna arrived, full teapot in hand.

"No more tea, then?" she asked as he passed her by.

"Thanks, but no," he said, heading for the door. "Gotta get back to the *Errant*."

"Hold it right there, McCabe."

At Jinna's command he froze, turned. "Is there a problem?"

"You left too much money. *Again*." As she spoke, she closed the distance between them.

"I did nae such thing." He stuffed his hands in his pockets as she tried to shove the damp bills into them.

"It's twice what you owe." She gave up and waved the bills in his face, which in spite of everything, made Rory grin.

"Consider it a down payment on my next meal."

"Rory. . ."

"Ach, will you look at the time," he glanced at the wall clock over the counter. "Best be off. Captain Pitte'll be pacing at the gangplank, he will." He backed up another step.

"John hasn't paced a gangplank in, *ever*."

"Aye, but it's been an odd day for the crew," Rory pointed out. "Well, you saw."

"I did, but none of that excuses you leaving too much money," Jinna insisted, even as he retreated.

"How about this?" he countered. "How about you keep it safe for me until I've need of it?"

Then, before Jinna could protest further, he reached back and grabbed the door handle, pulling at the same time as he turned—and walked straight into the door, causing him to see, he was sure, a talon of dracos flying around his head. "I'm all right!" he called, shaking the dracos away and, before anyone could say anything, stumbled out into a chill damp that was a too-perfect backdrop to his current mood.

CHAPTER 12

THE OUTBUILDING WAS A STABLE.

Or at least, Jagati figured the row of stalls and faint must of old hay indicated it had been a stable at one time.

She was just happy the place was empty, and happier that the stalls' exterior gave her an excellent view of John and Sameen as they approached the bow window she'd recommended.

It was her first sight of Sameen, and something about the petite blond had Jagati's jaw clenching. As she watched the woman slide around the desk in her fancy green gown, she couldn't stop the soft hiss or the muttered, "Viper."

"Odd, I was thinking the same thing," a familiar voice said from behind.

Jagati hissed again, then looked over her shoulder. "Why didn't I hear you come in?" she asked as Tariq stepped out of the shadows, shooter in hand.

"Like the fog, I move on little cat feet."

"That sounds like poetry. I hate poetry."

"Imagine how that distresses me. Ysabel," he murmured, and Jagati's eyes widened in surprise as Cheekbones slid through the stable door, her shock stick in hand.

"Hey," she greeted the other woman. "What's the buzz?"

"If you please," Tariq jerked his gun to one side, indicating Jagati should move from the window. "And leave the rifle."

She glanced over her shoulder, and reassured that John was, at least at the moment, blocked by Sameen, did as he asked.

Tariq handed his gun to Ysabel, who kept it trained on Jagati while he took Jagati's place.

Jagati looked at Ysabel. "I thought we lost you after the Hokey Pokey. How did you manage to find us?"

"I didn't. After I left Xanadu, I reported to Tariq, and we came here together."

Which made zero sense to Jagati. "If you weren't following us, why would you come here?"

"Because," Tariq said, his eyes locked on the library, "this is my house."

Jagati's jaw dropped. "Your house?" She let out a low whistle. "I guess crime really does pay. But wait, why would Sameen want Pitte to deliver the cargo to your house?"

"Presumably because it is her house as well," Tariq replied, adjusting the rifle's scope before adding, "Sameen is my wife."

"Whoa," Jagati said. "So, your wife hired us to rob you?"

"That is what I originally thought," Tariq responded after a beat. "But since the woman talking to your captain is not my wife, I seem to have been mistaken."

"And it just got weirder," Jagati observed.

Ysabel said nothing.

"They seem to be having a dispute," Tariq observed, then froze, eye glued to the scope.

"What's happening?" Jagati asked.

His response was a single word.

No, not a word.

A name.

"Izaldine."

Jagati's fists clenched. "And who on Fortune is—"

"Izaldine El Karim," the boy introduced himself to John, then looked at Mary. "We are not to have such toys in the house. Mama says so."

"Your mama is very wise," John observed.

"They won't let me see her," Izaldine said with understandable resentment.

"Never worry about your mum." Colin's dark eyes locked on John. "You'll see her as soon as Captain Pitte 'ere gives over the cargo."

"Izaldine is my son," Tariq said from where he stood, his eye glued to the rifle's scope.

"So your wife isn't your wife, but your son is your son?" Jagati asked before she could stop herself. "Sorry, but you have to admit, the situation is smogged."

"Smogged, yes," he eased back, studying the scene with his own eyes for a moment. "And dangerous."

"How . . ." Jagati began.

"How dangerous?" Ysabel asked at the same time.

"At least one shooter in there," he said. "It is aimed at my son. The woman is holding something as well. I cannot tell what, but I suspect it is a weapon."

Jagati stepped forward. "Let me take a look." It said something, she didn't know what, that he did step aside, allowing her access to her weapon.

"The woman's not moving," she said, peering through the scope, "but the man with your kid? That's Shiny," she glanced at Ysabel. "Your competition from Xanadu."

"I told you of him," Ysabel said to Tariq.

"He's pointing the gun at Pitte, now," Jagati reported. "And not—Sameen's moving and—shit!" The expletive came out as a hiss. "She's got a Cooper mini. I hate those things."

"It looks as if your captain is about to give them the satchel," Ysabel noted from where she had appeared at Jagati's left.

"And when they get what they want?" Tariq asked. "They won't need a hostage anymore."

"Actually," Jagati said, "that won't be the problem."

Inside the library, John watched Mary pull the battered allusteel case from his satchel.

"This doesn't look a thing like the box our client described," she said.

"That's because it isn't," he admitted. "My mechanic broke the original case, so he gave me one of the old toolboxes from his workshop. It isn't pretty," he said, "but at least it stays closed."

"And locked." Mary set the box on the desk and looked over to where John and Izaldine now sat on the couch, Colin covering them with his weapon.

John's shooter lay on the desk, well out of reach.

The situation might be dire, but Izaldine, having found his airship in the cushions, was now contentedly running wheels at the bottom of the gondola over his lap, over and over.

"Key?" Colin prompted.

"Jacket pocket," John told him, then indicated Colin's weapon. "I'd like some assurance I won't be shot when I reach for it."

"Life's full of risks," Colin pointed out.

"I suppose it is," John said, then slowly reached for his inner jacket pocket, withdrew the key and tossed it to the waiting Mary.

"What do you mean, he does not have the calculator?"

"Exactly what I said." Jagati didn't roll her eyes at Tariq's question, but only because she was still following the action in the library. "Once he saw what was in that box, Pitte figured Sameen was up to no good. Wait . . . looks like she's asking Pitte for the key."

"I need to get inside," Tariq said. "They may seek retribution on my son."

Jagati shook her head. "We need to wait."

"For what?" he asked.

"For the signal."

He didn't respond.

"Tariq?"

"Too late," Ysabel told her. "He's already gone."

"Smog it." Jagati toggled her rifle to active. "You'd better go after him."

"Why?"

"Because if you don't, he'll be getting a face full of signal."

A rush of footsteps in straw told her Ysabel had taken her advice.

"Okay, Pitte," she murmured, "whenever you're ready."

"Do you have any idea what's inside that box?" John asked as Mary put the key in the lock.

"I know it's worth a pile of starbucks," Colin rumbled.

"And that doesn't strike you as risky? Taking on an unknown retrieval?"

"You didn't ask me what I was sending you after," Mary pointed out, jiggling the key, which was sticky.

"An unusual lapse on my part," John admitted. "And after laying eyes on the cargo, one I regret."

"Naughty thing, looking where you shouldn't," Mary told him before letting out a pleased, "Ah ha!" when the lock clicked.

"Trust me," John said, "you do *not* want to open that box."

"Oh but I do," she replied with a grin. "I want to know what someone would pay a crystal bed to get back. Who knows?" she added, flipping up the box's latches, "Maybe it's worth two crystal beds."

At which point John was already turning toward Izaldine so he had the child under the cover of his body when Mary lifted the lid and the flash-bang Rory had set inside the toolbox went off.

Jagati closed her eyes just before the woman opened the case, waiting two seconds past the *boom* to open them and take aim.

Still wrapped around the boy, John rolled to the floor, then hunched, turtle-like, over Izaldine as he nudged him toward the door.

A few bursts of plasma, followed by an explosion of glass, told him Jagati was doing her job.

As was Colin, who leaped out of the smoke, shooter in hand, just as John and Izaldine reached the fireplace.

"Go!" John ordered the child as he spun and dove for Colin, grabbing the shooter and pushing it aside. He managed to get in a right hook that cracked against the other man's jaw.

Colin cursed but held tight to the weapon. Then he cursed again as Izaldine latched onto his leg, slamming at it with his airship.

"Bloody swarmin' gnat," Colin hissed before he shot his head at John in a classic Epsilon kiss.

John jerked back, avoiding a broken nose by a bee-wing's breadth, but also losing control of the shooter, which Colin turned back in John's direction before swinging John into the mantel.

"Keep it up, kid," Colin snarled as he took aim, "and your mate loses his head."

"I don't think that will happen," John said despite the red haze of pain exploding from his shoulder.

Colin grinned. "Why not? D'ya think the gnat's gonna give me any grief?"

"No," Tariq said, his own shooter live and aimed at Colin's head, "but I will."

"Papa!" Izaldine turned to his father with a gap-toothed grin. "Hello Ysabel," he added, waving to the tall woman at the door as if explosions and fisticuffs in the library were a natural occurrence.

At this point Jagati appeared at the window where, to John's amusement, she threw Izaldine a fist to the heart before stepping through the shattered glass.

Ysabel stepped forward to disarm and contain Colin, while Tariq turned to his son.

John was just easing away from the fireplace, meaning to give Tariq and Izaldine some privacy, when a soft *snick*, followed by an equally soft grunt, had him spinning to see Tariq slump to one side, the fletching of a small crossbow bolt sticking out of his shoulder.

"Jagati!" he called, at the same time Mary rolled out from under the desk, holding the Cooper mini.

Jagati spat a word that had Izaldine's jaw dropping in awe while giving Mary's legs a sweeping kick that dropped the woman flat on her back, right on top of the mountain of broken glass.

Mary yelped and started to scramble back up.

"I don't think so, sister," Jagati said, taking aim as John crossed to the desk.

Jagati glanced at John as he approached, but his glare was for the woman on the floor.

"There was no reason to shoot him, Mary," he said.

"True, but I was aiming at you."

"Do we need her?" Jagati asked between clenched teeth.

"For a few moments, at least," Tariq said.

John, Jagati, and Mary looked to where Tariq, one arm draped over Izaldine's shoulders, had joined the party, seemingly oblivious of the bolt in his shoulder.

"Oh good," Mary said. "You survived."

"You won't," Tariq countered, "unless you tell me what you've done with my wife."

"Oh," Izaldine said. "Mama is—"

Whatever it was Izaldine meant to say was interrupted by a *fwump* from outside, which had every head in the room turning to the window where a long, knotted length of several types of fabric had unfurled to the wet ground.

This was followed by a slim, dark-haired figure slithering down the makeshift jump line before coming to a shuddering halt in the decorative shrubbery.

"Sorry," the figure said, hanging tight to what looked like a counterpane. "Only, I heard all the noise and figured this was a good time to make the proverbial break for it."

"Mama!" Izaldine beamed.

"Does this mean I don't get to shoot Mary?" Jagati asked.

"Or him?" Ysabel said, eyeing Colin.

"Jagati," John murmured.

"Ysabel." Tariq shook his head, though his eyes remained locked on the woman hanging onto the bedding. "*Delbar-am*, it is good to see your face." He started forward but only made it one step before he stumbled and caught himself on the desk.

"*Delbar-am*," she repeated the endearment. Then her head tilted and her mouth quirked. "I see you've been shot. Again."

Though her dark eyes shone with mischief, there was something else—something lurking just beneath the levity—that had John looking away. Which was when his eyes caught on the crutches he'd spied earlier, and he looked back to where Izaldine's mother still clung onto the bedding, as if to hold herself upright.

"Oh," he said, then stepped around the desk, edged behind Jagati, and climbed through the window to where the woman waited. "If I may?" he asked, holding out his arms.

"Of course," she said with a grin and a little whoop of glee as John swept her into his arms and back through the window.

A moment later, he left Sameen perched atop the desk between her husband and son, who was clambering up to her lap, already explaining how he'd found his airship.

While Izaldine chattered, John returned to the window to pick up the crutches.

"Nothing like the killer we met in Dyar's Canyon," Jagati muttered, glancing at Tariq as John stepped to her side.

"No," he agreed, glancing at Mary, who was still on the floor, picking glass from the back of her arm before adding, "No one here is quite who they seem."

Then he rounded the desk to hand the abandoned crutches to Sameen.

"Thanks," she said, the smile turning over her shoulder to include Jagati, "both of you—whoever you are."

"Oh," John began, "that's a—"

"That's a long story," Jagati replied at the same time.

"One that can wait," Tariq said. "At least until I've dealt with these . . . people." His gaze fell on Mary who, for the first time, looked nervous.

"Will there be skinning involved?" Jagati asked.

CHAPTER 13

John wasn't the least bit surprised that Tariq didn't want to teleph the coppers, but he was surprised that he decided to release Mary and Colin.

Tariq did keep their weapons, at least, and made it clear that any further sightings in the vicinity of the El Karim family would lead to a much more permanent solution.

Mary had readily agreed. "Our only interest is the cargo," she said, then glanced at John. "Since our client is determined to get his property back, we'll be continuing our search elsewhere."

"I can suggest a few places to look," Jagati offered as Ysabel escorted Colin and Mary out of the house and, at Tariq's orders, out of the district.

The door had barely closed behind them when Izaldine turned to his mother to declare, "I'm hungry."

"Of course you are," she said. "Go on, then." He took off at a run, and she swung after him with a syncopated thump of her crutches.

John gave Jagati a look and jerked his chin after the pair, indicating she should go along with them.

She, in reply, jerked her chin at him, indicating *he* should be the one to follow Sameen.

In return, John cocked an eyebrow in reminder she'd given up her shot at being captain and Jagati, predictably, bared her teeth, thus informing him she'd follow the non-verbal order but that John should expect some very verbal repercussions at a later date.

Then she stomped out of the library.

"Do all your orders have such an effect?"

John looked at Tariq who had not only seen the entire non-verbal exchange but appeared to have understood every unspoken syllable. "Not all," he said, "but enough to keep things lively. Do you think they mean it?" he asked, indicating the door through which Colin and Mary had departed. "That they'll leave you alone?"

"As Mary said, their only interest is in the cargo." Tariq began to shrug but stopped as the motion pulled at the crossbow bolt still in his shoulder.

"The cargo," John repeated, studying the captain of the *Al-Djinn*. "About that . . ."

". . . if I'd known how much trouble the thing would be, I don't know that I'd have nicked the smogging lockbox in the first place," Sameen said as she poured boiling water from a steaming kettle into the squat brown teapot she'd set on a cart.

Jagati breathed in the scent of Avonian Breakfast tea as she set the mugs Sameen had pointed her to on the table and Izaldine, already seated, poked through a bowl of overripe apples and pears.

Having not eaten for some time, herself, Jagati considered grabbing a piece of fruit as payment for being social, even if the being social was meant as a way of learning more about the calculator.

Though it had been simple enough to steer the conversation in that direction while Sameen maneuvered around her kitchen, pulling biscuits from the cupboard, filling the kettle, warming the pot, filling it with leaves, not a motion wasted.

With the tea steeping, Sameen placed the pot, a pitcher of milk, and both her crutches on the cart, which she used as a support while she pushed it from the counter to the square table.

Unwillingly impressed, Jagati waited until the other woman eased into a chair next to her son to return to the main topic of the night.

"So, if you didn't know what you were taking, why would you take it?"

Sameen's smile returned, mischievous as ever, while she poured the tea. "That's rather my job, isn't it?"

"Your job is stealing unknown objects?"

"I stole a box with a tri-level Kairos lockset in the possession of an individual known to have technochrist leanings," Sameen said, unconcerned with all this talk of stealing, despite the fact her son was sitting right there, drinking it all in. "I didn't need to know what was in the box to know it would be of interest."

No doubt there was more to Sameen's story, but Jagati sensed this wasn't the time to press, so instead she asked, "And you never opened it?"

"Of course I opened it," Tariq said as he perched on the edge of the tub in the upstairs bath, where he'd led John after John noted it would be wise to remove the bolt from his shoulder. "Or rather Jacques, my mechanic, opened it. And proud of himself he was. Kairos locks are not for the faint of heart."

"So I hear." John took hold of the crossbow bolt with one hand and set the other on Tariq's shoulder. Before Tariq had the chance to say more, he yanked the bolt from the other man's shoulder while Tariq's knuckles went white on the tub's edge.

He dropped the shaft into the sink, lifted the flask of antibacterial wash, and held it up. "Ready?" he asked.

Tariq's answer was a short nod, so John did the needful and poured a hefty dose of antibacterial into the wound where it foamed vigorously.

"And it didn't bother you," John asked, poking through the medical kit for tweezers, "what was inside the box?"

"At first I thought it a joke," Sameen admitted, ruffling Izaldine's hair as he reached for his third biscuit. "It wasn't until Tariq had taken it out of Nike, and Colin and Mary arrived, that I learned otherwise."

"What about Colin and Mary?" Jagati asked as Izaldine slid her a biscuit. "Thanks," she said, then looked at Sameen. "I mean, did they say who they work for?"

Sameen shook her head as Jagati took a bite of the buttery, crumbly shortbread. "They didn't have to. We met him soon after Mary and Colin arrived. He told me," she continued, "that he'd seen me run off with his property, though I could have sworn the street was empty at the time."

"His name is Galileo," Izaldine made an icky face. "He smiled a lot, but I didn't like him."

"No, love," Sameen murmured, dropping a kiss on his head. "Neither did I."

"Galileo?" Jagati's brow furrowed. She'd heard that name before.

"He could see inside my head," Izaldine added with a longing gaze at the biscuit packet.

"So can I," Sameen told him before leaning down and whispering, *"Just one more."* Then she looked back to Jagati. "As Izaldine said, Galileo is a sensitive, and dead set on retrieving the calculator. He had a whole speech about the right to expand our technologies and how the keepers and the Accords were holding the citizens of Fortune hostage to ancient fears."

"Wait." Jagati straightened as the starbuck dropped and she remembered the conversation aboard the *Errant*, when she'd teased Eitan about his rebellious phase. And when she'd asked about the phase's name . . . it was . . . "This Galileo," she said, looking at Sameen who was watching her, brows raised in curiosity. "Was he very persuasive?"

"Crystal and comb for everyone," Sameen agreed. She pulled a medallion—the Broken Sapling, given to those wounded in service—from under her tunic and began to toy with it. "But my take?" she continued, her thumb sliding over the snapped tree. "He's in it for the money."

"I suppose you think us fools for even keeping the thing," Tariq said.

John followed him down the stairs, his knee throbbing with every step. "I have thought you many things since Dyar's Canyon," he replied. "Fool is not one of the terms that came to mind."

"I can imagine a few of the words that did," Tariq replied.

"I imagine you had a few choice words for us as well," John noted. "That said, I can't imagine anyone in the shadow trade— even fools—willing to handle an item as volatile as that calculator, yet you did." Then as he joined Tariq at the bottom of the stairs he added, "It makes me think."

"You strike me as a man who thinks a great deal," Tariq said, turning to face John. "Perhaps too much."

"You wouldn't be the first to say so."

"And what do your thoughts tell you, now?"

"They tell me you had a reason for stealing the calculator," John said, focusing on the other man's narrow features, which gave away nothing. "A reason other than money."

"And how can you know this?" Tariq asked, crossing his arms, wincing, and immediately uncrossing them.

"Mind the bandage," John cautioned. "And I know this because no one who looks at his wife and child the way you do would risk them for the sake of profit."

"Thoughtful and correct," Tariq said, after a beat. "We did not steal it for money."

"Then why take such a risk?" John asked.

"We were told to."

John took a breath, let it out, then decided he may as well ask. "By whom?"

"That," Tariq said, "is a long story, and one I cannot share."

"I see. No," John corrected himself. "I don't see at all."

Tariq's expression became pained. "Believe me, I take no joy in holding the truth from you but . . . it is complicated."

"Of course it is."

***

Since all the talk of illicit tech was putting her off her tea, Jagati decided to change the subject by indicating the medallion Sameen was still toying with. "Ex-Corps?"

Sameen looked down, as if unaware she'd been fiddling with the object. "Sorry, yes." She dropped the medal, lifted her mug, and took a sip before continuing. "I was on the UCAS *Maathi*'s jump team until my line fouled during a jump over Delta, back in '46."

"I was at Delta." Frowning, Jagati recalled the battle on Midas's northeast border, a confrontation of ground and air forces that, in the end, neither side could claim as a victory. She remembered mostly a lot of smoke, flak, and the crush of the infantry retreat her team had been supporting. "Not our best day."

"Mama got hurt," Izaldine said, not looking up from the toy airship he'd carried from the library, which he now seemed intent on ramming into his pear. "She was asleep for a long time."

"Izaldine was only three," Sameen said, ruffling his hair, "but he remembers more than I do. Honestly, I don't know how Tariq managed an invalid and a three-year-old at once."

"Don't make me rethink my opinion of the man who threatened to skin me . . ." Jagati groused.

"He what? To *what?*" Sameen looked at her son. "Papa has some splainin' to do."

"Like Lucy?" he asked, eyes wide.

"Just like Lucy." She turned to Jagati, "The Shakespeare Circus has a matinee repertoire based on a character named Lucy, her compatriot Ethel, and their escapades."

"Wait, wait! The women who ate all the candies?" A smile tugged at the corner of Jagati's mouth as she recalled the single play John had dragged her to that hadn't put her to sleep.

"As I recall, you actually enjoyed that one," John said as he and Tariq entered the kitchen, Tariq going immediately to Sameen and laying a hand on her shoulder, then looking at his son.

"Well then, have you left any tea for your poor papa?" he asked his son.

"Laying it on a bit thick, aren't you, dear?" Sameen murmured.

"I have been shot," he pointed out.

"Again," she pointed back.

"Lots of tea," Izaldine cut in, rising on his knees in the chair before admitting, "but not many biscuits."

John, meanwhile, came up on Jagati's side, took her mug from her hands, and gulped down half its contents.

"Hey!" she glared up at him. "Mine." She poked him in the side.

"Tasty too," he said, handing it back before accepting the crumbling remains of a biscuit from Izaldine. "Thank you," he said, devouring it in a bite. "Also tasty, but we'd best be getting back to our 'ship."

"Work, work, work." Jagati winked at Izaldine, who gave her another crumb as a trophy.

"You're just encouraging her," John said, making the boy grin, then looked to Izaldine's mother. "I feel I should apologize for our part in," he gestured vaguely around him, "all this."

"Sorry about the window," Jagati added before downing the last of her tea.

"Nonsense," Sameen waved that aside. "I count us lucky Mary hired you. There's many a crew wouldn't think twice about taking the money and no question's asked."

"As she said," Tariq agreed. "And as I said earlier," he looked at John, "I am in your debt."

"If you can make the arrangements we discussed," John said, "I will consider all debts paid."

"Arrangements?" Jagati looked at her captain.

"I'll explain on the way," he said while she scootched out from the chair.

"Don't forget to tell him about Galileo," Sameen reminded her.

"Galileo?" John and Tariq asked at the same time.

"Technocrat sensitive," Sameen said.

"Who might also have been Eitan's boyfriend, back in the day," Jagati continued.

John blinked. "What?"

"I'll explain on the way," she parroted his response, tossing a salute to Sameen and Izaldine and a grudging nod to Tariq before heading out of the kitchen.

John stood dumbly for a moment, then followed. "What?"

"I guess she got some splainin' to do too," Izaldine said as the pair departed.

CHAPTER 14

THE RETURN TO THE AIRFIELD WAS BOTH LESS crowded and less eventful than their journey out, and John supposed he should be thankful that Tariq was no longer an enemy.

But the fact was, the calculator still weighed heavy on his mind, and he knew they'd not seen the last of Mary and Colin.

And what of their employer? The mysterious Galileo, who may or may not have ties to Eitan but clearly had zero qualms threatening a child to achieve his ends. Everything so far indicated the man was both determined and ruthless—a treacherous combination, as John had long ago discovered.

The tram came to its rocking halt, pulling John from his musings to find they'd reached the airfield. He rose and followed Jagati as she slung the carryall holding her rifle over her shoulder. He exited the tram in her wake, and they wove through the half-dozen travelers waiting to board for the return trip.

Among them stood a pair of aeronauts, both wearing the Tenjin Corporation patch on their flight jackets, in the midst of a heated discussion.

"I'm tellin' you Ken," one of the two was saying, "all them sensitives are Force users. Just like in the ancient texts."

"Stories, Johnny," his companion replied. "Those is all stories. And if I'm in for a full night of you spoutin' conspiracies, I'll keep my starbucks and you can whistle down Goodyear Lane for someone to buy you a drink."

John and Jagati watched the squabbling pair board the tram.

"They're bad enough in reality," Jagati muttered as they continued on their way.

"What?" John looked up. "Who?"

She jerked her chin at the pair behind them. "Sensitives. Galileo. Barth Vader from that space opera deal."

"Darth," John corrected absently. "And Galileo is just one sensitive out of many." As he spoke, his eyes slid over the airfield, almost deserted by now. "Eitan has never shown himself to be anything but honorable."

"Exception that proves the rule," she said, hunching her shoulders.

"That's a remarkably Earthbound way of thinking," John noted.

"I'm just saying, a bomb is a bomb, whether or not the crystal-det has sparked."

"That is a point of view," he murmured. "But if it's all the same, I'd as soon continue to believe the best of humanity—including sensitives."

She opened her mouth to argue, but even as John braced himself, she closed it again, and they continued on in silence.

It was only after they arrived at the *Errant*'s berth, and found the cargo bay door—the one they'd left secured—wide open, that she spoke, again. "So much for the best in humanity," she said, pulling her rifle from its cover as she headed up the gangplank.

"There'll be no living with her now," John muttered, drawing his own shooter as he followed Jagati into the cargo bay to discover their 'ship seemed to have been searched by a battalion of rabid ferrets.

A quick scan of the lower decks was slightly reassuring; the destruction was cosmetic only—shelves torn down, loose parts spread across the deck, nothing to indicate any structural or mechanical damage, so far.

In silent accord, John and Jagati made their way up the starboard companionway to the fourth deck where, as soon as he stepped into the corridor—which smelled as if the entire spice cabinet had exploded and gone to war with the vinegar—John heard a rustling sound.

He raised a fist, warning Jagati they had company, then gestured aft.

Jagati nodded, raised her weapon, and both moved in the direction of the medbay, from which the noise emanated.

He looked over his shoulder. She nodded and, on a silent three count, both burst into the medical bay, blinking against the acrid odor of anti-bact gel.

"Stand down," John ordered the young man currently rifling through the 'ship's medicine cabinet.

"Hands where I can see 'em!" Jagati added as the youth spun toward the door.

"Here are my hands," he said, holding them out to show a tin of headache powder in one and a cold pack in the other. "Now if you'll please be quiet—"

"Quiet?" Jagati echoed, then looked at John. "Is this guy for real?"

"Quite real," another voice answered the question, and John, Jagati, and the youth all looked to the nearest cot where a much-the-worse-for-wear Eitan was halfway to sitting up, a blade shooting out of his left sleeve and his face drawn with pain.

"Stay down," the intruder ordered with a hint of exasperation before blinking in disbelief. "Is that a knife?"

"Are you all right?" John lowered his weapon and crossed the room, stepping over a collection of first aid supplies strewn over the deck, including a broken anti-bact vial. "What happened?"

"What did you do to him?" Jagati advanced on the youth.

"What?" The young man's eyes sparked with anger. "I didn't do . . ."

"Leave him alone," Eitan said, looking to John as if the mere act of speaking hurt. "He is with me."

"He is?" John asked as he and Jagati looked from Eitan to the intruder who had dark, shoulder-length hair and eyes, a complexion on the olive side of tan, and a face that certainly would get its fair share of looks.

"Huh," Jagati said, turning back to Eitan. "Kind of young for you, isn't he?"

"*He*," the young man said, glaring equally at everyone, "is standing right here."

The he in question, they soon learned, was Tiago Hama, and he was a medical student at Yousafzai University. "Class of '50," he explained as he administered headache powder, a cold pack, and some expertly applied acupressure to the patient while Eitan told them of his confrontation with Galileo.

"I've no doubt it was Galileo who broke into the *Errant,*" Eitan finished his report, the entirety of which he'd delivered with his eyes closed.

"No doubt," John agreed. "But to search the entire ship in so short a time, he'd have had help."

"So it *was* the old boyfriend," Jagati observed, then seemed to hear herself. "Sorry," she said.

"So am I," Eitan replied.

"Maybe you should clear the rest of the 'ship," John suggested, glancing at Jagati.

"Good plan," she agreed, then fled the scene.

John shook his head, then turned as Eitan let out a soft sigh, possibly due to the foot massage Tiago was currently administering.

"Your friends," Eitan murmured, then opened his eyes and looked at Tiago. "They said something about a meeting? No, an appointment."

Tiago's hands continued working at Eitan's pressure points. "It's nothing to worry about."

"I think it is," Eitan disagreed. "And my sorrow to inconvenience you."

"If I didn't want to be inconvenienced, I should have chosen a different profession," Tiago replied with a crooked grin, releasing the foot and rising from the cot. "But now that you're in recovery, it's time I got back to the city. I'm on the third shift at the hospital this month." As he spoke, Tiago collected a well-worn coat and battered satchel from one of the other cots.

"Thank you for your help," John said, drawing the few starbucks he had from his pocket. "I wish we could do more"

The dark brown eyes grew darker. "Doctors don't heal for profit."

"Of course," John said, hiding the insulting cash.

"Perhaps when we're next in Nike," Eitan took over, smoothly, "after we sort out this—situation—we could offer you dinner?"

"As long as Jagati is nae cooking."

The three men turned to the door to see a damp and wrinkled Rory eyeing the wreckage.

"Rory," John nodded. "This is Dr. Tiago Hama."

"Not quite doctor, yet," Tiago inserted.

"He came back with Eitan," John finished the explanation.

"Did he, now?" Rory assessed the dark-haired student, then looked to the man on the cot. "A bit young for you, isn't he?"

Once Tiago departed, John sent Rory to assess the damage done to the *Errant*, then he dug the rolling stool from behind an upended bed and parked it next to Eitan's cot, sat down, and leaned his elbows on his knees. "I'm sorry," he began.

"You want to know about Leo—Galileo," Eitan guessed, closing his eyes.

"We need to know what we're up against," John agreed.

Eitan nodded, then winced. "Jagati would have told you, he and I were close."

"She mentioned you were involved, and that he introduced you to the technochrists when you were at Chandrasekhar," John said.

"He was very passionate on the topic of technologies," Eitan murmured. "He was very passionate about a lot of things."

"Ah," John said.

"He was also—is also," Eitan amended, "an incredibly gifted sensitive." Then, as John listened, Eitan explained how Galileo could employ not only the "off switch" Eitan had used but also a kind of time-blank. "Beyond that, he can force a person to fall into a memory, or a dream," Eitan continued. "He did it to me while I was shadowing Rory, and for a time I was lost in the past. I don't know how long I might have remained lost, if Jinna hadn't broken through the illusion."

"That is impressive," John said. "And terrifying."

"Especially given Galileo has no qualms about using those abilities to advance his own fortune. Which is almost understandable," Eitan continued, "given where he came from."

"And where was that?"

"The easy answer is he came from Guinness."

"And the hard answer?"

"Abandonment, poverty, disease . . . death." Eitan paused, then took a breath and continued. "His father deserted them. His mother was—I think she suffered from depression, or worse," he said, sending a quick glance John's way before continuing. "But the worst was when Leo lost his twin sister to Midasian Fever."

"That would have been terrible," John agreed.

"More than terrible, given Syl was also a sensitive, and that Leo was—they were linked, you see, when she—"

"Wait." John straightened, suddenly cold. "You're saying they were connected, psionically, when she died?"

"That, yes."

John shook his head, trying to imagine that kind of shock, then trying not to.

"Exactly," Eitan said, as if John had spoken. "And that trauma . . ." He paused, then met John's gaze. "You know I am not the strongest of sensitives, but even I could sense that wound. It was almost as if . . ."

"As if what?" John asked when Eitan's voice faltered.

"It was as if, when Syl died, she took a part of Leo with her."

Despite the twisting of his heart, John heard himself ask, "Which part?"

There was another, longer, pause before Eitan at last replied, "The part that loves."

CHAPTER 15

John left Eitan with orders to rest, then joined Jagati and Rory in preparing for liftoff.

Rory was busy replacing the connector on the port aft pod, so John and Jagati played a quick round of Wasp, Keeper, Draco, which John lost with an ill-timed Keeper. That left a gloating Jagati to prep the bridge while John inspected the envelope.

Over an hour later, he descended through the midship hatch, dropping to the deck in time to spy Jagati exiting the bridge, one leg of the nav table in her hand.

"The envelope looks good, and all the cells are at optimal levels," he said. "I figured I'd check on Rory's progress with the engine pod."

"The bridge is functional," she reported, tossing the leg into a bin of other broken bits, "but it's a smogging mess."

He nodded, turned, and headed for the aft ladder.

"Hey," she called, and he stopped to look back. "Have you cleared the vent systems, yet?"

"After I talk to Rory." He waved and added the vents to his mental list as he descended the central ladderwell.

On reaching the fourth deck, he found Eitan in the lounge, returning the scattered books to their shelves.

"I thought you were supposed to be resting," John said as Eitan tucked a book into the crook of his left arm.

Eitan straightened, slowly. "The pain is gone. All that remains is—I suppose you might call it a kind of distance—as if I were walking in a dream. But I can walk. And carry." He nodded to the books in his arm, then met John's concerned gaze. "I have been through worse."

John believed him, though he wished he didn't. "Just don't overdo it."

"Yes, mother."

John managed a smile at Eitan's irreverent response, then continued on his way to the cargo bay, running over the checklist of tasks remaining before they could safely lift off.

Envelope and cells, check. Bridge, mostly check. Bilges and three out of four engines, check . . .

He paused mid-step.

Had there been something else? He frowned, then shook his head as the chill night air slithered up the ladder to remind him of the engines, and Rory.

Descending to the cargo bay, he found Nike's chill had moved in and set up housekeeping, prompting him to roll down his shirtsleeves on the way to the gangplank.

"Rory," he called as he hit the ramp. "Have you figured out what's going on with that engine yet?"

"I've got the connection rewired," Rory called back, "but there's another problem."

John felt the beginnings of a headache of his own. "I'm not sure we can afford any more problems with this job." He stopped halfway down the ramp as he saw Rory was not alone. "Oh. Pardon me, Jinna." He managed a smile for the young woman. "I didn't realize Rory had company."

Rather a lot of company, John noted, as he spied a girl of indeterminate age peeking from behind Jinna, her bedewed black curls springing madly over a deep fawn complexion and wide dark eyes.

And just past the girl, beyond the *Errant*'s running lights, stood another man, clad in the distinctive coat of the Colonial Infantry.

Habit had him nodding a greeting before continuing down the ramp to join Rory. "What kind of problem are we talking about?"

"Jinna's got some sort of trouble," Rory said, glancing over his shoulder. "This is John Pitte, captain of the *Errant*," he told the others. "John, this is Jinna's friend, Mia."

"Pleased to make your acquaintance." John's easy smile warmed further at the girl's answering grin.

"Sorry," Rory apologized as he looked at the soldier. "I didn't catch your name."

"I didn't throw it," the man replied, though his eyes remained locked on John.

Those four sharp words struck John like hooks, twisting through his memory and pulling him closer to the taciturn stranger.

Except, of course, it wasn't a stranger at all, because as John met the cold blue eyes, he spoke again. "Gideon Quinn," the soldier introduced himself. "Commander of the—"

"12th Company," John cut in, shuddering as the sound of Gideon's voice reopened the wound left by Jihan's sword, his knee exploding again as he dropped to the deck while Rand gave the order to fire on Gideon's company.

"John?"

Rory's voice had him blinking, shuttering the past, the better to focus on the man before him. "You kept the coat?" he asked.

Quinn's chin jerked in John's direction. "You didn't."

"No," John said. "It didn't feel right—"

Which was all he had time to say because that was when whatever slim thread of control had been containing Quinn snapped, and in the space of a heartbeat, John was propelled back so fast and hard his feet left the tarmac. The next thing he felt was the sick thud of his own head striking one of the gondola's ribs, followed by the sudden lack of air as Quinn's hands wrapped around his throat.

Jagati was stowing weapons on the bridge when a sudden, overwhelming surge of anger slammed into her with the force of a tidal wave.

Eyes darkening, she didn't think, just grabbed a shooter from the weapons locker and raced for the ladder.

By the time she reached the fourth deck, the wave had receded just enough to hear voices she didn't recognize shouting, along with a high-pitched keen that made the hair on her neck stand on end.

Teeth bared, she jumped the last few steps to the cargo bay and landed to discover Eitan was also racing toward the open gangplank, where he stumbled to a halt so quickly she almost ran straight into him "What?" she asked, sliding around his frozen figure to see John being strangled by some maniac in an infantry coat.

"Smogging Nasa," she muttered, starting forward even as Eitan shook off his stupor and raced to the tarmac, where he put his hand on the attacker's shoulder.

Good, she thought, knowing Eitan would have the maniac down and broken without breaking a sweat.

Except he wasn't taking the maniac down.

What the hells? she thought, even as the rage that had drawn her this far swamped her senses, icing her synapses so her vision frosted over and all she could see was John, not even fighting back.

Striding forward, she powered up her shooter, toggled it to single shot, and pressed the muzzle to the base of the maniac's skull. "Let him go, or I will be decorating the hull with your brains."

Somewhere to her left, she heard a young girl say, *"Gideon,"* but the red haze didn't fade.

"I won't bother to count to three," she said.

She couldn't say if it was her gun or the kid crying, but the maniac did as she ordered, dropping his hands and leaving John to slump onto Eitan's waiting shoulder.

Still, the frosted haze remained, strong enough that she reversed the shooter and cracked the maniac on the head, taking comfort in the shock of wood meeting skull.

"Jagati, that was hardly necessary."

"Were you without oxygen long enough to suffer brain damage?" she snapped. "That was absolutely necessary."

John ignored that and, though not entirely steady, crouched beside the unconscious man where Eitan was already assessing the damage.

"I told you he was trouble." She heard a semi-familiar voice and turned to see Jinna, Rory's old shipmate, looking way more pregnant than the last time Jagati had seen her.

"Except he's not," the girl who'd called the would-be killer Gideon said, wiping her eyes as if ashamed of the emotional display. "Not really."

"Uh huh," Jagati said and jerked her head toward the river. "I vote we see if he can float."

"Jagati," John rasped, his expression flat with disapproval.

"What?" She glared at him, then looked up to see the kid tossing her a look of pure defiance. "I was joking," she said, unwillingly impressed. "Mostly."

"Rory," John said, rising somewhat creakily to his feet, "see to the colonel, would you? And our guests, if you don't mind."

"Aye, captain." Rory jerked his head. "Mia, would you help me gather my kit?" he asked, sharing a glance with Jinna, who nodded and helped usher the girl aboard after him, despite the kid's obvious desire to remain with the unconscious maniac.

"Wait," Jagati said as John's words sank in. She looked down at the tall, spare figure who was, yeah, wearing the Infantry coat, but without the suns of his rank. "Colonel?"

"Colonel Gideon Quinn," Eitan said before John could reply. He'd come to his feet and was standing at her side. "My commanding officer, until Nasa."

At the same time, something flapping and big and annoyed came swooping down to land near Gideon's shoulder, giving Jagati her first view of a tame draco.

"Wow," she said as a slightly breathless Rory appeared, first-aid kit in hand and Mia at his heels.

"Where is Jinna?" John asked.

"We set her up in the galley," Mia said. "She's knackered." Then the girl copped a squat next to the draco. "He'll be all right, Elvis," she said, rubbing the creature's head. "He will be all right, won't he?" She gave Rory a stink-eye Jagati found admirable.

"He'll be right as rain," Rory assured before casting an eye at the misting night. "Of which we've plenty."

As Rory cracked open his medical kit, Eitan eased up next to Jagati. "A word?"

"What?" she asked, but he was already moving away from the small crowd. Frowning down at Gideon one more time, she turned and followed him to the relative quiet next to the gangplank.

"How did you know to come outside?" he asked.

"What?" She blinked. "Why do you ask?"

He studied her a moment before responding. "I came down

because I felt the colonel's anger. It was—is—deep, and terrible, and cold."

Jagati thought of tidal waves but said nothing.

"So much so," Eitan continued, "that it struck me like a blow, even inside the *Errant*. Only I didn't know it was him until I spied him." He paused, took a breath, released it. "That is why I hesitated. I was trying to reach him psionically."

"You shouldn't have tried." She shook her head, momentarily distracted. "Not so soon after that backlash . . ."

"It's done," he replied shortly. "And as you saw, I failed. I also failed to protect you from that rage, and my sorrow for that."

She actually snorted at that. "I don't need protection."

"Not even from yourself?" He paused as she shifted, boots sliding on wet tarmac. "I think it is time for you to accept the truth that you are a sensitive."

Her breath expelled as if she'd been punched. "What on toxic Earth makes you think I'm a sensitive?"

Because the anger you experienced minutes ago was not yours. It was Gideon's. I sensed it from both of you, at the same time.

"No," she said, shaking her head. "I was angry because Quinn was trying to kill John."

Perhaps. But that does not explain how you are hearing me, now.

He continued to look at her, his expression patient.

Her jaw dropped because not only had he spoken to her mind-to-mind, he'd done so without touching her. "I thought you could only connect during physical contact." The words were an accusation, and they both knew it.

"Usually, but sometimes, with another sensitive, I can speak mind to mind."

She threw her hands in the air, the forgotten shooter waving. Then she stomped away, then stomped back. "So what do I do about this?" she asked. "Dammit, I don't even *like* sensitives. A bunch of toxic wasps." She paused, thought about what she'd just said, and made another face. "Sorry."

"Some are toxic." He let out a slow, foggy breath. "That said, unless you wish to become toxic yourself, some training will be necessary." He paused, and both looked back to where Rory was ministering to Gideon. "And you never noticed? All this time . . . ?"

She gave a sharp, almost painful, shrug, then holstered the shooter. "I thought it was instinct. Following my gut."

"What happened here goes well beyond instinct," he said.

She wanted to argue, and might have, but the slap of boots on wet ground made her turn to see John approaching.

"Rory says we need to replace the T-connector in the aft port pod," John told them both. "If you could head to the dock master's," he said to Jagati, "the night watch should be able to supply what we need. Rory listed a few other supplies as well."

"You just want to get me away from Quinn, don't you?"

"It seems wise," he agreed. "But also, we need the supplies—and some information."

"What kind of information?" she asked.

"Anything you can dig up on District Minister Killian Del," he said, holding out a small piece of paper and what she figured was the last of his cash.

"A minister?" Eitan straightened.

"Why do we need to know about him?" Jagati asked.

"He's the man Jinna is running from," John said.

"It just gets better and better," she muttered but took the money. Then, as their hands met, she decided to test Eitan's theory with John, and damned if she didn't pick up the edges of pain, exhaustion . . . and a burned toast sense that she immediately recognized as irritation.

Probably, she thought, with her.

"Sir, yes, sir," she said, pocketing the starbucks and snapping a fist to her heart before stalking off into the airfield's dark mist.

"That went well," John said as he watched her depart, then turned with Eitan to where the party surrounding Gideon seemed to be stirring. "Perhaps I should offer Jinna and Mia some tea," he continued, "while you and your CO get reacquainted?"

"Of course." Both men started back to the airship. "You know he will want to speak with you, after."

"After," John said, "I'll be ready."

CHAPTER 16

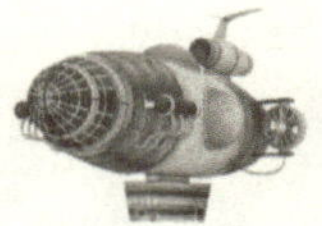

John wasn't surprised Mia didn't want to leave Gideon, and it wasn't until she looked at the draco and received a dip of the head from the small creature that she consented to follow John into the airship.

Even under the current circumstances, John found himself delighted by the exchange.

He was less delighted to see Rory popping up to follow them. "What was that you said to Jagati about Killian Del?" he asked, angling around to face John and Mia both. "Your voice carried," he added.

"That toxic bastard." Mia spat. "He thinks Jinna's babe should be his."

"Sounds like him," Rory muttered, glancing at John. "Half the reason Liam joined up was to get away from his da."

"Jinna says Liam was nothing like the old codger," Mia nodded.

"Which is all well and good." John continued to usher the girl along. "But—"

"He's been after Jinna for months," Mia continued over him. "Wouldn't take no for an answer, but tonight he stole the hive."

"Months?" Rory asked, his expression going still. "How did he steal the hive?"

"He came into Kit's, loaded with muscle and meanin' to take Jinna to his house and keep 'er there until she had the baby. Can you feature it?"

"No," Rory said, looking up the gangplank, as if he could view Jinna inside the *Errant*. "I can't."

"Neither could Gideon." Mia nodded her agreement. "You should'a seen 'im! He knocked the honey outta all three Ohmdahls before they figured they was working for a toxic—"

"Bastard, yes," John said, wrestling the conversation back to the present.

"I need to see to Jinna," Rory said, starting up the gangplank.

John stepped in front of him. "You need to see to Colonel—to Quinn. Then you need to see to that aft pod, or we won't be able to lift off, and if we can't lift off," he continued before the fire in Rory's eyes became an argument, "Jinna will still be on the ground, in Nike, where Minister Del can reach her."

Rory's jaw twitched and his eyes, which always seemed to grow larger when he got angry, continued to spark. But he jerked his head once and turned back to where Eitan crouched next to Gideon.

John let out a foggy huff of breath and turned to Mia. "Shall we?" he asked.

She shrugged and started up the gangplank. John followed and found himself hard-pressed to keep up with the nimble street thief as she sprang up the ladder to the galley, where they'd left Jinna.

"She's a nice airship," Mia called over her shoulder as they headed up the corridor toward the sound of water on the boil, "excepting it looks like the Coalfarts dropped a plasma barrel on it."

"Yes," he said as the tea kettle's whistling softened, "I'm aware."

"Hey," Jinna's head popped out of the galley's starboard door, "this place is a mess."

"A little misunderstanding regarding a piece of cargo," John said, following Mia.

Jinna's head tilted. "The same cargo Galileo was after?"

"Who?" Mia asked.

"Possibly," John said to Jinna. "You wouldn't know him," he told Mia.

"I hope not," Jinna murmured, then raised her voice. "I've got the water going, but I can't find the tea in," she waved at the wreckage, "all this."

John, having seen the galley, wasn't surprised. "I'll loo—"

"Books!" Mia burst out, racing forward to where the books John had last seen in Eitan's arm were scattered in the passage. Stooping, Mia sorted through them with the care and fascination of an antiques expert opening the footlocker of a first lander.

Recognizing a kindred spirit, he joined Mia and, crouching, caught the look on her face as she caressed the spine of one of the books. "That's odd," he said, tapping the thick, many-times read tome. "I didn't realize we had two of this one. I have another edition of this book in my quarters." A surreptitious glance told him Mia had almost shuttered the longing in her expression. He frowned and straightened, with a slight wince for his knee, as if considering some deep problem, then looked at Mia. "I don't suppose you'd care to take it?"

"I—are you sure?"

"Quite sure," he said. "It's bad form, keeping extra non-essentials on an airship."

"Oh," she said, her expression wavering between glee and pride as she accepted the novel.

John looked away to find Jinna standing in the passage, watching.

The little mother offered a wan smile and an approving nod

before looking away and, to John's distress, bending over to retrieve another fallen book.

Rushing forward, he snapped up the book before Jinna could finish crouching.

She raised her brows, then narrowed her eyes as she read the title. "Oh," she said, reaching for the thin tome. "I know that one."

"*Explosives, Accelerants, and Detonators?*" John read the title as he handed her the book while checking on Mia, who was now sitting cross-legged in the passage, pouring over her new treasure.

"A reminder of the old days," she said, flipping the pages. "Read this front to back in basic. And then back to front, then sideways."

"That's right," John recalled. "Rory said you were in demolitions."

"Small hands, flexible fingers." She held one hand up and waved. "Good for disarms."

"And now you're cooking in a diner?"

"It's all chemistry, isn't it? Until the soufflé explodes. Then it's a party."

John laughed, then coughed as the laugh tickled his abraded throat.

"I bet you could use some tea too."

"You would not be wrong," he replied, glancing one more time at Mia before leading the way back to the galley.

"I'm surprised you didn't offer her the whole library," Jinna murmured, following.

"Given her circumstances, I doubt she'd be able to keep it. I've learned a bit about a dodger's life over the years," he explained as her brows rose in question.

"Me too," she admitted. "I still consider it a personal triumph I got Rory to teach me to pick a lock."

"Impressive," John said, not hiding his surprise. "He's not one to share much of his childhood."

Then again, neither was Jagati, or Eitan, or himself, for that matter.

He thought of the child reading in the passageway. "What are the chances Mia would be willing to come with us when we raise anchor?"

"Slim," she admitted, after a beat. "I've been trying to get her out of Ellison's hive for months, but even if she dared walk away from him, she said he'd find her, or us." Her eyes narrowed. "I'd have liked to see him try."

"I bet you would," John said. "Then again," he observed as he began to search the wreckage for any usable tea, "perhaps Colonel Quinn and his draco will be able to convince Mia there's a better way."

"Maybe," she said, then looked at him.

"What?"

"Why aren't you mad at Gideon?"

"Because he has every right to his anger," John replied.

"I suppose," she said, then started tidying the counter before asking, "And you don't?"

To that, John had no answer.

Nor did he, later, when Jagati returned with Rory's T-connector, the news Gideon was awake and less inclined to commit murder, and the suggestion they lift off as soon as possible.

Since lifting off required the parts, he sent Jagati to find Rory while he, Mia, and Jinna finished drinking the mint tea Jinna had made from a packet he'd found under a chair.

Afterwards, all three made their way down the gangplank, Mia and John talking about the book and Jinna protesting she didn't want to be any trouble.

"So you've said," John told her, as he'd said before over tea. "But lately, trouble is pretty much the *Errant*'s stock in trade." At which point the port aft engine sputtered, whined, and ground to silence.

"I'm on it!" Rory's shout filtered from within.

"Really," John said, "it always works out. Eventually."

"It'll be fine," Mia promised, giving Jinna a bolstering nudge.

"Sure," Jinna said.

"I'll take care of Del."

At the sound of Gideon's voice, John turned to see the other man had joined him.

"Oh, but—" Jinna began.

"It'll work out," Gideon cut in before looking at John. "So, you're okay?"

"I've had worse," John replied, clearing his throat as he glanced at Eitan, then turned back to Quinn. "I should have taken care of Rand," he said. "If I was going down for insubordination anyway, I should have taken care of him."

"Not to worry," Quinn said softly. "I will."

"Del *and* Rand?" John said. "That seems a tall order."

"Not for the commander of the Dirty Dozen," Eitan said.

Gideon's lips quirked, and he turned to Eitan. "Do you want in on this?" he asked, causing John to hold his breath.

He could never argue with Eitan's right to confront General Rand, but the timing—

"I wish I could," Eitan said. "But I have obligations here." He glanced up at the *Errant*, then back to Gideon. "But please, feel free to give General Rand my regards."

"You can take that to the apiary," Gideon promised, while John tried not to look *too* relieved.

Then the port engine sparked to life, and Elvis, Gideon's draco, jumped from the gondola to land on Gideon's shoulder, reminding John it was past time to get the *Errant* off the ground.

CHAPTER 17

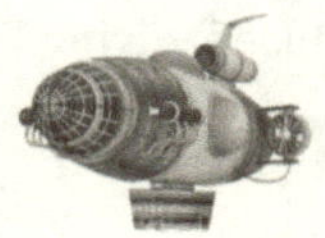

Once the 'ship was safely aloft, Rory retreated to his cabin and found it as thrashed as the rest of the airship.

Cursing, he toed off his boots and kicked them in the general direction of the closet, next to a pile of laundry that had been dumped from the hamper which had, in its turn, been pulled from its slot in the bulkhead. Snarling at the wreckage, he yanked down his suspenders, stripped the damp shirt straight over his head, and dropped it on the mound of rumpled clothes.

Twenty minutes, he thought, turning toward the head. Ten, even. Just long enough to get out of the cold wet clothes and into a hot wet shower, and then—maybe—he could face . . .

"Rory, we have to—oh—ah . . . *Hmmm.*"

He spun to see Jinna frozen halfway through the cabin door.

The cabin door he'd neglected to lock because no one ever came into his room without knocking.

"I'm sorry," she said, even as he turned back toward the bath. "I didn't realize you'd be . . ."

The sentence trailed off, and he now looked over his shoulder to discover her eyes were fixed on his back. Or, more accurately, the marks on it.

All twenty-nine of them.

"It's fine," he told her, turning so she'd not have to look on the mass of scars.

"No, it isn't," she said, her voice thick with anger. "What Rand did to you? And to John, and to Gideon and his company? It is so *not* fine."

Now *he* blinked. "I meant, it's fine that you've come barging into my room."

"I didn't barge—yes, I did," she backtracked, her eyes dropping. "I wanted to apologize for not telling you about Killian Del sooner. I just didn't want you to—"

"Didn't want me to what?" he cut in sharply. "Care? Be there for you? What?"

"This." Her eyes shot up. "I didn't want you to be—*this*." She gestured at him. "All—snippy."

"I am not snippy," he snapped, though even he could admit he sounded a might snippy. "What I am is angry."

"And I didn't want you to be that, either."

"Well, pity it is that you can't always have what you want."

Her hands fisted at her sides. "It's not like I—"

"*You never said a word*," he said, his voice so low it hurt to speak. "Mia says that smogging bastard's been after your babe for months, and you never told me. Not one word, not one telgram, not a single ping on the radio. Why? Did you think I'd not come?"

"No," she said. She shook her head once, with an expression he remembered of old. Chin tilted up, eyes cool, the pride of Pride. "I knew if I called, you'd come."

The jolt of her words scored as deep as the whip had scored his flesh back in the day, so it was a moment before he could speak again. "But you didn't."

"No," she said again.

"Because you didn't want me to come?"

"No," she said for the third time, "I didn't." Her gray eyes were as enigmatic as a Campbell mist. "Can you think why?"

Because you're stubborn? Because you're convinced there's naught you can't handle on your own? Because you know how I feel and can't return it? "Because I'm not Liam?"

"Because," she said, her voice suddenly thick, "you don't know the answer to that question."

And because he didn't—he truly did not—he could think of nothing to say as she walked out of the room, slamming the door behind her as she went.

"You know what you are?"

John looked up from the baking dish he'd only just retrieved from the floor to see Jagati entering the galley. "I'm quite confident you're about to tell me."

"You are a self-sacrificing, honor-blind moron with a martyr complex who won't be happy until he gets himself killed!"

"Put that way, I sound like an overachiever." John set the dish on the table and ducked down under it to collect the pieces of a broken mug.

"I'm not kidding." Jagati ducked down as well, so they were both under the table, wedged between the chairs John had recently righted.

"Have a care of that shard," he told her, reaching for the broken bit of crockery before she could rest her hand on it.

"See?" She waved that hand around instead and whacked a chair leg. "*Dammit.* That's what I'm talking about. Here I am yelling at you—"

"I'm deeply aware of that."

"—and you're all, 'don't cut your pinky, dear.'"

"I don't believe I said anything of the sort."

"You're watching out for me, even when I'm ready to finish

the job Quinn started and throttle your over-principled neck until you're blue in the face!" Absently, she retrieved a tin of tea and a lone chopstick.

Since they'd been short a chopstick for over a week, John didn't think its presence on the floor was related to the search. "I fail to understand how you routinely find fault with my watching out for you," he said as, hands full of broken mug, he eased back from under the table and straightened.

"I don't find fault with that." She popped up on her side of the table.

He looked at her.

"Okay, I do find fault with it, but that's not why I'm yelling at you this time."

"My apologies; please carry on with whatever it is you are yelling at me for, this time." As he spoke, he carried the mug's detritus over to the trash niche and dumped the bits.

"How can you *not* know why I'm yelling at you?" she yelled. "That thing with Quinn? That's like, the fifth time I've come along to find someone trying to kill you, and you not doing a smogging thing to stop it!"

"Not all of them were trying to kill me."

"Eitan was," she said shortly. "And he'd have done it. If I hadn't shown up and convinced him to take a half-second to read you, he'd have done it. And that was after the kid in A Fine Mess, which was after that Lau woman from the 12th Company came close to shooting you after the court-martial." On this last she waved her hands and almost poked herself with the chopstick.

"Mind the utensils," he said, crossing over to remove the offending piece of wood, and the tea, lest she chuck it at him.

"Stop that." She batted at him. "Stop taking care of me."

"If I did that, would you stop taking care of me?"

"I don't take care—"

"Would you walk into a situation where I was being killed, maimed, or damaged and just let it happen?"

"Of course not."

He looked at her, one eyebrow raised.

She glared at him, both eyebrows lowered. "I'm just saying—again—that Nasa was not your fault. You are *not* the one who killed those soldiers. I know it. Eitan knows it. Hells, even Quinn knows it now. So," she continued, pointing at John, "what makes it so impossible for you to accept that on that one day there was a bigger dog—a bigger, rabid dog—and *that* day the big rabid dog won?" Her voice lowered, though he'd not say it became soft. "You did everything you could to stop Rand. It's not on you that it wasn't enough."

"Perhaps not," he murmured as, once again, he felt the cold intrusion of Jihan's sword, heard Rand's voice ordering the cannons to fire.

"You're thinking," Jagati said, her voice slightly off. "Stop that."

"Now that is asking the impossible." He turned away to put the tea in its proper cabinet and the chopstick in the sink with the rest of the surviving kitchenware. "You've never willingly taken to command," he noted, turning on the water, pleased to see it running hot, and tossed a handful of crystals from the soap canister into the basin with the dishes.

"What does that have to do with . . . ?" She gritted her teeth. "No, I haven't."

"Which is understandable," he said, turning the spigot to the right so it could fill the rinse basin.

"How?" Joining him at the sink, she snapped a towel from its hook on the wall.

"Because with command comes the acceptance that every life lost is on you—"

"That's complete aurochs sh—"

"It's the truth," he cut in shortly, digging through the water until he found the sponge and, once he did, applying it to one of the plates he'd rescued from the compost bin—an act of pure spite on the searcher's part. "An uncomfortable truth, but there it is. And there's another truth," he continued. "A corollary to the first, that the life of the captain is held in higher value than that of her crew." He slid the plate into the rinse water and looked at Jagati. "I imagine that's what really kept you from ever accepting the captain's chair, the fact others would die for you."

"Stop turning this back on me," she said, automatically retrieving the plate and starting to dry it. "I'm not the one who'd allow myself to be murdered because of some misplaced sense of responsibility."

"I just finished explaining why it isn't misplaced." He dredged the bowl he'd been washing in the soapy water before moving it to the rinse. "But for you, well . . ."

"Well, what?" As his voice trailed off, she set the plate on the counter and pulled out the bowl.

"Let's say, I don't believe you'll ever be comfortable with the idea of someone else placing a higher value on your life than you do." This he said to the chip on the mug he was washing. "Possibly because, as far as I've seen, you value your own life at a pin's fee. Shakespeare," he explained at her confused glare. "You remember, from when I took you to see *Hamlet*?"

"I remember sleeping through most of it." She turned her scowl down to the bowl. "What is it even supposed to mean?"

"It's supposed to—it *does* mean that I have never seen anyone more likely to throw herself in front of the plasma, whether there's something to be gained by it or not." He looked up to see she'd gone still, the bowl dripping in one hand and the towel hanging limp in the other, her face unreadable. "It means," he said to that expressionless mask, "perhaps you're right, and I shouldn't allow myself to be blamed for what Rand did, but by the same quarter star, perhaps you should accept that your life has more worth than you give it."

Still she didn't move, nor did her expression change.

"Any road," he turned his attention back to the dishes, "whatever your thoughts, the answer is no, I will not stop taking care of you, if only because you can't be bothered to take care of yourself." With that, he dipped the mug into the rinse and held it out to her.

Jagati looked at the mug, then at the bowl in her hand, then at John.

In the end, he supposed he was lucky she decided to throw the bowl into the bulkhead instead of his face—though he imagined this was only because the sound of ceramic breaking against bamboo was more satisfying than the dull thud of a bowl to the nose.

By the time an unusually cross Rory relieved him at the helm, Eitan was more than ready to take the rest his crewmates had tried to force him to earlier.

On entering his quarters, however, he found his mattress had been slashed open and left on the floor.

Could be worse, he reminded himself, considering how many years he'd spent sleeping rough, both in the Corps and after.

Still, looking on the wreckage, he felt what little energy remained slipping away, like the edges of a waking dream.

Closing the door behind him, he unbuckled Rory's spring-blade and set it on one of his emptied shelves—the last thing he wanted was to stab himself in his sleep—and dropped heavily onto the bed's frame. Here he sat, staring blankly at the books strewn over the floor, the desk empty of everything but his sword, which should have been hanging on the wall above, and his clothes, scattered over the deck.

His head tilted on noticing a shirt near his right foot, the sleeve of which had ended up half-wrapped around the bottle of Tendo red that had been on the desk, as if cradling the wine.

Idly he reached out and lifted the bottle, holding it up to the light gleaming from the bulkhead.

Maybe just a sip.

Tucking the bottle under his left arm, he worked out the cork and set it aside. With his hand now free, he took a long, welcome swallow.

No one, he reflected, made wine like the keepers of Tendo. The cool, moist climate and rich hillside soil provided grapes the rest of Fortune envied.

Without thinking, he took a second drink and then a third.

Enough, he told himself with a shake of the head that set the room to spinning. More than enough, he thought as, with exaggerated care he set the bottle on the deck before retrieving the cork and putting it back in the bottle.

Except he didn't, because the cork missed the bottle entirely, and Eitan's hand slid down to hit the deck.

"Tired," he muttered, wondering why his tongue tasted like cotton.

He tried to cork the bottle again and failed again.

"Smog it," he said, dropping the cork and slumping against the bed frame. To his befogged brain, the hard bamboo felt like the thin mattresses used by the Chandrasekhar dormitories.

"Trust me," Galileo said, stepping from the bathroom to crouch at Eitan's side, "the bamboo is more comfortable."

Which was wrong, because Leo shouldn't have been there.

"Of course I should," Galileo said, clearly reading Eitan's thoughts. "Your captain invited me when he stole my calculator."

No, Eitan thought.

"Yes," Galileo said as Eitan's eyes, heavy with the morph Galileo had slipped into the wine, finally closed.

CHAPTER 18

After Jinna left Rory, she tried to cool down in one of the spare berths, but stomping around an empty room wasn't as soothing as she'd hoped, so she gave up and headed back to the galley, thinking she could excise her temper with some housecleaning.

Unfortunately, she discovered someone had beat her to it.

"Smog it," she muttered, glaring at the tidied space but, in fact, still seeing Rory's expression shifting from anger to blank to hurt just before she left his berth.

But how on toxic Earth was she supposed to tell him what he refused to *see*?

Worse, how could she explain just how much they'd both lost when Liam's airship crashed in that storm over the Amazons?

Even as she thought of Liam, she recalled that night in The Frayed Rigging, the night when everything had changed.

The war had ended, and she and Rory and Liam were celebrating together until Rory had left with John and Jagati.

She remembered watching Rory walk out the door, and how, afterwards, Liam had taken her hand and led her through the crowds.

She remembered his kindness and the warmth of his touch.

She remembered the sadness in his moss green eyes as he'd quietly pointed out, "I'm not him."

And she remembered, with an ache that went down to her bones, the kiss, and what came after when she'd said, "Neither am I."

Blinking away the tears that always accompanied the memory of that one, fateful night, Jinna almost turned to leave the galley but paused mid-step because, really, where else did she have to go?

At which point the baby danced a jig. "Hungry?" she murmured, then looked at the newly cleaned galley, then thought, *why not?* and crossed the room to poke through the cupboards and cooler.

Her quick inventory uncovered a stash of pasta, dehydrated tomatoes and mushrooms, a few leaves of kale, a jar of olives, a tin of beans and a lump of hard cheese.

No fresh herbs, but some dried basil, garlic, and thyme in Corps-stamped containers huddled behind the tea stash.

Not quite Kit's larder, but she could work with it and, pleased to see the *Errant*'s water tanks read as full, engaged in her favorite form of therapy.

***

Since the fight with John and murdering one of their few surviving bowls, Jagati had been prowling the 'ship like a bear dog, cleaning up more of the wreckage and generally avoiding people.

Her wanderings eventually brought her back to the fourth deck, where the sound of activity filtered out of the galley. Shoulder to the door frame, Jagati peered around the corner and huffed out a breath. "Jerk."

At the sound of Jagati's voice, Jinna spun toward the door, spoon held up like a weapon.

"Sorry," Jagati said, holding her own hands up. "My fault for jumping at shadows."

"Understandable," Jinna said after a pause, then grimaced at the wooden spoon before turning back to her work.

"What are you making?" Jagati came the rest of the way into the galley, where she snapped up an uncooked piece of pasta and sat down at the table, where she started to crunch it.

"The poor aeronaut's version of Penne from Heaven," Jinna said, looking over her shoulder at Jagati's guffaw, then tipped her head as Jagati crunched down on another piece of pasta. "How does that taste?"

"Like nothing. It's all about the crunch." Then she smushed the bits together to form a pasta-spit patty to show to Jinna.

"Ach!" Jinna said, but she was smiling as she grabbed the cutting board and started to chop the dried veg she'd collected. "Just be ready, because when this one's a toddler," she jerked a chin down to her swollen belly, "I'll be bringing them to learn from the master."

"As long as you wait until it's a toddler," she replied as Jinna minced the shriveled lengths of tomato to smaller bits, then started on the mushrooms Jagati had ignored the last time she cooked. "Those tiny balls of flesh freak me out."

"There's an image." Jinna shuddered, then tossed the tomatoes and mushrooms into the pan at her elbow, where oil had already been heating. A small pile of dried herbs followed, emitting a fragrance that had Jagati's mouth watering. Jinna gave the veg a quick stir, then began to chop the kale before she spoke again. "I haven't spent any quality time with babies since before I joined up," she admitted as she tossed the kale into the pan, then added a couple handfuls of pasta to the water she had boiling. "My cousin had twins, though, and they were as volatile as a crystal det mine, without the fail-safes."

"It isn't the volatile that freaks me, it is the 'I could drop and break it' that does. Small, squishy, I hear that they have a soft spot on their heads and if you drop them on it or hit it against something you break 'em." She nodded to herself.

"So no squishy, breaky babies for you; check," Jinna said, turning to stir the pasta and poke at the veggies.

"Breaking things is my skill set," Jagati said, leaning back in her chair. "Mostly that's why I joined up. That and Dodge getting the smog bombed out of it."

"Same here," Jinna said. "I mean, the getting bombed out part. Except it was Macintosh instead of Dodge. Up the Fordians."

"Up the Fordians," Jagati echoed. "You were Airborne during the war, weren't you?" she asked. Rory didn't talk about much of his time on the *York*, but she knew he'd met Jinna while he served on the troop carrier.

Jinna nodded. "Part of the 72nd, up through the final push in Cervantes," she named one of Allianza's northern territories.

"The *Desmos* fought at Santandar," Jagati said, referring to the airship she'd been posted to after Nasa.

"Practically next door to each other," Jinna said, after a moment of silence for those final battles. "Still, all in all, I've found I prefer making food to building mines. Speaking of, do you know where the tin opener is?" She glanced over her shoulder toward an unopened tin of cannellini beans.

Jagati grunted and stood, moving to Jinna's left to root around in one of the drawers where she quickly found the opener, and in a few moments was removing the lid from the tin.

As she presented the beans, she looked down at the exceptionally pale woman beside her, noting a blueish tinge to her lips.

"Hey." Jagati set down the tin and squinted at a blue vein showing in Jinna's neck. "Are you okay?"

"What?" Jinna looked up. She'd been lowering the heat source under the water, which had hit a turbulent boil. "I don't . . ." She looked again at the water, now boiling over despite the lowered heat. "That's not right," she said. Then she looked up, patting a hand over her heart. "What's our altitude?"

"We generally cruise at about 2,000 meters," Jagati said. "But even if Rory took us higher, the pressurization would . . . should compensate." But even as she spoke, Jagati's head tipped up, her ears tuning in to realize she couldn't hear the familiar burr of the vents. "Uh-oh . . ."

The thud of boots in the corridor heralded company. She looked up to see John poke his head through the starboard door. "I think there's something wrong with the—"

Jinna's knees buckled and she dropped.

"—ventilation system," he finished as Jagati caught the other woman and lowered both herself and the unconscious Jinna to a sitting position on the floor.

"Get the water," she said, looking up and wondering why John appeared to be covered in little black dots. She blinked and watched as he altered his course for the stove and killed the heat under both pans, then took the boiling pot and thrust it into the sink where it could pose no further threat.

Finally, he turned and crossed to the port arch, where the airship's radio hung. "I'll check with Rory on the bridge," he said, his own breathing labored to Jagati's ears. "It may be Galileo's people sabotaged the altim—the alt—" he paused, blinked, shook his head and looked back at Jagati, huddled on the floor with Jinna because it was too much trouble to try and move.

"I'm sorry," he said, blinking, "but are there two of you?"

Wondering if Jinna could be heavy enough to be constricting her breath, Jagati sipped in some air. "What?" she asked.

"What?" he asked back, blinking owlishly. "Never mind."

Then, as she watched, he reached for the hand piece, missed. Reached again. This time he caught the hand piece, which made him smile giddily at Jagati right before he dropped to the deck, taking the radio with him, ripping the cord from the box.

"Ahhh, crap." Jagati said, then looked left as another figure appeared. *"Whoa,"* she gasped out as a blurry figure wearing a breather walked her way. "Who?" she asked, then shook her head, then wished she hadn't as the blurry shape wavered, then faded, then . . .

Galileo watched the woman slump, then risked a quick sensing to confirm all three of the crew were, in fact, unconscious.

He was pushing himself, far enough that he felt a telltale buzzing in the base of his skull, a buzzing which could expand to a migraine if he wasn't careful.

But no one else could have psionically pressured Rory into bringing the *Errant* to 3,400 meters while Galileo's newest hireling disabled the ventilation system.

At least it had taken only a few minutes for Pitte and his crew to succumb to hypoxia.

"This the last of 'em?" Colin, his own rebreather in place, entered the galley.

Galileo nodded. "Who is on the bridge?" he asked, his own voice hollow under the mask.

"Mary. The mechanic's out," Colin assured. "He won't cause no trouble."

"Very well." Galileo gestured to John, then Jagati. "Lock them up as we discussed. Quickly. As soon as you have them contained, we can restart the ventilation system."

"You got it, guv," Colin said and moved off to deal with John.

Galileo crossed to where the two women were slumped together.

Crouching, he reached out to brush aside Jinna's red-gold hair.

Syl's had been wavy, he recalled, and a few tones deeper, for she'd taken after Da, while Galileo favored their mother.

Light and shadow, my babes, Mum had said.

Except Syl was gone, and Mum with her, leaving Galileo a lonely shadow, hovering over this echo of his twin.

"Little sister," his deep voice rang hollow through the breather, "I wish you weren't here."

With a sigh, he removed his breather and placed it over Jinna's blueing lips. As soon as the roseate bloom on her cheeks began to ease, he adjusted the rebreather over his shoulder and lifted her into his arms. "Come along, then," he told her, rising with the barest show of effort, "we'll get you settled somewhere safe until this is over."

And as he carried her out, he began to whistle a tune, an old one, that Syl had always loved.

CHAPTER 19

John woke not so much with a start as with a slow, unenthusiastic sally.

As consciousness poked him back to reality, he noted the aching head, tingling limbs, dry cottony mouth, and the labored breathing of hypoxia.

Except hypoxia generally occurred when flying at high altitudes without pressurization.

Something that should not have happened.

Not on the *Errant*.

Not with his crew.

As he came more fully awake, he also recognized the lack of engine noise.

Engines shut down, he thought, while the gentle sway of the deck told him they were still aloft, most likely at high anchor.

Another poke, this time from someone's finger, had him peeling one eye open to see Jagati drilling her finger into his shoulder. "Please stop."

"I wouldn't need to poke you if you'd woken up when I said your name the last thirty-two times."

"Did you count?" John began to sit up, then froze as he realized his right arm hung over his head, secured by a shackle, the chain of which ran through one of the D-rings used to secure cargo nets.

On the other end of the chain, a second shackle held Jagati's left wrist.

He met her gaze, a cold ball forming in his gut. "Where is everyone else?"

"Haven't seen Rory or Jinna, but Eitan's over there." Jagati jerked her chin past John's shoulder, and he turned to see the soldier slumped against the pallet of emergency water rations, his right arm suspended by a length of rope tied to the bar holding the barrels in place.

"Shouldn't he be awake by now?" John asked.

"He may be out a while longer."

A deep voice carrying the lilt of Guinness had both John and Jagati turning to see a tall, dark-haired man descending the ladder. "I might have used a heavy hand with the morph," the stranger continued as he reached the deck.

As one, John and Jagati shoved themselves to their feet.

"Where's Jinna?" Jagati asked, rattling the chain as she pounded at her left arm while John tried to rub the feeling back into his right. "And Rory?"

"The little sister is safe," the man told her. "As is your mechanic."

"And I'm guessing you're Galileo?" John said.

The man nodded.

"How?" John asked, then cleared his throat. "I mean, where were you hiding? We searched the airship, top to bottom."

"Actually, you didn't," the man said. "No one looked in the deck two mechanical room."

Where the ventilation systems were housed. "I was supposed to run pre-flight on the vents," John muttered.

"And would have, if I hadn't discouraged you." Galileo tapped the side of his head.

"You influenced me?" John asked, then tamped down the nausea accompanying that realization. "You invaded my privacy."

"That tracks," Jagati said, her voice casual enough, but John was certain he *felt* the waves of her anger battering at him. "No wonder you're Eitan's *ex*-whatever."

"A great deal more than whatever," Galileo murmured.

"You certainly made me believe that."

Now all three turned to see Eitan easing to his feet while pressing the stump against his temple. "Did you have to use so much morph?"

"I wanted to be sure you couldn't kill me on sight," Galileo told him, then turned to John. "Where is my property?"

"Yours?" Jagati asked before John could reply. "Like, 'I found it, so it's mine' or like 'I made it'?"

"Like, 'I made it'," Galileo told her.

"Well, that changes everything," Jagati said, then—at John's confused glance—sighed. "If he found or stole the thing, it's about the money," she explained. "Creating the thing means it's about more than a handful of starbucks."

"Actually," Galileo said, "it is about the money. Mostly."

"Galileo has never allowed ethics to stand in the way of his desires," Eitan observed.

"And it's easy to be ethical when you never have to worry where your next meal is coming from," Galileo told Eitan, then turned to John. "Meanwhile, I'll thank you for telling me where to find my—"

"Oy! Mind the steps!"

All three of the *Errant* crew straightened as an agitated Rory tumbled down the last few steps and onto the deck.

"Rory!"

"How are you?"

"Are you all right?"

"Ow," Rory said, rolling onto his back and staring at the

rafters as a woman stepped lightly down the ladder, sword in hand.

"The mechanic is awake," she said as John and Jagati shared a look, then turned back to stare.

"*Ysabel?*" Jagati said.

"What are you doing here?" John asked.

"You and this wasp have met?" Rory asked, easing up to his elbows.

"She works for Tariq," John explained.

"*Worked* for Tariq would be the operative term," Galileo said. "Now she works for me."

"Mary convinced me Galileo offered superior opportunities," Ysabel said, hauling Rory to his feet and shoving him toward the starboard bulkhead, where another set of shackles hung from another of the D-rings.

"Where did all these shackles come from?" Jagati wondered.

"Colin always travels prepared," Galileo told her, even as the man himself appeared in the companionway, holding Jinna by the wrist.

It was at this point that Rory, making a sound unlike anything John had ever heard, rammed his shoulder into Ysabel's sternum, grabbed her sword, and flung himself across the deck, sweeping the blade wildly to keep Galileo back as he raced toward Colin, who reached under his coat.

John, taking a breath to call a warning, felt that breath catch as Rory came to a juddering halt.

"What?" Jagati asked as the mechanic's fingers went slack, and the sword dropped to the deck with a dull, dead sound.

Then, as John watched, his body jerked, and jerked again, and his breath gasped out, and then again his entire body wracked as if someone or something were striking him, over and over and over again.

Which was when John caught on, but only because he'd been

present the first time he'd seen Rory flogged, back on the *Kodiak*, over six years ago.

Instinct had him searching the room for the culprit, but he only found Galileo, standing mid-deck, his eyes fixed on Rory.

Galileo who, as Eitan had told John, possessed the ability to send a person back in time.

"Stop," John called, pulling at the chain so hard Jagati hissed. "Dammit, he's disarmed, make it stop!"

"Leo," Eitan added his voice. "Please. This is not who you are."

"Are you so certain?" Galileo asked, but as he spoke, Rory gave one last convulsive shudder, then crumpled to his knees.

As he fell, Jinna twisted her arm out of Colin's grip and rushed to kneel at Rory's side.

Even as Colin strode after her, Galileo stepped in front of him. "I told you, she is not to be harmed."

"McCabe . . ." Kneeling at Rory's side Jinna's voice was low, but everyone heard the tremor in it. "Are you all right?" She put a hand to his cheek, leaned over. "*Rory* . . ."

"Come." Galileo stepped up and offered her a hand. "You are upset. It is not good for the babe."

Jinna's gray eyes shot up, sparking as she slapped his hand aside. "Don't play the hero with me," she told him. "I've already seen what you are."

"Attagirl," Jagati tossed in.

"Leo," Eitan said while, on either side of the young couple, Ysabel and Colin waited for some sign of what they should do. "You remember what it was like, to be young and hurting."

Galileo's eyes flashed up to meet Eitan's. "That I do, all too well."

Silence fell as another fragment of the past lodged between the two men.

"Oy, then," Rory's voice slurred its way through the tension. "S'aright," his hand half-lifted and fell again. "Everthin's fine an' dandy." His eyes opened and, despite the vestiges of remembered pain, his brown eyes were clear and for Jinna alone. "See?"

"Yes," she nodded and knuckled at the tears already falling before thumping him in the shoulder with a vehement, "Dammit, Rory!"

"Wait! What did I do?"

"The same thing you always do." She waved the thumping hand and then thumped him again. "Putting yourself in front of the plasma for me."

John glanced at Jagati, who absolutely did *not* return the look.

"I do not always—" Rory protested.

"Of course you do. You did it on the *York* that time my line frayed while I was handling a midair disarm. You did it at Cervantes when you were dead sure I was about to step on a mine—as if I can't tell the difference between a mine and a mushroom!"

"Obviously Rory couldn't," Jagati murmured.

"I only wanted you to be safe." Rory started to sit up.

"Really?" She pushed him back down. "Why?"

"What d'ye mean, why?" Bafflement danced over the young man's features, and John felt a stirring of pity for him.

"I mean," her hands flew to her sides, *"why?"*

"Because we're mates." He glared down, apparently fixated with her knees. "I'd do the same for any of my mates."

"Really?" Jagati whispered.

"Bollux to that," Jinna said, borrowing Rory's term. "Why," she leaned forward, a pale fury with fire for hair, "do you keep putting yourself between me and the wasps?"

Rory hissed, then looked up to meet her gaze. "If ye must know, t'was for Liam's sake."

"Liam," she echoed the name, which dropped like an anchor between them.

"Who's Liam?" Colin whispered.

"Baby's father," Jagati whispered back. "Shhhh . . ."

"Aye." Rory tried and failed to meet her accusing gaze. "For him. Because . . ."

Jinna filled in the blank when his voice faltered. "Because he was your friend. And because you think you owe him something."

"I do." He looked up, his eyes more fierce than even when he'd been charging at Colin. "I did. After Nasa? I'd have been rotting in the bact-tanks or sent to the Barrens as a deserter, for I was that close to jumping 'ship before he raised me out. So yes, I do . . . owe him."

"Liam didn't think so," Jinna said, her expression softening.

"No?" Rory shook his head and let out a sigh. "Well, he wouldn't. But he *did* ask me to look after you while he was gone, and then . . ." His voice trailed off, and John could almost see the shadow of Liam Del fall between the two young people. "He asked that one thing of me, and then he died," Rory finally said. "So I owe it to him to keep you safe."

"Okay," she said. "I understand that. Except Liam wasn't asking you to keep me safe for him."

"What?" Rory said, looking up. "*What?*"

"I'm not sure what Liam told you," Jinna shook her head, and the red-gold of her hair glowed under the overhead lamp, "but he and I were . . . we weren't a couple."

John heard the hitch in Jinna's voice and wondered what she wasn't saying.

"Really?" Colin snorted. "Because where I come from, a queen inna royal jelly says otherwise."

"Do you mind?" Jinna's eyes shot in his direction.

Colin held up his hands and stepped back a pace.

She turned back to Rory. "It's true, Liam was over the moons because he wanted—really wanted—to be a father. But he also knew how I felt about you. And . . ." Again her voice faltered, and again, John wondered.

"But he—and you—" Rory's face paled and reddened and

paled by turns. "You never said anything. All this time—*years!* I thought the two of you mad in love!"

"And all this time, *years*," she countered, "you kept throwing Liam at me and me at him. We thought you weren't interested!"

"Because I thought I had no chance!" he protested. "And besides, *you* never said anything," he echoed the original protest whilst rising to his feet.

"Neither did you!" she pointed out as she tried to do the same, then held up a hand so he could pull her up next to him.

"Well," he spluttered, and shoved his hands in his pockets. "I suppose that makes us both bleedin' stupid!"

"I guess it does," she tossed her head and, literally, bellied up to him, gray eyes snapping with fury.

"Fine!" he snapped.

"Good!" she snapped back.

"All right, then." And now Rory's hands came out of his pockets, and he grabbed the girl by the shoulders and yanked her in for a kiss.

She let out a surprised curse that softened to a sigh, and Rory's grip eased. His hands slid down her shoulders to hold her hands and, as he deepened the kiss she gave a little gasp.

John cleared his throat and looked away, then nudged Jagati, who was watching like they were at a matinee of *I Love Lucy*.

"I believe that's quite enough of that," Galileo said, and Colin and Ysabel each stepped up to collect one young lover apiece.

Ysabel pulled Rory back to the starboard D-ring, this time wasting no time fitting shackles around both his wrists while Colin waited with Jinna, who was standing quietly, hands clasped together and staring at Rory as if uncertain what she saw.

"Now that young love has been requited," Galileo said, "it's time to get back to the business of my property."

"Why bother to ask when you can creep around in people's heads?" Jagati asked.

"I wager he cannot," Eitan observed, turning to Galileo.

"You've been busy, tonight," he noted. "Even for you, the energy you have spent masking yourself and your team, delving into other people's memories, influencing Rory—it carries a price."

"You would know," Galileo replied. "How is your head, by the way?"

"Never better," Eitan said.

"Liar," Galileo murmured. "Fortunately for me, I have more than just a few psi-tricks up my sleeve." And as he spoke, crossed to where Ysabel had just secured Rory and held out a hand. "Your sword."

"No." Jinna started forward as Ysabel handed over the short, lightly curved blade, but Colin held her back.

"While it is true I would never harm Jinna," Galileo explained, placing the tip of the sword under Rory's chin, "I have no issue at all with killing *him.*"

"Whoa, hold up!" Jagati exclaimed.

"The cargo is on the *Errant,*" John said at the same time.

"We searched the *Errant,*" Galileo replied.

"I didn't say it was *in* the *Errant,*" John said quickly, then as every eye in the bay turned on him, explained, "It's attached to the starboard aft engine pod."

"Now that is clever," Colin said as Galileo stared.

"When did you put it out there?" Jagati asked.

"Right after Rory opened the box," he told her. "I left the galley, harnessed up, and went outside."

"So to be clear, you left my prototype calculator secured on the engine pod of an airship?" Galileo asked, though he did lower the sword.

"What's a calculator?" Colin asked Jinna.

"No clue," Jinna replied.

"It is very well secured," John said to Galileo.

"It had better be." Galileo drew a thick key from his pocket and held it up. "So, who's to fetch it?"

"I'll—" Rory began.

"I'll do it," Jagati said at the same time.

"Nonsense," John said. "I'll go."

"Years leading jump teams," Jagati pointed out.

"I got it out there," John said. "I can get it back. And beyond all that," he pointed at himself with his right hand, thus pulling Jagati's left, "*Captain.*"

"*First Mate.*" She imitated his tone and pointed at herself with her left arm, pulling at his right. "As such, it is my duty to lead any off-ship retrieval while you safeguard the vessel."

John felt his eye twitching. "I should never have taken you to see *Star Trek, The Musical.*"

Her eyes gleamed. "But ya did."

"Except that's fiction," he pointed out.

"Didn't you *just* finish explaining to me how the life of the captain is considered more valuable than that of their crew?"

He hissed, hearing his words from the galley thrown back at him. "I was speaking of life in the Corps," he said, "and you know it."

"This is taking too long," Galileo said. "Ysabel, unlock the cap—"

And then Jagati shifted her weight and slammed her boot into the side of John's bad knee.

Shouts of surprise from Rory and Colin underscored the curse John let out as, sweating and furious, he gripped their shared chain to hold himself upright.

Galileo, meanwhile, returned Ysabel's sword to her, then crossed to John and Jagati to unlock Jagati's shackle.

She moved away, shaking her arm to life at the same time Colin led Jinna over to take her place.

"Really?" John asked.

"It's not like she has anywhere to run," Jagati added.

"I prefer to take no chances. Apologies," Galileo said to Jinna as he slammed the shackle closed on her left wrist with metallic clunk. "I'd rather you not put yourself in any further danger."

Once Jinna was secure, he glanced at Jagati. "Get into your harness. I would like to finish this business before the suns rise."

"So say we all," Rory tossed in as Jagati crossed to where the jump lines and harnesses hung near the bay door.

"Jagati," John said, waiting for her to look in his direction. "*I* value it," he said, "at far more than a pin's fee."

He saw, by the flash of surprise followed by resentment, she remembered the other part of their conversation in the galley.

CHAPTER 20

While Jagati donned her harness, Galileo spun the lock on the bay door and hauled it open. Once it was latched to the bulkhead, he lifted the *Errant*'s boarding axe from where it was secured nearby. "No funny business," he said, hefting the weapon.

"You have trust issues," she told him, her breath puffing in the chill air flowing from outside.

He leaned close, his eyes near to black and, she thought, not entirely sane. "So do you," he murmured.

She bared her teeth, grabbed a carryall, and secured it to the harness before tugging on her gloves. She stepped up to the door, triple-checked that her line, fixed to a ring in the deck, was secure, then turned so she was facing the bay. With her left hand, she toggled on the harness torch and leaned back. "Three, two, one . . . go," she murmured, then stepped backwards into the air.

John held his breath as Jagati dropped out of sight, then exhaled into the silence that fell over the assembled.

Galileo remained near the open door, both hands gripping the boarding axe while the chill night air swirled into the bay and Colin and Ysabel roamed the deck, eyes darting from their prisoners to Galileo and back.

Next to him, Jinna made a small sound and shivered.

"Cold?" John asked.

"A little," she said.

"Here." He held up his free arm and she slid under it as he sent an apologetic glance Rory's way, only to see the quickest flash of a wink.

Odd, he thought, then looked down to see Jinna opening her hand to reveal one of Rory's lock-picks.

Which was when he realized that the earlier kiss may well have been a celebration of young love, but it had also been Rory's way of getting the lock-pick to Jinna.

"Would you like me to fetch you a coat?" Colin asked.

"No one is going anywhere to fetch anything," Galileo snapped, still staring out the door. From the direction of his gaze, John figured Jagati was halfway to the pod junction. "Radio Mary on the bridge, she can bring something down."

"Oh good," John murmured. "Mary is here too."

"It's all right," Jinna said as Colin crossed to the bay radio. "I can handle a little cold."

"No trouble," Colin assured and crossed to the bay radio. "This bird ain't goin' anywhere, and if I know Mary, she's already bored."

Jinna closed her hand over the pick while John glanced at Eitan and, when the other man met his gaze, tipped his chin at Colin.

Eitan dipped his head and waited for Colin to deliver his message. "So your name is Colin?" he asked as the other man replaced the mic.

"Aye." The mercenary shot a suspicious glance Eitan's way.

"And what do you need? A pillow? Someone to scratch your back?"

"Neither, though I will keep you in mind should I have an itch."

John watched Colin swallow.

"I am merely curious," Eitan continued, "how a man such as yourself chose this life. You have skills, initiative, looks . . ." Again the smile, drawing Colin another step closer to Eitan. "Fortune could be your apiary."

"You'd think," Colin agreed, running a hand over his smooth golden-brown scalp. "But you know how it is. War ends, the Corps don't need the extra bodies, and what's a demobbed infantryman to do? I spent my life onna lines, pushing the smogging Coalfarts back to their side. S'what I'm good at, pushing trouble back to the other side."

"And no one does it better. Colin's a queen's dream when it comes to combat."

John turned to see Mary descending the companionway. She'd lost the gown, he noted, but had replaced it with a pair of Rory's trousers, Eitan's shirt, Jagati's spare boots, and John's own jacket.

"I can see why you wanted a wrap," she said to Jinna as she crossed the deck. "It's as cold as Stolichnaya down here." Mary held up a blanket, taken from John's bed, as she walked over to tuck it around Jinna's shoulders.

"Hello, Mary," John said, drawing her attention to him.

She looked up, smiling. "I told you we'd keep looking."

"I recall."

With Jinna covered, Mary glanced about the bay. "So this is the airship you're so keen to hold on to?"

"It suits us," John told her.

"It's a bit empty," she pointed out. "I'd have expected a freighter would have more freight."

"Depends on the client, doesn't it?" Rory tossed in from his side of the bay. "The job you hired us for's right wee, but you should have been here for the bees."

"Please," Eitan held up his arm, "let us not speak of the bees."

"He hated the bees," Rory confided to Colin.

"Shut it, everyone," Galileo snapped.

At John's side, Jinna pulled the blanket around to cover both their hands.

Outside, Jagati was working her way aft, swinging from grip to grip along the gondola's hull.

At least John had chosen the pod closest to the door. Especially given it was smogging cold out here, and her flight jacket, while sufficient inside the 'ship, wasn't enough to keep her from shivering as she eased down the gondola's length, letting out the excess line as she went.

To pass the time, she hummed a tune that had wormed its way into her skull soon after being introduced to Quinn's draco, and had just gotten to the first chorus, and the sappy lovers crying in the gloom of Heartbreak Hotel, when she reached the pod junction, a thick appendage from which the pod itself extended from the main hull.

For most repairs, Rory could access the pod via that junction. For outside repairs, he—or whoever pulled the short straw—used line and harness and the rungs built into the gondola, though usually those repairs happened while anchored in an airfield.

"He had to put it on the bottom of the engine," Jagati groused as she reached the bulbous pod. "Couldn't have hidden it on top." She unlooped a little more line and made a one-handed bowline through one of the grips.

With the line secured, she re-checked her harness at all points and then let herself drop to swing beneath the pod. As she swung, the circle of light from the harness torch at her shoulder danced along the underbelly, brighter than the slivers of moonslight peeking through the clouded night.

Even as dark as it was, she quickly spied the cargo, securely fastened just fore of the vent.

Very securely.

With, like, a mile of envelope tape.

Unbelievable.

After venting a steady stream of curses, she leaned back to shout, "A knife would be helpful!"

"I should have mentioned the tape," John observed as Jagati's demand filtered through the door.

"You think?" Colin growled, then he, Mary, and Ysabel headed aft to confer with Galileo.

"Hold still," Jinna murmured, taking advantage of the distraction.

John said nothing but kept an eye on Galileo, who was handing a second harness set-up to Ysabel.

Across the bay, Rory shifted, rattling his chains so that, when the lock on John's shackle clicked open, it went unnoticed.

Jagati wasn't sure what to expect, but it certainly wasn't Ysabel sliding down on a line with the ease of experience. She waited while the other woman caught the nearest handhold and climbed over to the pod. "You need something cut?" she asked, her own torch flaring over the pod as she dropped to join Jagati.

"You have no idea," Jagati replied. "I considered using my teeth, but your boss is in a hurry."

Ysabel looked at the lump illuminated by Jagati's torch and grimaced. "It would be bad if the package were to fall."

Both glanced down. Through wisps of cloud cover, they could see the ridged shadings of what Jagati guessed were the protected wilds of Lycos.

"Would you rather ask Galileo to land?" Jagati asked.

Ysabel's face twisted in a rare show of disdain, then she anchored her feet on one of the low bars and wrapped one arm around her line.

Jagati did the same. Once she was as secure as she could make herself, she put her hands under the package before giving Ysabel a nod, then waited as the other woman drew a utility knife from her belt and began sawing through the patching tape.

Sooner than she would have expected, the package fell into her hand. "Gotcha," she said, then shoved the troublesome bit of tech into the carryall on her harness.

Once it was secure, both women climbed up the pod's side before Ysabel held out her hand.

"Seriously?" Jagati asked.

Ysabel simply arched a brow.

Jagati huffed, then unhitched the carryall and handed it to Ysabel, who hooked it to her harness before both women began the laborious process of edging their way to the main hull.

Inside the bay, Eitan was waiting.

For what, he wasn't entirely certain, but John clearly had something planned though, at present, the captain remained quietly huddled with Jinna, eyes on their captors.

Eitan followed John's gaze to where Colin stood mid-bay with Ysabel's sword in hand, while Mary leaned against the ladder rail.

Galileo was pacing in front of the open jump door.

At last, Eitan turned back to John, who turned to meet Eitan's gaze and dipped his head once before tapping Jinna on the shoulder.

She took a deep breath, let out a pained hiss, and then looked down before saying, "Uh oh."

"What?" John asked, all his focus suddenly on the young woman at his side, his voice tight with worry. "What, uh oh?"

"I think," she said. "I think I should sit down . . ."

And then she went limp.

Everyone jumped, Eitan included, as John caught Jinna with his free arm.

But it was Galileo who moved the fastest, rushing to Jinna's side, projecting a concern so sharp that Eitan felt it like a blade to the heart.

"Little one," Galileo said, letting the axe *thud* to the deck so he could help John support Jinna. "*Deirfiúr?*" he murmured, dropping his lips to her hair.

Hearing the Keltican term for 'sister,' a surge of alarm shot through Eitan.

"Please," Galileo was saying, his voice harsh, "don't go."

"I won't," Jinna murmured, her eyes easing open. "Wow," she said, her skin flushing as she met Galileo's gaze. "I almost feel bad about this."

"Bad?" Galileo asked, brushing her hair aside. "About what?"

"About—"

John's left elbow snapped out and across Galileo's temple, stunning him long enough for John's right hand, free from its shackle, to deliver a cracking uppercut that sent Leo to the deck.

"—that," Jinna said as John swept up the fallen axe and turned toward Eitan while a shout from Colin echoed through the bay.

CHAPTER 21

Outside, Jagati waited for Ysabel to reach the pod junction before following.

Despite years of experience on the lines, her arms were trembling from the exertion. Dangling in the cold, holding her weight with one gloved hand, was no longer a daily experience.

Still, the muscles remembered, and she soon joined Ysabel on the hull, where both began the laborious task of edging their way toward the open bay door.

They'd gotten about halfway to their destination when a shout emerged from inside, followed by another, followed by the distinctive sounds of metal striking metal.

While Colin and Mary raced toward the center of the bay, John swung the axe down on the dowel holding Eitan and the emergency water rations in place. He felt the thunk of metal chopping through wood all the way to his shoulders.

"Here they come," Eitan said, grabbing hold of the dowel.

John, nodding, moved to his other side, already raising the axe, but by that time Colin was in range.

"Ah," John turned.

"I have it," Eitan assured, and dropped into a reverse bow to sweep his extending leg at the mercenary's ankles.

Unprepared for an attack from that quarter, Colin tripped and stumbled backwards, losing his grip on Ysabel's sword.

Mary was right behind Colin, and only hesitated long enough to pick up the fallen blade.

"Incoming," Eitan warned as John finished chopping through the heavy doweling on the other side. Spinning, he raised the axe to block Mary's overhead cut while, to his right, Eitan and Colin rolled to their feet, Eitan brandishing the dowel and Colin drawing a shock stick from under his coat.

At least it wasn't a shooter.

"Twenty starbucks says Eitan breaks that stick over your skull," he heard Rory call as Mary danced forward, blade in hand.

<hr>

Whatever was happening in the cargo bay, Jagati decided this was a good time to even up the odds.

Since Ysabel wasn't an idiot, she clearly held the same opinion because as their eyes met, Ysabel was shifting toward Jagati.

With an unholy grin, Jagati shot out a kick, which Ysabel dodged.

Jagati angled away, her left hand and foot still on the hull, her right hand taking the line.

A meter away, Ysabel mirrored the action, down to the bared teeth, making Jagati realize that if the other jumper weren't a swarming turncoat, she might have actually liked her.

Rory, still locked to the starboard bulkhead, looked from the fallen Galileo to where Eitan swept the unwieldy dowel in a series of arcs, spins, and jabs to drive the muscular Colin across the deck, shock stick sparking against the dowel, the bulkhead, anything but its actual target.

A rattle from across the bay had Rory turning back to see Jinna tugging the shackle's chain through the D-ring to free herself.

"Brilliant!" Rory called as she sidestepped past the fallen Galileo. "Only you wouldn't have that lock-pick would you?"

Jinna froze mid-step and looked behind her. "I think I dropped it," she said as John ducked a whistling swipe from Mary's sword and Eitan's staff at the same time.

"Pardon," Eitan called, reversing the swing.

"No worries," John replied, parrying the next swipe, and the next.

"It is for me," Mary said, huffing. "I want you all to myself."

Rory and Jinna shared a grimace, then both looked at the pallet of water casks which, lacking the dowel Eitan was even now spinning like a bo staff, was open on one side.

"I've got—" Rory began.

"I have an idea," Jinna said, and they grinned at one another before she crossed the deck to the pallet with a clank of chain.

"Don't overdo, now," he cautioned.

"Are you kidding?" she asked, crouching next to the nearest cask.

"Right, sorry, forgot myself. Carry on."

She carried on, using her legs and center to muscle the cask to one side. Her face reddened with the effort because, though the barrels weren't large—they had to be hauled up to the ladder to be of use—they were still heavy.

"But truly," he said, "don't . . ."

Her glare made him clamp his mouth shut, and the spark of metal on metal drew Rory's attention from her efforts to where

John had just caught Mary's arcing blade in the crook of the axe. As Rory watched, John twisted on the haft, using the sword itself as a lever to pull Mary close before, with another twisting jerk, he sent the sword clattering to the deck.

John slid one hand to the axe end of the handle to form a bar which he used to press Mary against the ladder.

A blur of motion to his left called Rory's attention to where Eitan enveloped Colin's shock stick, twisting it out of the mercenary's hand and sending it flying across the bay before delivering a short, sharp backswing that struck Colin across the shoulders with a meaty thunk and sent him slamming into the starboard bulkhead aft of Rory, who felt the juddering from meters away.

"Do you need help?" Eitan asked Jinna, but Colin, growling, pushed himself off the bulkhead.

"Eitan!" John snapped the warning as he looked up from where he held Mary.

But because John was focused on Eitan, he didn't see Mary's left hand twitch.

But Rory did, just as he saw a flash of silver drop into Mary's hand. "Knife!" He shouted the warning only a second before the cask Jinna had been shoving went tumbling across the deck, straight toward Colin, who made a stumbling leap to get out of the way.

The noise caused Mary to start, giving John time to catch Mary's wrist before the blade could do anything worse than slice his arm.

Rory turned to where Colin tried to recover his balance at the same time Eitan swept forward, using the staff to crack across Colin's cheek, reversing it to slam into his gut, and reversing yet again to smack him across the back of his smooth pate, dropping him to the deck.

And as Colin fell and Mary held her hands out in surrender, Jinna's cask continued to roll aft until it struck Ysabel's sword and changed direction to starboard, toward the open door.

"HEADS!" Rory shouted as loud as he could, hoping Jagati would be able to hear the warning.

Jagati and Ysabel both looked up as Rory's warning split the pre-dawn air, then they watched the cask tumble out the open door.

Without hesitation, both dropped line and swung aft in an arc wide enough to prevent a fatal collision with the barrel before swinging back, each clambering for a hand hold.

"Feeling the urge to switch sides again?" Jagati called over as both fought their way to the hull.

"Please." Ysabel's teeth flashed. "I have seen your 'ship; you have nothing to offer. Besides," she indicated the satchel over her harness, "I already have the prize. If any of the others die, it only increases my profit share."

"Wow," Jagati said, reaching for the hand grip now to her left, "that is cold."

"You say that as if it is a bad thing," Ysabel countered before, without warning, releasing her grip on the hull and swinging for Jagati.

"That was a little extreme," John said as Mary's knife clattered to the deck.

"Just part of the job," she said, glancing at the warm red staining his sleeve. "It's not personal."

"How nice," he said, then he dropped the axe and, even as she began to smile, stepped back and delivered a left cross that knocked her senseless. "That might have been a little personal," he murmured as Mary slumped to the deck.

I beg to differ, a deep lyrical voice shivered through the bay—

no, through John's mind—sending a chill down his spine and freezing his limbs in place. *This is quite . . . quite . . . personal.*

As Jagati turned to face the swing, she saw Ysabel had her knife to hand and was swiping outward—not at Jagati, but at Jagati's line. "Really cold," she muttered, kicking off the hull and torquing her body so she immediately swung back in, legs locked forward in a double kick that caught Ysabel in the hip, sending her against the hull with a thud.

Hissing, Ysabel spun and bunched her legs up to push off again while Jagati grabbed on to a hull grip, took a deep breath, and pushed off, meaning to arc behind her opponent.

Except that Ysabel, mid-swing, caught Jagati's line and, as both twisted into each other, started sawing.

Turn around, John.

John turned, slowly, as if moving through honey.

What he saw first was Colin, out cold on the deck and, to Colin's left, Eitan on his knees and head bowed low, the staff hanging loose from the rope on his right wrist.

He saw Rory, still shackled, but John didn't think it was the chains holding him frozen, not the way his grief-stricken eyes stared, fixed on some unseen point.

At last, John faced Galileo where he stood, a bruise marring his temple where John had struck him. Standing next to him, her small, capable hand draped unresisting in his, stood Jinna.

The young woman's expression was neither fearful nor angry, but a terrible blank.

It looked to John as if no one was living inside.

"What's wrong with them?" he asked. "What have you done?"

I've done nothing. 'Tis you, John, who've done this. If you hadn't resisted, they'd be fine and proper. But you did, so now they're each living their worst nightmares. Over and over and over again.

"That's not possible."

Isn't it?

And then Galileo was at his side.

John hadn't seen him move, but he was there, and then he was picking up the axe and turning for the door and John's body would . . . not . . . move . . .

Then Galileo raised the axe and brought it down, and the line holding Jagati parted and John's world tumbled a thousand feet down . . .

CHAPTER 22

Jagati couldn't help but appreciate how sharp the other woman kept her blade.

Even more, Jagati appreciated that she herself was already swinging up behind Ysabel so that, even as her own line gave way, she was latching on to the other jumper's back like a baby sloth.

Ysabel responded by reversing her blade and stabbing Jagati in the thigh.

"Sonofa . . . !" Literally howling mad, Jagati elbowed Ysabel in the skull, which distracted her long enough for Jagati to remove the knife from her leg and hold it up against Ysabel's throat. "Think fast."

"Let them go."

Inside the cargo bay, Galileo turned from John, who was watching the nightmare of Jagati's fall—she had died four times by now—to meet Rory's angry, impotent glare. "Best be grateful you are locked up," he said, nodding at Rory's shackles, "or I'd have you reliving that flogging again."

Rory's response was a furious shake of his chain, but Galileo ignored the mechanic's tantrum and turned to where Eitan knelt on the deck, his breath coming short and sharp as he waded through blood and death for the pleasure of his captors again . . . and again . . . and again.

Satisfied Eitan and John were both lost in their nightmares, he glanced Jinna's way.

She lay curled quietly on the pallet, dreaming of holding her child.

Despite her part in the attempted coup, Galileo could no more harm her than he could his own sister.

A jerk of breath from John told him that Jagati had died for the fifth time.

And that was the glory and wonder of the mind, Galileo thought; a person could die, or lose their dearest love, or endure tortures beyond imagining a thousand times in the space of minutes.

"Not what I'd call a wonder, Leo."

Galileo looked down to see Syl looking up from where she sat, cross-legged on the deck, her serious gray eyes peering through the tumble of red-gold hair.

"Not a wonder, then," he said, "but it is a necessity."

Her eyes widened, then narrowed. "And how can causing so much pain be necessary?"

Galileo frowned and looked away, toward the door, through which he expected Ysabel and his calculator to appear at any second. "You wouldn't understand."

"And why would I not?"

"Because, Syl, you're dead."

"Dead I may be," she replied popping to her feet, "but your excuse I'll not."

"Excuse?" he looked down into her flushed cheeks, noted the rash climbing up from her throat. "For what?"

"For doing harm to good people," she said with a short, sharp cough. "For breaking the law—"

"The law." He waved that off even as he shuddered to see her body wracked by the fever. "The law's nothing more than a way to keep the likes of us in our place."

"Now there's a conceit." Syl took his hand in hers, which was burning hot. "To think all those centuries past, our forebears came to Fortune and decided, on the spot, to make a law against tech because *that'll* keep those wretched Kanes of Guinness in their place."

"Syl," he sighed over the laugh, for no one had, not once, made him laugh the way she could. "You know what I mean."

"I suppose I do." She pressed his palm to her cheek and looked up. "But I also know that what you're doing is wrong, and you'll forgive me if I'll have no part of it."

"Syl, don't . . ." But she was already fading, as she'd faded before. "Don't go, Syl."

"Syl isn't here."

"What?" Galileo turned from the empty space his sister had occupied to see Eitan standing behind him.

Shaking, yes, and with a bruise forming on his cheek, but his eyes were clear and very, very angry as he added, "She was never here."

Rory stood next to Eitan, holding his mangled left hand close to his chest which, Galileo thought, explained how the mechanic had escaped the shackle dangling from his right wrist. No doubt it was that shackle which had bruised Eitan's cheek, waking him from the arena of his nightmares.

"So clever, you are," Galileo said to Rory as the pain of the younger man's broken thumb rippled the aether between them. "I should have killed you in that alley."

A low sound, more animal than human, emerged from Eitan.

Galileo turned to face him, already diving deep, deep into his ex-lover's mind to where the chains of Adia waited to bind him, again.

"No," Eitan said. "Not this time."

And as he spoke, those cage doors closed with a psionic *clang* that rocked Galileo back on his heels.

"This time," Eitan continued, taking a trembling step forward, "there is only you, and I, and *now*."

Then Eitan raised the staff to which he was still bound and cracked the wood against Galileo's cheek, sending him to the deck where the staff slammed into his spine and then his ribs.

Then Galileo was lying on his back on the cold, cold deck, his body and mind a firework of hurts, and the staff was hovering over his face, and the next blow, he knew, would be the last.

Jagati held her breath until Ysabel raised her hands, signaling surrender.

"Good," Jagati said. "Great." Then she tucked the knife through the back of her belt.

"Now what?" Ysabel asked.

"Good question," Jagati replied.

They swung in silence for a moment, listening to the sounds of action up above diminishing.

"You better hope that your crew came out on top," Jagati observed.

Ysabel's shoulder moved in a shrug. "Even if your people win, I doubt they will kill me—well, maybe the one-armed wolf," she amended. "But I have confidence your captain can hold him back."

"Eitan!" John, freed from Galileo's waking nightmare, raced across the deck even as Eitan's staff rose. "Stop!"

"Do not get in my way," Eitan warned.

"You know I have to." John skidded to a halt before adding, "This isn't who we are."

"But it is," Eitan told him, every muscle trembling as if desperate to be unleashed. "As Leo reminded me, just now."

"He showed you shadows," John said as Jinna let out a soft cry. "Specters of the past."

"Yes," Eitan agreed. "*My* past. *My* actions. Things *I* have done." He glanced up. "Things no one should ever do."

"Then don't—"

"Don't listen to him," Galileo said. "Finish it." As he spoke, he looked up into Eitan's eyes. "You never played the coward before; don't start now."

"No," John whispered as Eitan raised the staff and, with an animalistic roar, slammed it down again.

"That didn't sound good," Jagati said, looking up at the loud crack that had emerged from the door.

"For whom?" Ysabel asked.

Jagati had no idea.

The line creaked, the sky began to turn pink.

CHAPTER 23

GALILEO, FLAT ON HIS BACK, STARED AT EITAN'S STAFF, planted on the deck mere millimeters from his face. "You should have done it," he whispered as tears streamed to mix with the blood. "I wanted you to do it."

"Why would you want such a thing?" Syl asked, stretching out at her brother's side.

"Because I've lost," he told her, brushing a hand over her hair. "Everything I wanted for us . . . it's gone."

"There is no us," Eitan, his expression a perfect mix of fury and confusion, pulled Galileo's eyes from Syl's.

"But we have each other," Syl pointed out, and Galileo dismissed Eitan to focus on his twin. "'Tis all I ever needed, to have you at my side."

"Oh but I've missed you, love," Galileo said, blinking at the tears.

"I'm not . . ." he heard Eitan begin to speak.

"Sure you've no reason t'miss me." Syl pounded at Leo's shoulder with a familiar thump. "I've been right here all along, haven't I?"

Galileo's breath caught as her face, which would never suffer the blights of age, brightened with an impish grin.

And with those words, that smile, all the cares—the ambition and anger and resentment which had moved Galileo since Syl died in their thirteenth year—washed away.

Syl was at his side.

The rest was just . . . noise.

As he thought this, she snuggled close, just as she had when they were children together, and as when they were children together, she started to sing.

"I walked deep in the lea 'neath a lonely sun . . ."

It was one of Fortune's oldest, saddest songs, but she had always loved the tune.

It was then, as the tune wove through Galileo's soul, that Eitan, by now kneeling at the fallen man's side, released his grip on Galileo's shoulder, so that the ghost of Syl faded.

But the echo of her song remained.

"Maybe we should remind them we're still out here," Jagati said, looking upwards.

"I think they know," Ysabel offered as a silhouette appeared at the open door.

Jagati squinted but couldn't make out any detail. "Can you see who it is?"

"No."

The shadow disappeared, and the line jerked and they started moving upwards.

"I have twenty starbucks that say it's my team," Ysabel said as they ascended.

At that, Jagati laughed. "You're on."

Then both heard something odd and turned their heads up.

"Is that . . . singing?" Ysabel said.

"*. . . deep in the lea 'neath a lonely sun . . .*"

"Sounds like Jinna," Jagati murmured, tightening her grip on Ysabel as the line jerked and slipped down a few feet. "Hey! Watch it!" she yelled up to the door.

"Sorry," John called down.

"What he said," Rory added, and she felt Ysabel tense as they creaked upwards.

"*. . . to gather honey for my love . . .*"

"There are two of you," Jagati complained as soon as they reached the lower edge of the door. "How hard can this be?"

Then they were at the door and Rory, with John, pulled both women up and inside.

Which was when Jagati realized exactly how hard it could be as she spied John's bleeding arm, then Rory's broken thumb, and within a heartbeat of seeing the two injuries, was slapped by a swamping wave of fear, anger, guilt and, oddly, grief.

"*But the meadow it was parched, and no flowers grew . . .*" Jinna's song continued as the thick stew of everyone else's emotions roiled in Jagati's gut.

"Keepers," she muttered, then yelped as John gripped her upper arm hard enough to bruise.

"Are you all right?" he asked, staring at her with an intensity that told her where the fear was coming from.

"I'm fine," she said. "It's good. I'm good. We're all good." Then she tapped his hand on her arm.

He looked down and immediately eased his fingers from her bicep. "Sorry."

"It's okay," she said, then turned to find Ysabel holding out two ten stars, which Jagati took with much less enthusiasm than she'd anticipated, thanks to the aforementioned fear, anger, guilt, and grief.

Peering over Ysabel's shoulder, Jagati found Colin and Mary both locked in the port side D-ring that had first held John and Jagati.

Colin looked dazed, but Mary was wearing a disgusted expression—anger, Jagati thought—and her own heart went pitty pat as she saw the bruise on Mary's cheek.

She looked away from Mary to where Eitan stood.

His arms were crossed tightly over his chest, and he was staring down at Jinna who knelt next to an unmoving Galileo.

Guilt, Jagati thought, though she couldn't imagine why.

"*. . . they fell by the score, to gather no more . . .*" Jinna continued to sing the ancient dirge of Earth's ending, composed sometime in the first century after landing.

"Is he . . . ?" Jagati looked from Galileo to Eitan. "Did you . . . ?"

"No," John said, moving back to the open door. "He's alive. He's just not . . ."

"He is not here," Eitan, still staring at Galileo's inert form, finished the sentence for John.

"Then where is he?" Jagati asked.

"I'm not entirely certain," John murmured.

"I am," Eitan said.

"*. . . though all's quiet in the glen, sleep will . . . will . . . come no more . . .*" Jinna's voice hitched as the ballad came to a close.

Rory almost dropped the shackles he was awkwardly looping through the starboard D-ring, but Eitan was already kneeling next to the little mother, taking her hand, helping her to her feet.

"Thank you," he told her.

Jinna shook her head, knuckling at her eyes. "Why that song?"

"It was his sister's favorite," Eitan explained, and there, Jagati thought, was the grief.

She let out a ragged breath as a *whirr-chunk*, along with a sudden lack of breeze, told her John had locked the bay door.

"I imagine you want this," Ysabel said, and Jagati saw her holding the laden carryall out to John.

"*Want* may be too strong a term," he said wryly, but he

accepted it. "Now, if you don't mind?" He gestured to starboard, and Ysabel turned and strode to where Rory waited. She joined him, looked at his left hand.

"Don't be getting any ideas," he told her, then glanced at Eitan, then back.

"Wouldn't dream of it," she said.

"Told ya we'd win," Jagati said, waving the starbucks Ysabel had given her before shoving them in her pocket.

"Are you twelve?" John asked, slinging the carryall over his shoulder.

"Sometimes." She shrugged and began to walk away, but her leg buckled. "Shit," she muttered, even as John appeared at her side, his eyes haunted, and again there was the bitter wave of fear from earlier.

"What happened?" he asked.

"Knife," Jagati said, adding a 'no big deal' shrug for good measure.

"It is a big deal," he countered, as if she'd spoken aloud. "You need to get to the—" he began when a soft sigh emerged from Galileo, followed by a sniff from Jinna.

"Sorry," Jinna said as everyone looked her way. "Hormones. Mostly."

"No worries," John said, then as Jagati started to sidle away, added a soft, "*Stay.*"

"Who do you think you are?" she hissed.

"Your captain," he hissed back, before looking up. "Rory, can you head to the bridge and radio the *Al-Djinn* for our landing coordinates?"

"Aye to that."

"The *Al-Djinn*?" Ysabel asked.

"Yes." John looked at Tariq's former crew member. "While you were selling yourself to the highest bidder, your captain and I were making our own arrangements."

"Clever," was Ysabel's response.

"Yup, making you look not so smart, isn't he?"

"At least I am willing to take a risk for what I want," Ysabel said.

"What on toxic Earth does that mean?" Jagati demanded, but Ysabel had apparently used up her words for the day and simply relaxed against the bulkhead.

"Rory?" John tilted his head toward the companionway. "To the bridge if you please. Eitan," he looked at the soldier, who was still looking at Galileo. "Perhaps you could keep watch down here? Jinna . . ." He paused. Likely, Jagati thought, because he didn't know what to do with her.

"I'll go with Rory, if it's all the same," Jinna said. "Be an extra hand until we get his fixed."

"Of course, and thank you both," John said to Rory and Jinna. "That bit with the lock-pick saved all of us."

"Looks like I missed a lot of the fun," Jagati noted as the two young people started for the ladder. John's eyes shot to hers, and she felt something odd twisting inside, but rather than address it asked, "Do you have orders for me too?"

"I . . ." He paused, still staring.

"You . . . ?" she prompted, poking his arm. "Spit it out."

"Oh, the hell with it," he grumbled, and then his arms were around her and his lips on hers and somewhere in the near distance Rory's voice was rising in a cheer, but none of that mattered because *smogging toxic Earth*, the man could kiss.

Who knew, she thought, then the kiss deepened and she stopped thinking altogether while everything and everyone else dissipated into a soft, welcoming fog.

It would have been lovely, were it not for the sick welling of pain from her leg, the cold spreading through her limbs and, finally, John's terror-stricken voice following her all the way down into the dark.

CHAPTER 24

JOHN TUGGED THE SATCHEL HIGHER ON HIS SHOULDER as he stepped off the gangplank onto the soft, springy grass of the Linconao Keep airfield.

The keep itself was built on a plateau set against Mount Apu, which overlooked the Oracle Ocean on one side and the Lycos wilds on the other, so the air tasted of a mix of saltwater and Avonian pine, while the sounds of crashing waves underscored the birdsong from the forests.

At any other time, he might have enjoyed the location, but the last few hours, spent dashing between the cargo bay, helm, and the medbay had left him feeling stretched and brittle, so the colors were too bright, the birds cries too loud.

Even fresh air was an affront, after breathing in the odors of blood and infection from Jagati's wound.

John suppressed a grimace and glanced to his right, where Tariq's *Al-Djinn* sat at anchor, her sleek hull gleaming under the late afternoon suns.

Beyond the *Al-Djinn* sat a light scout 'ship flying the keeper's colors.

At last, he turned his attention to the welcoming party gathered nearby, where Tariq stood, a black-coated accent to the scarlet and saffron of the keepers surrounding him.

John counted a dozen keepers altogether, ten of them armed rangers.

But it was the woman standing next to Tariq, who wore the scarlet-on-scarlet of a Senior Master, who drew his eye. Her elaborately braided hair was silvered, her complexion the same golden brown as Tariq's and, as John neared, he noted the Senior Master's eyes were the same deep amber as the *Al-Djinn's* captain.

"Captain John Pitte," Tariq said as John came to a halt, "may I present the Senior Master of Linconao Keep, Shohreh Nazri, my immediate superior . . . and my mother."

Which, John thought, explained the eyes. "Senior Master." John bowed his head in respect before adding, "Your grandson favors you."

"Captain," Shohreh greeted him with a faint smile, then gestured to the rangers behind her, who split to form two files of five each. "My son tells me you have some inconvenient passengers."

"Inconvenient," John echoed. "A circumspect description."

"As my son will have told you, I live in a very circumspect world," Shohreh replied.

"He has." John shot a glance at Tariq. "Just not in so many words."

<hr>

"No," John said.

He was standing at the base of the steps in Tariq's house, where he'd come to a stop because Tariq had just suggested the Errant *crew retain possession of the calculator.*

"If you will just listen—" Tariq began.

"I have listened. And I am telling you, no. You can't expect us to keep

the damned thing."

"Then who? I can hardly keep it," Tariq pointed out. "I have no doubt Mary and Colin's employer will be watching my family. If they even suspect I lied about having the device in my possession . . . I am not willing to risk them again."

"I don't suppose we can deliver it to the local authorities?" John asked.

"Not unless we are prepared to spend our remaining years in the Barrens," Tariq replied.

"We have hammers aboard the Errant," John pointed out before the same logic he'd used against Jagati's earlier destructive suggestion reared its reasonable head.

"Exactly," Tariq said, as if John had spoken aloud. "I, for one, do not wish to spend the rest of my days avoiding retribution. But there is one other option," he added, meeting John's eyes.

"You want to set a trap," John murmured.

"It is the only way."

"And supposing we succeed," John said. "The calculator will still exist, along with the person who developed it. I won't be party to murder," he added, quickly.

"We might be able to avoid bloodshed," Tariq said, though his expression wasn't hopeful. "I will contact my superior and arrange for you to deliver the device to a place of safekeeping."

"For all I know, your superior is a Midasian boffin with aspirations toward starting the war again."

John wasn't certain, but he thought Tariq's eyes came near to a Jagati-level eye roll. "I swear, by my wife and child, the party I report to will not put the calculator to any ill use. Or any use, come to it."

Now, standing in a meadow, faced by a Senior Master and her rangers, John looked over to Tariq.

"I did swear," Tariq told him.

"So you did." John returned his attention to Shohreh. "There are four inconveniences aboard. One, the leader, is in our medbay. The others are being held in the cargo bay. Your son will know them." Here he glanced at Tariq. "Including Ysabel."

Tariq, who'd already learned of Ysabel's betrayal, said nothing.

"We will see to them," Shohreh said, and at her gesture, the ten rangers strode toward the *Errant*. "Our doctors will also see to their leader—Kane you say he's called?"

"Galileo Kane," John agreed as the rangers' boots thudded up the gangplank behind him. "Though he may be more in need of a cog—one familiar with sensitives."

"Keeper Constantine has some experience in the area," Shohreh said. "And Tariq says you have wounded of your own?"

"A leg wound that took infection," John told her, clearing his throat before continuing. "A broken thumb, and a pregnant woman who suffered a bout of hypoxia."

Shohreh glanced at the young keeper at her side. "Fetch Ngozi and Eduardo," she said. The young woman gave a fist to palm bow, then raced to the massive granite structure that seemed to grow out of the cliff against which it stood. "Doctors Tshibangu and Xicale are quite skilled. Your crew will be well cared for."

"Thank you," John said.

"It is the least we can do." Shohreh replied. "That being said, I believe you have something for me?"

"Of course." John reached into his satchel and pulled out the calculator, still wrapped in fabric and patching tape, and held it out.

Tariq, brow cocked at the wrapping, stepped forward and took the bundle. "Do I want to know?" he asked, indicating the remains of the patching tape.

"I can assure you, you do not," John told him as the young keeper came trotting back with two others in her wake, both in the red with saffron trim of Masters, both carrying medical satchels. The two doctors sent the Senior Master a nod and proceeded into the *Errant*.

John turned, meaning to follow.

"Captain," Shohreh stopped him, and he looked back. "I would be grateful for a word in private . . . once your crew is settled."

John knew Shohreh was being polite; saying no to a Senior Master of the keepers wasn't an option. "Of course," he said, then returned to his 'ship and his crew.

Later, John trailed the same young keeper who'd fetched the doctors into Shohreh's office and found her seated at a low desk, around which a garden of colorful cushions had been scattered.

The Senior Master was pouring out the second of two cups of tea, which gave John time to take in the collection of thick woven rugs and a detailed map of the Linconao protected regions on the walls.

A fire crackled on the hearth, and overhead a solar lamp glowed softly, gleaming off the teapot Shohreh held. Beyond the hexagon-shaped window behind her desk, the sky was already darkening.

His eyes caught on a rich green tapestry hung next to a crowded bookcase.

"Thank you, Anya," Shohreh dismissed the young keeper, drawing his attention to the desk.

He glanced at the teapot Shohreh was setting over the warmer and the bright red cups filling the air with the aroma of hyacinth.

"I am pleased to see you again, captain," Shohreh said as his eyes came to rest on hers. "I trust your injured are on the road to recovery?"

"Yes," he said, not even trying to hide his relief. "Jagati—that is, my first mate—is past the crisis and sleeping comfortably, and Dr. Xicale says Rory's hand will heal completely."

"Eduardo has a great deal of triage experience," Shohreh said, gesturing John to sit. "And your mother-to-be?"

"Jinna is well," he said, folding himself onto one of the cushions. "And the child also. And your Dr. Tshibangu . . . I wasn't aware sensitives had the ability to make that sort of determination."

"Not all can."

"An amazing gift," he murmured. "But it would also be something of a burden. Is that why she chose a life in the Keep rather than a city posting?"

"Perceptive of you, captain." Shohreh handed him a cup, then took the other. "And yes. While Ngozi's skills would benefit any hospital, the strain of so many injuries, so much pain, so much death, might well have driven her mad."

"But not here," John guessed, sipping the citrusy tea.

"Not here, no. Though we have our share of traumas, and the Keep provides ample fodder for a family practitioner, as Tariq could attest."

"Should he be in the mood to converse," John observed, sipping at the tea, savoring the tart hyacinth before asking, "Did Tariq grow up here?"

"Here and in Nike, with his father," Shohreh replied.

"Forgive me." John set the cup down with a gentle tink. "I didn't mean to pry."

"If I believed you prying, I would not have answered." She smiled. "Not every liaison is permanent," she explained. "Sayyed and I began as friends, and friends we remained until his death. And though officially I was required to oppose his choice of career, *unofficially* we came to an arrangement that suited us both."

"Sayyed was in the shadow trade," John guessed. "And Tariq kept up the family business?"

"On both sides," Shohreh nodded. "And, as with his father, while I cannot *officially* recognize his work in the shadows, I can make use of his skills and connections for the general good. Plus, it makes the First Landing Day reunions less incendiary if we can all get along."

"I imagine it would," John said, turning his cup around on itself. "Only," he began, then stopped himself.

"Go on," Shohreh prompted, raising her cup for a sip before returning it to the desk. "If you tread too close to the hive, I won't sting."

"Very well," he said. "Only I wonder, what do you mean when you speak of the general good?"

"I would think that obvious."

"Yes, but no." John pushed his cup aside and rubbed a hand over his knee, which was aching. "Take this business with the calculator."

She crossed her hands one on the other atop the table. "What of it?"

"From what I can piece together," John said, "Sameen stole it on your behalf."

Shohreh nodded but said nothing.

"Except, how did you know it existed?" Here Shohreh's lip twitched, and John wondered if he'd stepped too near the hive, but he kept on. "Perhaps," he suggested, "not all keepers wear the saffron and scarlet?"

The barest dip of her head might not have been an admission, but neither was it a denial.

"And if that's the case, perhaps such a keeper spent some time with a radical technochrist . . . but no." His brow furrowed as he considered the angle. "Galileo's sensitivity would have made that difficult."

"Galileo is not the only technochrist in Nike," Shohreh offered.

"Of course. So, the theoretical keeper in technochrist clothing learns of—"

"Suspects," she offered.

"Suspects," John corrected himself, "the existence of a piece of illegal tech." Here he leaned forward. "Why not inform the local authorities? Let them make an arrest and put an end to the affair?"

Now she leaned forward. "Why do you think?"

"Because then it would be real," John said after a beat. "The public would be aware the calculator had been created. And if it could be created once, it could be created again."

"And that would be only the beginning," she confirmed. "The technochrist movement to date has remained on the fringes of society; even in the Coalition states they are barely skin on the pond, but that would change the moment theory became practice. The movement would grow and push for a repeal of all laws against advanced tech."

"And those seeking to profit from the advances would add their weight to the technochrists," John followed the track. "Those in opposition would step up, and we'd see dissent throughout the Colonies, and likely the Coalition as well."

"If Earth's history has taught us anything, it is that greed devours conscience. Dissension would be the best scenario," Shohreh mused, sitting back and taking up her cup again.

John considered that. "So the keepers, through Tariq and Sameen, appropriated the calculator to pre-empt the possibility of a civil war."

"Having yet to recover from a decidedly un-civil war between the Colonies and Coalition, can you blame us?"

"No," he said, tapping the desk lightly. "No, but I wonder if there isn't more you could have done."

"Oh?" She sipped, then set the cup down with the gentlest of *clinks*. "What sort of more?"

"As you said, greed preys on the conscience, but greed is often the byproduct of want." Certainly that had been the case with Galileo. Poverty, starvation, the loss of a beloved sister—dark seeds planted in the youth and come to fruition in the man.

"Poverty is the source of many ills," Shohreh agreed.

"So why allow it?" John asked, meeting her gaze. "Your mandate is to uphold the Apian Accords, your rangers rival many a standing army, *and* you have representatives in every major city on Fortune. And yet you stood by while the Coalition waged war on the Colonies, while ristos climb to power on the backs of commoners, and while children die in their brothers' arms—"

Her brow arched, and John cleared his throat. "It may sound like the plot of a melodrama, but I have a young woman on my airship who is, in fact, fleeing a man so powerful he believes he can take her child from her without consequence."

"That is dreadful," she murmured.

"It is an outrage," John countered. "So why, if keepers care so much for the people—"

"But we don't," Shohreh cut him off, though not unkindly.

"I beg your pardon?" John managed, staring.

"We don't care for the people," she explained. "An understandable misconception, as we do provide humanitarian aid when and where possible. But as a whole? We are not here to make a better world *for* humanity. We are here," she continued, "to keep this world safe *from* humanity."

"But," John began, then stopped because he had to search for the words. "Then why intervene at all? If you've no concern for the people of Fortune, why send Sameen after the calculator?"

"For the same reason the Apian Accords forbid advanced technology in the first place," she told him. "To prevent the destruction of Fortune by those who inhabit it. At the present state of technological development, we have equilibrium. Certainly, there were some thorny decades after crystal was discovered, but its sustainability and volatile nature prevented it shifting the balance too far. Yes, the Coalition may attack the Colonies over crystal rights, or there may be riots in the slums of Guinness, and Midasian Fever can strike at any time and people will inevitably die, but—and this is key—the planet will survive.

"Introduce one piece of advanced tech, however," she continued, "and, as we just discussed, we are in danger of following the same geometric progression that led to Earth's demise. And that," she said, pouring fresh tea into both cups, "is why I asked Sameen to steal the calculator."

She finished speaking, and after a beat, John's eyes dipped, watched his hands reach for his refreshed cup. The hyacinth tickled his nose, and the bright tea danced on his tongue.

As he swallowed, he felt the warm liquid fail to break through the ice forming in his sternum.

"You disapprove," Shohreh guessed, studying him.

"Not entirely," he said, though his voice was uncertain. He glanced up. "About the calculator."

"What about it?"

He put the cup down. "I strongly suspect Galileo had a buyer for it, which means there is at least one other person who knows it existed."

"I believe you are correct," Shohreh agreed. "But we don't yet know who that buyer is." She paused, considering him. "On that note, the keepers could use another set of eyes out there, should you be interested."

"Thank you," John said, "but on the whole, I believe Errant Freight is better suited to working for the people you don't care about." As he spoke, he pushed himself to his feet. "Maybe, if we messy humans do a good enough job watching out for each other, you won't need to watch us so carefully." As he spoke, he shot a meaningful glance at the green tapestry by the bookcase.

Shohreh followed John's gaze, and allowed a small smile. "I look forward to observing your efforts, captain," she said, then nodded her dismissal.

Once John had bowed himself out, Shohreh waited for the door to close behind him before drawing another cup from the tray under her desk.

By the time Tariq pushed through the green tapestry, she had his tea poured.

"I told you he would say no," Tariq said, kneeling opposite his mother.

"So you did." She eased back on her heels as he lifted his cup. "Still, the crew of the *Errant* may prove useful, should the need arise. Meanwhile, on to more important matters." She tapped the desk. "When are you going to bring the family up for a visit?"

CHAPTER 25

and that her leg hurt.

Oddly, it was the lying down part that had her eyes popping open before she shot upright, only to come face to chest with John, who was sitting on the edge of the cot.

Cot.

Medbay.

Right.

She frowned, thinking back.

Obviously, she had passed out from blood loss down in the cargo bay.

Also obviously, lack of blood had caused her to hallucinate, because there was no other reason for her to be remembering John's arms around her and the spark that hit when his lips . . .

"Back." John interrupted the hallucination by setting a hand to her shoulder and giving a push that, while gentle, had her plopping back to the pillow. "Rory cleaned the wound, but not fast enough to avoid infection. You're on bedrest until the antibiotic finishes its job."

"Damn it to smogging Earth and back," she swore because she really hated lying around doing nothing.

"You're worried about missing all the excitement."

"I am not," she grumbled, crossing her arms over her chest.

"Just as well," he said with a smile. "Because you've already missed it."

"What? Why?" She started to sit up but, at his raised eyebrow, settled back with a grunt. "What exactly did I miss?"

"Quite a bit," he said, idly straightening the bedding over her, which was when Jagati realized she was in a sleep shirt and nothing else.

"Such as?" she asked, tugging the coverlet out of his hand.

"Such as we left the calculator, along with Galileo and company, at Linconao Keep. You've been out for over twelve hours," he added, studying the edge of her pillow.

"Linconao—I what?" She struggled upright again. "It was nothing. A smogging puncture . . ."

"It was not nothing," he countered, pushing her back again. And while his tone remained light, looking more closely, she could see the dark circles under his eyes and the lines of strain in his face. "You lost a great deal of blood, plus the infection, plus you hadn't fully recovered from the altitude sickness before heading outside to retrieve the calculator." He paused, took a breath, released it. "You were a mess, and we were lucky the keepers had a trauma specialist *and* enough antibiotics to spare."

Jagati crossed her arms over her chest again. "Getting old," she grunted, and glared out of the port.

"No more than the rest of us." John patted her arm lightly. "So, do you want to lie here and sulk? Or would you like to hear why we're not being shipped to the Barrens for dealing in illegal tech?"

"Didn't even cross my mind to worry about that," she said with a hitch of her shoulder. "I figured you could honey talk us out of any kind of sentence."

"As much as I appreciate the sentiment, it's Tariq you can thank for our freedom," he said then he explained what had happened at Linconao, and who Tariq worked for.

"His *mother*?" She said as his story wound to a close. "I didn't think he had one."

"Ha."

"I'm serious!" But she was also, unaccountably, nervous. "So, what happens to them, now? Galileo and his drones?"

"I'm assured Senior Master Shohreh will handle the details. It's possible Mary, Colin, and Ysabel will face some jail time. That, or they'll end up working for Shohreh."

Jagati made a *pfft* noise and waved her hand. "I can't see a Senior Master taking on a pair of mercs and a woman more interested in starbucks than loyalty."

"I don't know." John's expression went distant. "The Senior Master is nothing if not practical. Plus, any sort of incarceration would require a trial . . . and testimony, which wouldn't be optimal for us—or the keepers trying to keep the calculator a secret."

She frowned because, on principle alone, she wanted to see the wrongdoers suffer. "Politics," she muttered.

"Exactly," he agreed.

"A'ight. That covers the three lackeys, what about the mastermind?"

"Galileo will remain under keeper care," John said, and though his expression remained thoughtful, she caught the fluttering edges of his anger before he, looking at her, tucked it away.

The fact that, thanks to the sudden onset of sensitivity, she knew he was angry *and* capable of hiding it from her, was just one more layer of irritating. If there were any justice on Fortune, she'd be able to rid herself of the sensitivity, or bury it, or—

She thumped the bed in frustration, then realized it wasn't the mattress she'd hit.

"Ah," she said as John's gaze dropped to where her hand had landed on his leg.

After a stutter of heartbeats, he raised his eyes to meet hers, but still he said nothing as the silence shifted from companionable to not in a few breaths.

"What?" she snapped. "Have I got something on my face?"

His jaw gave a familiar, pre-smile twitch. "No."

"Then what?"

"I enjoy your face," he said as the smile arrived. "I particularly enjoy seeing it after it's been kissed. Then again," he continued, "I've only seen it post-kiss the one time, and then you passed out, so perhaps the expression wasn't a response to the kiss but lack of blood?"

She felt her admired face heat up as she realized the kiss hadn't been a hallucination. "Ummm . . ." she began, then faltered.

"Take your time."

"Let me tell you what I'll take—"

A knock at the doorsill cut her off, and both she and John turned to see Rory stepping in. "Sorry t'interrupt—whatever." He waved at them before focusing on John. "There's a telgram from Nike to your attention."

"Of course," John said and looked down at Jagati, who'd removed her hand from his thigh the second Rory appeared. "Get your rest," he told her, rising from the cot and crossing to join Rory at the door. There he stopped and looked back. "Jagati, regarding the topic we were not discussing just now?"

"Yeeaah?" Her tone was a little befuddled and a lot wary.

"The queen's in your net."

With that, and a nod for Rory, he was gone.

Rory watched him leave before turning to the impatient patient. "He'd be talking about the kiss, wouldn't he? Because it was quite the—"

"Get. Out."

Two days later, John and the rest of the *Errant* crew, plus one, settled at a table in The Frayed Rigging.

The pub, a favorite of Nike's aeronauts, was as crowded as ever, though the Rigging of the past had included more uniforms. Nowadays, the blue and black of the Air Corps had been replaced by the civilian gear of coveralls and battered flight leathers.

John took a sip of his dark nutty ale, breathed in the mix of pineapple leather and alcohol, and felt the tensions of the past few days melt a little bit more.

The warming process had begun on reading the telgram Rory had reported, which turned out to have been from Gideon Quinn, informing John that Killian Del was no longer a threat, and hoped that Jinna would join both he and Mia at the Elysium Hotel on her return.

Gideon's message also indicated that his and John's "mutual problem" had been resolved, but didn't say how, leaving John to assume that Gideon's dealings with General Rand were not something to be mentioned in public.

With no recourse but to wait for more information, John had set course for Nike where, upon arrival, Rory suggested a trip to The Frayed Rigging, Jinna had immediately agreed, and now here they were.

He lifted his glass again, bumping into Jagati's shoulder as he did. Not that she noticed as she, Jinna, and Rory were all entranced by Eitan, who was on the dance floor with a handful of others, arms and hips moving as one with the music, the fingers of his hand snapping, his body interweaving with six other dancers into a twining, sinuous strand.

Then, in tune with each other and the musicians, the strand broke apart, again becoming seven disparate individuals following the drums into a sudden stamping, whirling crescendo which just as suddenly stopped.

Applause broke out while dancers and musicians shared hand grips, embraces, and the occasional formal kiss on the cheek.

"I could never move like that," Jinna observed, sipping her tea. "Not even before I got pregnant."

As she spoke, the band stood up for a break and the dancers splintered off to find their parties.

Eitan returned to their table, slinging himself into the chair Jagati had been guarding against all comers.

"Is there nothing you don't do well?" Rory asked.

Eitan didn't answer at once, but first took a drink of the ale they'd all been guarding. "Knit," he said at last, setting the glass on the table.

"Ha," said Rory.

"No, but truly," Eitan said with the faintest of smiles. "In primary school I was the despair of my textiles instructors."

"Same here," Jinna chimed in. "I can't get through a single row on a bunting without dropping at least three stitches." With which statement she threw a curious glance Rory's way.

"Alas, I had no such fancy schooling," he told her. "'Twas all locks, dips, and grifts for me before the Corps."

"I ditched textiles," Jagati admitted with a shrug.

Everyone looked at John. "As a matter of fact," he said, "I was quite the knitter back in the day. And I find spinning an excellent way to clear a busy mind."

"Of course you do," Jagati said into her glass.

"I'll know who to beg for help when it comes to baby gear," Jinna said, then yawned. "Sorry."

"No need for that," Rory told her. "I'm knackered, myself, and with half as much reason." As he spoke, the arm he'd rested over Jinna's shoulder curled in, and his other, unbandaged hand joined hers where it rested atop the table, causing her to look up at him.

The gesture and the look were both so new and so perfect that John was compelled to turn away, which left him facing Jagati, who'd also averted her gaze from the shared tenderness in their midst.

She rolled her eyes, a move so predictable it made John smile.

"We'd best be off home." Rory's voice broke into the moment, pulling everyone's attention back to where he was rising from the table. "Unless you'd prefer your flat?" he asked Jinna. "Because I can take you to your flat. Or to that hotel where Mia's staying. Or—"

"The *Errant* is fine." To everyone's relief, Jinna cut him off. "Tomorrow's soon enough to figure out the rest," she added before yawning again. "And yup, the tired tree has fallen."

"The *Errant* it is, then," Rory said, beaming like a new crystal lamp as he helped her from the chair.

"Sleep well," Eitan said as the remaining three rose in respect.

Jinna thanked him with a smile, said good night to the others, and then she and Rory, with his arm circling her, made their way out of the pub.

Jagati took advantage of the extra space by stretching her legs out under the table and hefted her beer toward the departing couple. "I have to admit, I didn't see that coming. Did you?" she addressed both men. "Know he had a thing for her?"

"I suspected Rory might have feelings for Jinna that went beyond friendship," John said. "But I'd no idea they were so serious, or that she returned them."

From Eitan's chair, the silence was deafening.

"Oh, come on," Jagati kicked at his chair's leg. "You're not telling me you *knew*."

"Sensed." He took another drink, set the glass down, and met her accusatory gaze. "It was not deliberate, but," he shrugged, "some feelings are less subtle than others."

John took another drink, careful to avoid looking at Jagati. "So, you were aware they were in love with one another?" he asked, setting the glass down. "The whole time?"

"Again, some feelings are—"

"Keepers, man," Jagati cut in, "why didn't you save us all the —" Her hands waved in what John assumed an indication of Rory's emotional state over the past few days. "—and tell him? Her? Them?"

Eitan's brow arched. "For the same reason sensitives cannot give testimony in a criminal case."

Jagati's brow furrowed. "Which is?"

"Because the psyche is not a book," he explained with the patience of an instructor.

"No shit," she replied with the irritation of the impatient.

Now came Eitan's smile—along with several spilled drinks from that smile's line of fire. "What I mean is, thoughts and emotions do not remain still, waiting quiet on a shelf until they may be opened and read."

"So what are they like?" Jagati asked, sitting up and leaning forward.

"Sometimes they are like a murmuration of starlings," he replied. "Sometimes a blizzard. Still others it is like being in the midst of a great battle, all smoke and noise and confusion."

"That is so not helpful," Jagati complained.

John sipped his ale and waited.

"Let us try it this way," Eitan said, leaning forward. "Think of everything you experience in a single day—or even a single hour —and also what you think of those experiences. And then there are the older, deeper, buried thoughts those experiences waken. A woman accused of murder may be innocent but experience guilt for not liking the victim. In the same way," he continued as Jagati's frown deepened, "one moment of contact with Jinna might reveal a tenderness for Rory that, had I touched her five minutes later, would have been subsumed by anger, or sorrow or irritation."

"Well, it is Rory," Jagati said, then added a quick, "Sorry. Habit."

"Mm, well," Eitan tapped the table in time with the drums

which had begun to beat anew. "The point is, every one of those thoughts or emotions would have been true in that moment, but to conclude from the one contact, in the one moment, that it was a lasting truth, *and* to share it as such, would be irresponsible at best. At worst?" His shoulder lifted, and he met her gaze. "Would you risk it?"

"I guess not," she said, flicking a glance at John, then away again.

And in that moment, in the hollow space beneath his heart—the same space he'd lived with for all the years he'd loved her—John felt a murmuration.

He blinked and realized Eitan was watching him. But if there was a message in his nearly black eyes, John couldn't read it, so he turned his attention to the dance floor.

There, an aeronaut was already moving to the beat, her hips swaying, hands twining in an intricate pattern and her cloud of deep black curls floating in syncopation.

Up on the stage, the oud player, eyes on the dancer, began to pick out a tune, then the fiddle slid in, and John couldn't tell if the dancer followed the music or the music followed the dancer.

At his side, Eitan took a last drink from his glass and thumped it to the table. Rising, he wove his way back to the dance floor to join her just as the tempo increased.

Watching, John saw the woman turn, noted the flashing of burns along the right side of her face.

His eyes moved over the pub, taking in more burns, more scars, and more than a few spaces where an arm or leg would be.

Over a year of peace, but the spoils of war were still much in evidence.

"Think she'll take him home?" Jagati asked.

John looked over to see her still leaning forward on the table, watching the dancers. "If he doesn't, half the pub will be following him back to the *Errant*."

At that she grunted, and John settled back to observe as she turned her glass around on itself a few times.

"So—" he began.

"I think we should—"

They both stopped. "You first," he said.

"Ugh." She stopped turning the glass and rapped her knuckles on the table. "It's just, all that talk about sensing and emotions and that minute in the cargo bay and . . ." She hissed and shook her head. "Listen, sure, for kids like Rory and Jinna, it's simple,"

"Young they may be, but Rory and Jinna are both seasoned veterans and have lived a life. And Jinna is carrying a child of her own under what could best be termed trying circumstances. I can't think of anything less simple."

"Yes. Fine. Whatever," Jagati said. "But they're still both younger than we are."

"Yes, they are." Oh, but how he enjoyed seeing the cool Jagati O'Bannion flustered. "Which means we have less time to waste."

"Exactly! Wait," she frowned. "That's not what I meant."

"Oh?" He raised his glass, much as Eitan had earlier, and took a drink before asking, "And what did you mean?"

"Sometimes I hate you."

"I know." He smiled and leaned in, so they were face to face, close enough he could see the gold flecks in the dark of her eyes.

She didn't lean back.

"So . . . about the queen being in my net," she began.

"Yes?"

There was a soft huff of breath. "I think I might keep it."

His right brow rose. "I don't know what that means."

Her eyes narrowed. "You aren't going to make this easy for me, are you?"

"It's not easy for me," he said, his own huff of breath displacing a curl that had fallen to her cheek. Without thinking, he reached up to brush it back, noticing she not only did *not* slap his hand, she still didn't back away, so again he looked into her eyes. "I want to know what you want."

"I thought I was being clear." Her nose wrinkled in frustration. "I want . . ." Another huff of air. "I want—"

"Excuse me."

At the diffident greeting, John and Jagati both straightened like marionettes on a puppeteer's strings and looked up to see an older man with weathered copper skin dressed in clothes as well made as they were ill-used.

"I apologize if I'm interrupting," the man said.

"Oh, you're not interrupting," Jagati waved off the idea.

"Of course not," John agreed.

"Nothing happening here," she added.

"I see," the man's expression shifted from diffident to amused. "In that case, might I ask if I have the pleasure of addressing Captain Pitte of the CAS *Errant*?"

"Only if you're not planning on thrashing him," Jagati said.

John's glance slid her way, then back. "I'm Captain Pitte. How can I help you, Msr . . . ?"

"Doctor, in fact," the man introduced himself with a slight bow. "Doctor Alain Natsiq, and I'm in need of an airship. I was told you might have one to hire?"

John met Jagati's gaze. She sighed and nodded.

"That we do," he said to the doctor. "How may the *Errant* serve?"

* * *

The Errant *Crew will return in* Change of Fortune.

PREVIEW: CHANGE OF FORTUNE
AN ERRANT FREIGHT NOVELLA

"How may the *Errant* serve?"

It wasn't the first time Jagati had heard John ask that question, but it was the first time she'd heard it with mixed emotions.

Plus side, they could use the cash a new job would bring in.

Minus side, she was pretty sure she'd been about to kiss John again.

By all rights, she should have been relieved by the interruption.

She was relieved.

Mostly.

Smog it, she thought as the doctor waved to someone on the other side of the pub.

"Just letting my associates know I found you," Natsiq explained as he dropped into the chair John offered.

"Associates?" she asked, turning with John to spy a tall, slender figure with coppery skin and ink-black hair weaving through the crowded tables.

They were followed, Jagati noted, by someone of much shorter stature, the only visible feature being a mop of brown hair lightly touched with silver.

"Well, two of them," Dr. Natsiq explained. "Dr. Panesar is still at the airfield, inventorying our supplies. The other two came with me. My eldest, Kallik." Natsiq indicated the taller of the approaching pair with visible pride. "They are also a doctor."

"Two Dr. Natsiq's?" Jagati focused on the elder physician. "Doesn't that get confusing?"

"It would," Alain agreed, "but Kallik uses their full name, Natsiq-Corvais."

"I try to," the young doctor in question said as they arrived at the table, a goblet of red wine in hand and a twinkle in their dark eyes, "but generally our patients give up and call us Dr. A and Dr. K."

"They do not," their father replied.

"They do when you're not listening," Kallik said with an infectious grin.

The elder doctor rolled his eyes. "And this is Pyotr Aaberg," he continued as the last of the party broke through the crush, carrying two pint glasses.

Jagati, turning to the newcomer, felt a sense of shock.

Why, she couldn't say as, aside from his stature, the man was about as innocuous as they came.

Then she glanced at John just in time to see him schooling his features, and realized that it wasn't *her* shock she felt, but *his*.

Smogging empathic woo woo, she thought, and gritting her teeth, she reinforced the internal walls that Eitan—who, unlike Jagati, had a lifetime of knowing he was a sensitive—had helped her construct.

"You forgot your ale, Alain," Pyotr said in a heavy Stolichnayan accent, pushing one of the two pints he carried across the table.

"Oh, thank you." Alain accepted the drink. "Pyotr, Kallik, may I present Captain John Pitte and . . ."

Jagati filled in the expectant pause. "Jagati O'Bannion."

"Jagati is the *Errant*'s first mate," John explained.

"A pleasure to meet you," Pyotr said, climbing into the chair next to Kallik.

"And are you a doctor as well?" John asked Pyotr.

"Not me, no," Pyotr waved John's question aside. "I am merely an administrator."

"Pyotr is far more than that," Alain said. "As the team admin, he handles all the tedious details, so we in the medical staff can focus on our work."

"Interesting," John said, then glanced at Jagati before asking, "And what work do you do, precisely?"

"Nothing illegal, I assure you," Alain began.

"Just a little insane," Kallik added.

That had both Jagati and John turning to Alain, who raised his hands as if in acceptance of the judgment. "Are either of you acquainted with the organization, Medics Beyond Borders?"

"Sure." Jagati shrugged. "We've come across MBB camps a few times over the years."

"The organization does an excellent job filling in the gaps left by the keepers, with none of the same protections the keepers enjoy while doing it," John added.

"Like I said, a little insane." Kallik raised their glass in a toast to their companions.

"Not so insane this time," Pyotr said.

"We're flying to the eastern border of Stolichnaya—in February," Kallik pointed out.

"Keepers," Jagati said, then shrugged as everyone looked at her. "Not a fan of cold weather."

Alain sighed. "Unfortunately, neither was the captain of the airship we had originally chartered."

"It wasn't the cold she objected to," Kallik said, their voice taking on an edge.

"Is that so?" John glanced at the younger doctor.

"Captain LeVeau has opinions on just who Medics Beyond Borders should be helping," Alain explained. "In that she believes we shouldn't be helping anyone outside colonial borders."

"Talk about missing the brief," Jagati muttered as, from the other side of the pub, the musicians transitioned to a louder, faster piece.

"No succor to the enemy?" John guessed, pitching his voice up to be heard over the clapping that accompanied the music.

"Never mind that there are as many MBB members in the Coalition as there are in the United Colonies," Kallik pointed out.

"Which is why we came looking for you," Pyotr added, glancing at John.

Alain nodded. "After LeVeau cancelled on our contract, we went to the airfield office, and a fellow named Alvaro mentioned the *Errant* had just returned to Nike and might suit our needs."

"We might," John said, his eyes darting to Pyotr and back to Alain. "But there are some matters to discuss, first."

"We have the fee," Alain said before naming a sum that Jagati judged as just on the right side of doable.

"Which is good to know," John replied, "but money isn't the only issue."

"Please," Kallik held up their hand, "if you're going to turn us down, do it fast so we can start looking for another airship."

"We're not turning you down," Jagati said, glancing at John.

"Not at all," he agreed. "We merely like to go into a deal with a certain amount of transparency."

"Meaning?" Pyotr asked.

"Meaning, the *Errant* is an older 'ship," Jagati explained. "Like, liquid-aluminum battery old. No crystal power."

"Oh, if that's all . . ." Alain appeared ready to wave that off.

"Not entirely," John said.

"We've also got sparse guest furnishings," Jagati said.

"And a dodgy engine pod," John added.

"Not to mention the twenty-year-old bact-system, so water rationing is a necessity," Jagati continued.

"Basically, the *Errant* isn't the fastest, or most comfortable, transport on the airfield," John concluded.

"Forgive me," Alain said, "but this still feels as you are turning us down—just more politely."

"It's more that we like to under promise and overdeliver," John said.

"There's a reason we carry freight more often than passengers," Jagati added before picking up her drink. "It can get a little boring and a lot ripe."

"You realize we work in aid camps, don't you?" Kallik asked.

"Fair point," John admitted, then met Jagati's gaze.

She glanced at the doctors, and Pyotr, then back to John. She dipped her head, and he turned to the waiting clients.

"And it looks like we have an understanding."

"Excellent," Alain smiled. "Pyotr, you have the contract still?"

"Right here," Pyotr patted his coat while Jagati rose from her chair to wave wildly at the dance floor.

"Figure we should get Eitan in on the conversation," she explained at John's questioning glance. "Eitan's one of the crew," she said to the others. "Our mechanic already called it a night, but you'll meet him soon enough."

"Smog it to Earth and back," Pyotr swore, then looked up, sheepishly. "I seem to have dropped the contract somewhere."

"Possibly at the bar?" John asked.

"Seems most likely," Pyotr said, sliding off his chair.

"I'll—" Kallik began.

"I'll help you look for it," John cut in, popping up from his seat. "We'll be back soon," he promised.

"If you're sure," Kallik said, though they sounded perfectly happy to remain and enjoy their wine.

"We will be fine," Pyotr promised as first John, then he, turned to push through the surrounding tables.

"I hope the contract isn't on the floor," Alain said, eyeing the sticky floorboards.

"Did you say something about another crew member?" Kallik asked.

Jagati looked back at the dance floor and realized Eitan hadn't noticed her earlier hail.

"Hold on a sec," she said, jumping from the chair and heading toward the rhythmic crowd.

Halfway to her goal, she huffed out a breath and decided to try something different.

Standing still, she focused all her attention on Eitan's enthusiastically spinning figure and was rewarded by the sudden flick of his head in her direction.

As soon as their eyes met, she jerked her chin, which afforded her a quick nod from Eitan who immediately broke away from the dancers to join her.

"Possible job," she explained, leading him back to the table.

"One you seem less than pleased by," he said, reminding her he could sense more than her summons.

"The job is fine," she replied. "But there's something off about Pitte."

"You know, he has a first name," Eitan murmured, but as they had reached their table, she didn't have time to hit him.

"Eitan Fehr," she flicked a hand at her crewmate as the two docs rose from their chairs, "meet Dr. Natsiq and Dr. Natsiq-Corvais."

"Pleased to make your acquaintance," Alain said before relaxing back into his chair.

"Please, call me Kallik," the younger Natsiq inserted smoothly, reaching out their hand to grasp Eitan's.

Sweet merciful keeper's hive, she thought, as the smile Eitan gave Kallik nearly made Jagati's head swim.

"Both doctors, you say?" Eitan asked as he, Kallik, and Jagati took their seats. "Are either of you acquainted with Tiago

Hama? He is a friend, about to graduate from Yousafzai Medical."

"We haven't met, but then, we both graduated from Oronhy-atekha, in Moosehead," Alain explained.

While the Natsiqs and Eitan made nice, Jagati thought about the way John had been so eager to help Pyotr find the missing contract.

Something's up, there, she thought, tapping her glass.

But what?

John remained silent as he moved through the crowded tavern, dodging the occasional swinging mug or wayward elbow as he went.

He did not stop at the bar but rather turned in the direction of the tavern's entrance and then through the door.

Stepping out onto the Rigging's sheltered porch, he took a deep breath of the chill night air before leaning against a pillar, crossing his arms, and staring out into the street. "It's been a long time," he said as the other man came up alongside him, "Pascal."

"Long enough for you to improve your poker face," the man who'd been introduced as Pyotr Aaberg said. The Stoli dialect had been replaced something close to John's own Mooseheadian accent. "And it was already a good poker face. Civilian life looks well on you."

"Does that surprise you?" John glanced down, saw the green eyes flash with a quick hint of amusement in the light from the tavern window.

"A little," Pascal admitted, shoving his hands in his coat pockets and turning his gaze toward the rain-spattered road. "You were very keen on the Air Corps. I suppose I thought you'd be a lifer."

"I might have been," John replied. "But as you probably heard, that choice was taken away from me at Nasa."

"I did hear about that," Pascal agreed. "But not until a few years later. I was occupied . . . elsewhere."

"Of course you were," John murmured as a rickshaw came spinning down the street, spraying water everywhere

Someone inside the tavern had started singing "The Last Time I Saw Guinness" and a rush of voices joined in.

"You probably don't know this," Pascal continued, "but Special Operations opened a quiet—very quiet—investigation into Nasa soon after the event. I know one of the officers assigned, and he is nothing if not tenacious. The truth will come out."

"Some of it may already have," John replied, thinking back to his recent meeting with Gideon Quinn—another officer blind-sided by the events at Nasa.

"That's good then," Pascal said. "Still, I was sorry to hear of your part in it."

"I had no 'part' in any of the affair," John said tightly. "I was attempting to follow regulations, and I was stabbed in the back —literally—before being court martialed and my crew demoted and scattered throughout the fleet, all at the whim of the armchair general who commandeered my 'ship to commit murder."

At John's outburst, Pascal cleared his throat.

"Forgive me," John said as, with some effort, he bundled the familiar rage up like an old carpet, to be dumped back into the mental closet where it lived.

"Nothing to forgive," Pascal said evenly. "Though I believe the Air Corps owes you and your crew more than an apology."

"I'd as soon have nothing more to do with the Air Corps," John said, dragging his eyes back to Pascal's before adding, "Or any other part of the Corps, come to that."

"Ah," Pascal said. "Now we come to it."

"I don't want my 'ship, or my crew, involved in any of Special Operations' activities," John said.

"What makes you think I'm still with Special Ops?" Pascal asked, but quietly, as a couple stepped out of the pub and, sharing an umbrella, dashed down the sidewalk in the direction of the tram stop.

John waited for the amorous pair to turn the corner before replying. "You mean, besides the fact your name isn't Pyotr Aaberg, you're not from Stolichnaya, and you've never shown the least interest in charitable works?"

"You wound me." Pascal clutched a hand to his heart. "I've given generously to several charities over the years."

"Pascal . . ."

"Fine. Yes. I am on an assignment. And no, I can't tell you what it is."

"And what about the Natsiqs?"

"Oh, they're quite real. Real doctors, really working with MBB. As is Dr. Panesar."

"Panesar? Oh, the one at the airfield," John said, recalling Alain's earlier mention of a third associate. "But tell me, do you, or General Satsuke, or anyone in Special Ops, care what will happen to the good doctors or their organization if your cover is blown?"

"Please." Pascal scoffed at that. "There is not an intelligence agency on Fortune that hasn't embedded their operatives in various and sundry rescue organizations. In fact, I can guarantee there's at least one Midasian spy working on the Fordian border, right now."

"And how many innocent doctors will be arrested by the Colonial Corps should that Midasian operative be discovered?" John asked. "How many will be interrogated?"

"Are you implying the Corps tortures their prisoners?" Pascal's question was undercut by one of the new crystal-powered autos speeding past at what had to be thirty kph.

"Did I mention I was stabbed in the back on my own bridge while a general of the Corps looked on?" John asked in return. "More to the point, we know several of the Coalition states *do* torture their prisoners. Can you say, with one-hundred percent certainty, that those three doctors on your team won't suffer if you are discovered?"

"My cover has never yet been blown," Pascal said. "But, assuming such a catastrophe were to occur, I've been assured that the rest of the team will be protected—and yes," he added as John opened his mouth to protest, "I believe it. Not that I blindly trust the brass, but I do know they aren't willing to weather the public smog storm that would erupt if something happened to a group of volunteers under our watch."

"Vague and political," John observed. "How very Spec Ops."

"Something you would know well given that even after you left Spec Ops, you continued to be one of Satsuke's operatives."

"I was nothing more than a courier," John pointed out. "Like almost every fleet captain out there."

"You were more than that. I read the report on that Midasian cell you uncovered in Dodge. And the exfil in Isroa."

"And look where all that got me."

Pascal sighed, looked up. "Stabbed in the back?"

"Exactly."

"That won't happen this time," Pascal said.

"You can't know that."

"Perhaps not, but I do know that the northern refugees truly need aid. It's just your bad luck the *Errant* is the only available transport. So the only question remaining is if your resentment of all things Special Operations is great enough to prevent civilians on both sides of the border from receiving food, shelter, and medical care?"

Both men fell silent as the tavern door opened again, this time to an aeronaut who paused, blinked owlishly at the rain before shrugging, clomping down the short steps, and splashing her way in the direction of the airfield.

"John?"

He turned back to see Pascal's gaze—open, earnest, and as innocent as a murder hornet. "Fine. We'll take the job."

"Thank you."

"Just see we get paid," John said as he straightened. "And don't include my name in your reports."

"You have my word."

"For what that's worth," John muttered as the other man produced the "missing" contract from his inner pocket. "But before we rejoin the others, you should know that keeping your secret from the crew won't be easy."

"I think you forget how good I am," Pascal said, leading the way back into the pub.

"And humble," John pointed out, following the other man into the wall of heat and noise. He leaned down so Pascal could hear him. "But what I mean is, two of my crew are sensitives."

At that, Pascal came to a halt. "You couldn't have mentioned that at the start?"

With the barest hint of a smile, John patted him on the shoulder. "I imagine you'll be fine if you avoid Jagati—and whatever you do, do not let Eitan seduce you."

"Please. I'm a professional," Pascal scoffed, once again using Pyotr Aaberg's Stolichnayan accent.

And then they reached the table where the rest of their party was waiting.

Which was when Pascal set eyes on Eitan Fehr for the first time. "Why, this is hell," he muttered.

"*Professional,*" John reminded him, sotto voce, before announcing, "We found the contract."

Change of Fortune is now available.

Follow our Outrageous Crew on Ream for free to read the short story, *Errant Rising*, delving into the origins of Errant Freight.

As a follower, you will find complete novels, new stories, exclusive to Ream content and fellow lovers of quirky science fantasy.

Scan the QR code below to begin reading!

Acknowledgments

First of all, **thanks to you,** for reading this second book of the Fortune Chronicles (and giving John, Jagati, Rory, and Eitan a place in your bookish heart).

Double thanks to everyone who takes time **to leave a review,** which helps other readers who love character-driven adventures to take flight with the ragtag crew of the *Errant*.

We must also acknowledge Lori Drake and Cameron Coral for the morning writing/editing sessions, as well as Lori Diederich and Youness Elh for making the Fortune Chronicles readable and pretty, respectively.

Thanks, always to our families, both blood and chosen, and thanks also to all the other storytellers for daring greatly to share your work. This is a hard road, but it's all the better for having company.

ABOUT THE AUTHORS

A believer in the fun of fiction, Kathleen uses her history in theatre and fight choreography to create immersive adventures for fellow lovers of found families, outrageous escapades, and chaotic choices.

In addition to keeping the *Errant* crew flying, Kelley recently returned from five years of teaching acting in Shanghai. She now serves as an adjunct professor, teaching voice and directing at Mary Baldwin University in Staunton, Va. During the summers she teaches acting for the New School at New York University.

Both Kathleen and Kelley can be found hanging out at Ream Stories, growing more outrageous adventures featuring flawed heroes, chosen families, and all the snark you care to entertain.*

*Don't let the placid smiles fool you. The two K's have Statler and Waldorfed their way through many a stuffy gathering.

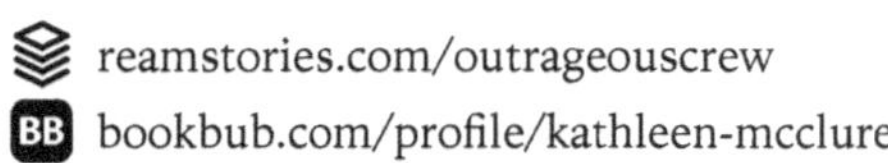

reamstories.com/outrageouscrew

bookbub.com/profile/kathleen-mcclure